In the Land of Birdfishes

In the Land of Birdfishes

Rebecca Silver Slayter

HarperCollins*PublishersLtd*

Published by HarperCollins Publishers Ltd

First edition

HarperCollins books may be purchased for educational, business,
or sales promotional use through our Special Markets Department.

HarperCollins Publishers Ltd
2 Bloor Street East, 20th Floor
Toronto, Ontario, Canada
M4W 1A8

www.harpercollins.ca

Library and Archives Canada Cataloguing in Publication
information is available upon request

ISBN 978-1-44340-737-3

Printed and bound in the United States
RRD 9 8 7 6 5 4 3 2 1

For, and because of, Conrad
and this is the wonder that's keeping the stars apart . . .

There are things that cannot ever occur with any precision. They are too big and too magnificent to be contained in mere facts. They are merely trying to occur, they are checking whether the ground of reality can carry them.

—Bruno Schulz

Mara

~

early 1960s

ONE

WHEN I HAD EYES, I saw my sister's hair (yellow), my mother's back, small rocks that the water took out and in from the shore with gasps of its deep ocean lungs. I remember my own hands, how tiny they were beside my father's. One day he put my hands in his and showed me how they disappeared, like that, inside his fist. Both my hands: gone. I lost all this—lost everything—but slowly.

Our mother was from Scotland, like my father's father, and most of the people and ancestors of the people in our town. She'd hardly been in Canada a summer when my father, the minister, and one of only seven single men in the town, asked her to marry him. He built her a house on a hill by the sea where she liked to walk, and I guess he thought that was enough. It looked like happiness, that little house with a blue roof and a window that looked without blinking at the shore. It looked like the end of the road—a small place where a life would grow, a family born out of the salt soil, stuck fast like stones in dirt. This was a small town, remember, and it's true what you've heard about them. Your dreams are small—no bigger than your head—in a small town, where there's nothing to look at and want that for yourself. Only what you can imagine in your own brain at night on the pillow, or a longing that gets you in a stomach that's fed but wants when you push your chair back from the table.

So think of this man coming home of an evening and seeing this woman, who by all accounts was pretty, sitting sewing something or another—put a candle in the room, though of course there was electricity, even on the north far shore of that godforsaken rind of the world, but just look what it does to her hair, how under that glow it becomes brass. Let every thing, every stick of wood, every door, the cracked glass of every window make a sound that is all its own. Let the wind pass through on winter nights and make a hollow howl against the roof, let the door squeak open for lack of grease, let the kettle whistle, let the boards on the floor by their bed creak every morning as they pull themselves out of it. Let them know every sound in the house. And let him love it, love watching her with her glowing golden hair and her belly swollen with twins, and the aching cry of the chair as she rocks back and forward and the crackle of fish oil in the lantern (make it a lantern!) beside her. And let her slowly go crazy in that house on the hill by the sea.

In the years after our birth, my father was rarely angry. He and my mother only spoke to each other in soft voices, and my sister and I were quiet children. Sometimes, if Aileen or I laughed, I would see both my parents turn their heads as if surprised to find us in the room. There was only ever one time that my father showed us the man he would later become.

It was twilight and my mother had left us, closing the screen door quietly behind her, and we'd all known she was going down to the shore. My father began washing dishes, and Aileen said to me, "Let's go with Mother." We slipped out the door and down the hill, Aileen's hair a yellow sail in the evening sky behind her.

When we reached the rocky beach, we could not see her in either direction and it was already darkening around us. Then we heard a splash in the water, and saw, far in the distance, a figure appearing and disappearing behind the waves. The water was rough—on this side of the hill, the land faced the open sea, and it was without end. From the other side of our house, you could walk down the road to a bay, where the water was always quiet and flat at sundown. That was the beach I loved.

"Mother," called Aileen. "Mother!" She began wading into the water.

"Wait," I said. I followed her. Aileen could swim already but I still hadn't learned. I would get frightened when Da said, "I'm going to let go of you now." I would cling to him because I wasn't ready for him to let go. (Let him hold me forever, and I'll kick my arms and legs the way he taught us and look up at him smiling down, and know his hands will never loosen at my sides.) Aileen began moving through the water, in the clumsy stroke Da called the doggy-paddle.

"Wait!" I said. The water was strangely warm in the cool air, but I shivered. I could feel rocks, broken shells, sand under my feet—there was life in the water. I knew it. I knew in the daytime how little animals, fish and things in shells travelled beneath the surface. Starfish slept and dreamt of rocks and the bellies of boats to wrap five arms around. All these sea creatures were in the dark sea water around me. I could feel the water moving as they stirred. I began crying. The eelgrass made slippery coils around my legs. Aileen kept paddling farther away from me, and I couldn't see Mother anymore.

"Aileen!" I took a few steps forward and my knee hit a rock, I stumbled and was suddenly on my back in the water, crying for my mother, for Aileen, and then hands closed under my arms and lifted me back out into the cold night air.

My father carried me back to the house in silence, wrapped me in a towel and sat me on our bed. He shut the door and was gone, but I knew I wasn't to move. A little while later, he returned and threw Aileen onto the bed too. She was crying. His face was such I hardly recognized him, this tall man who could lift both my sister and me like we were nothing, who had eyes like he could hurt us just as easily, toss me into the sea as pull me out of it.

"You are never, never to go to the water on your own.

"You will not swim at night.

"You will not leave the house at night alone.

"And you"—he knelt on the floor and grabbed Aileen's arm with both hands—"you will never leave your sister behind."

And then I remember Da telling us about drowning. I remember the names of every child in our town who had drowned since the ship *Hector* reached its shores and poured out the people whose descendants would one day become our neighbours and friends. I remember being asked to imagine water in the lungs where air should be. I remember closing my eyes and imagining it so hard my breath stopped for several moments and when it came again it was like water on a dry tongue, it was what the hungry word *grateful* would call up in my mind years later. And then Da got up and left, closing the door, with a look in his eyes like he had to leave the room or do us harm.

Da went back to his soft voice again and Mother stopped leaving the house after dinner. Sometimes she would stand by the window instead for hours at a time or sit on the couch with her hands in her lap, not looking at anything at all.

Don't look for Mother in this story. If you look at this hole I have made for her and see only the blurry lines of a sad woman who has no story at all, that is because that is what we saw. That is what we knew; a zero in a column of numbers that added up to an incomprehensible arithmetic. If you wonder what made her sad, what she was like when she wasn't watching the sea, what the thousand details were that make a person something more than a fissure in a family that broke—please ask those questions of someone who can answer. Tell me what they say. When my father asked her out for the first time, he showed up at her door with a jar of silver dollars. Every birthday or Christmas his grandmother had sent him a dollar, and he put each in a jar, and kept them until he was twenty years old and felt a pull in his heart for a woman who was new in this country. He drove her two hours to the city. They ate dinner with the jar beneath his seat, and left a silver column on the bill as they walked out into the starlit city streets. I think of those coins, and of the simplicity of my father's math. How the stack of coins might have looked to him like the shape of a female figure, of a woman who was polite from the other side of the table and let him kiss her when he took her home. How before they left the restaurant, he must have looked at the coins on the table and her across from them, and seen a divine intelligibility in things. My father's math failed him, and it failed my sister and me, and it failed my mother. She became incalculable; the hole in the centre of a zero that everything gets lost inside.

The last day I saw is the day I remember best of all. Was everything more beautiful that day? Was the sky as blue as the ten thousand skies I would never see? Were the colours, the shapes of things, complicit with the loss that was coming?

It was May and the pageantry of turning seasons was at work everywhere. The last plates of ice in the bay had pulled loose and turned to water. We were between seasons and closer, in truth, to winter than to summer, but in recent days, our family had begun to remember something. Now, suddenly, we recalled that there would be days when the hills would be filled with the warm, green, thriving smell of leaves and grass and the yellow hearts of wild roses, and Aileen and I would return at dinnertime red-fingered from strawberries eaten in the field. That memory was more sure than the dirty snow still clutching the roots of trees in the darkest parts of the woods. It was more plausible than the nights when water left in the kettle would freeze there. It was a vision so clear that we couldn't see anything else.

That morning I was awake before anyone else and sat on the porch steps, surrounded by the bustling smell of water turning against itself, its salt and sneer. The push of tides against the sand. The thrust of green, the whistle in the grass. I still wore my pyjamas, but had pulled rain boots on because the grass was always damp in the mornings, like Aileen's hair when she'd had dark dreams in the nighttime. Though the sun had only just appeared over the treetops behind me, I could feel its warmth on my neck and thought that maybe, all at once, spring had arrived.

I'd discovered an anthill that had just begun stirring after the long winter, and was watching the incredible industry of each ant, hurrying in and out of the little holes. Aileen and I used to wet peppermints with our tongues and lay them, damp and glistening, on anthills, horrified and fascinated by

8

how quickly the armoured black bodies would cover the pink candy and begin the slow work of carrying it home, particle by particle. Even the ants seemed not to trust the weather, and only a few moved on the surface of the hill. I watched the halting travels of one until he disappeared down into his subterranean kingdom.

"Mara," said my mother. "You're up early."

I smiled up at her. I think I thought my mother was beautiful. She'd become so vague—even now I see her face more clearly than I could then, and only now can I think that I loved her, thought her beautiful. At that time, she was in the process—though of course I didn't know it then—of untying herself from us. That day she was at the end of a very long rope, already far away and almost free, delivering herself to something that is as unknown to me now as then, as unknown to me as the substance of the rope she was untying, which I did not see or understand until she showed it to me later that day.

"Come here, little one. Let's go for a walk."

I held her hand and we walked not to her favourite beach but to the bay down the road. I was anxious to keep up with her even though my rain boots were loose. (They were pretty flowered ones given to us by a great-aunt in Halifax who always brought us clothes too big or too small when she visited. She only ever watched us from the corner of her eye, and from that perspective, we must have seemed bigger or smaller than we were.) But she walked slowly for me, which only later I remembered was strange for her. She never used to wait for us. We were always stumbling behind, desperate to catch up but sure we never would, while the pale gold of her hair, her narrow shoulders beneath the sweaters she'd knitted, which were all the same colour of blue, disappeared before our eyes. We loved our mother's back.

She didn't speak a word as we walked to the bay. And then, after a little while, she began to hum, and I didn't recognize the song she hummed, but it made me afraid. I looked down and saw she wasn't wearing shoes. Her feet were streaked with mud and she seemed not to notice when she stepped on the sharp stones buried in the dirt road, though I flinched to see her walk across them, feeling in my own feet how deep they dug into her flesh. As we approached the water's edge, I came to understand what I had not until that day. Though my mother had consented to live with us and, in her way, love us, she was another sort of creature altogether than what we were. She was not pained by the things that hurt me, and the smile she offered when my sister or I succeeded in making my father laugh was only something she had learned to do to please us. Her true smile would only be shown to creatures of her own kind and I did not know what those were.

"Are you going for a swim, Mother?" I asked as we stood there at the shore. She didn't answer me but stopped humming. By the rocks far at the east end of the shore, gulls were circling.

"It's Sunday," I whispered. "Won't Da be getting up soon? Won't we be needing to go to church?"

The sun was well above the trees now and shone down over the bay, lighting a golden path along the channel that connected it to the sea. My mother turned her face up to the sun, looking straight at it the way she had told us never to do.

I tried to turn my gaze, like hers, to the sun, but it was too bright to look at. Even my mother's face now seemed ablaze with yellow fire.

I stared at the sand beneath our feet, bowing my head and

wishing I had thought to wake my sister when I left the house that morning. If she were here, I knew I would not be frightened, because she was never afraid.

And then I saw the shadow my mother left behind her on the ground. When I looked at it first, it seemed to be a proper shadow, a hole in the light cast by the sun that matched the shape of my mother before me. But then, as I watched, it grew. It stretched, like something uncoiling, to reach down the beach and back to the road we'd walked on. And then the shadow began to flicker, its edges losing precision, rippling, as if the darkness that composed it was itself disintegrating.

And suddenly it burst apart, and I saw that what I'd taken for my mother's shadow was instead the shadow of a thousand birds, which all at once took to the air, breaking my mother's shadow into a thousand fluttering pieces that flew apart in every direction. I recognized the shapes of starlings, pipers, cormorants, and then they were gone—the dark shape of my mother was gone from the sand, dissolved into the flight of a thousand birds. And though I stared into the sky, into the trees and out across the water, I saw no wings or beaks to cast the shadows that I'd seen, only an absence. Only a departure. Only an empty sky.

And I understood then that the world was not knowable. The mysteriousness of my mother was the mysteriousness of all things, and I felt a crack run through, the seams pull apart, as if something were behind or beneath or between everything I'd known.

I did not speak or cry. I watched my own shadow on the sand, which had the size and shape of me exactly. And I felt terribly, terribly sad to see that my mother left no mark at all behind her in the sand.

11

And then she turned to face me and she wore a smile I'd never seen before. Perhaps it was her true smile she showed me then. And there was nothing to be done. Because our mother was a bird, or something like that. At any rate, she was not one of us. She reached down and took my hand in her own cool one that was as soft and smooth as a human hand.

"Let's go to church," she said.

At home, Aileen was still sleeping, and Da was at the kitchen table reviewing his sermon.

"I'm not feeling very well," my mother said to my father. "I think I'll have to stay home today."

Da was worried and took her temperature, but it was normal. He frowned at the thermometer and then at the clock on the wall, looking unsure.

"Don't worry about me," she said. "You'll be late. Mara, get your sister up. The choir will already be there by now."

When we left the house, my mother stood at the door, leaning against the frame. I waved to her from the truck, but she did not wave back. I realized she wasn't looking at us.

Aileen and I sat in the front row, as we always did, and the women from the choir smiled down at us as they always did. Aileen fussed beside me, scratching her knee and fiddling with her hair, while I tried to sit without moving even my toes in my shoes, which were too tight.

Da was reading about Jesus our saviour, and said that when people looked at him they saw a man of poverty and filth, when it was God himself who stood before them. Their eyes looked upon God but they did not see him. "*He was despised and forsaken of men, A man of sorrows and acquainted with grief; And like one from whom men hide their face He was despised, and we did not esteem Him. Surely our griefs He Himself bore, And our sorrows He carried."*

When he was finished, the choir sang in round, full voices that made me less sure of what I had seen on the beach. Beside me, the heels of Aileen's Sunday shoes clattered against the bottom of the pew. Though she didn't know what had happened to Mother's shadow, I was comforted by her fearlessness, her oblivion. And I decided not to think any more about it.

We rode the pickup truck home, Aileen in the middle and me against the window with the air rushing through and unravelling my braids. Da turned the radio on and smiled at us, his hands tapping out rhythms against the wheel.

There was something in the back of the truck. I think of it now and can't remember if it was paper or books or tanks of gasoline. But Da stayed behind us, unloading something. Whatever it was, I wonder sometimes what might have happened if the truck had been empty and Da had walked ahead, leading us into our house. But he stayed behind in some labour or another and Aileen and I ran up the hill, Da calling behind us that we'd better not slip in our Sunday dresses.

Aileen opened the door first.

I was second.

She was not a tall woman. Somewhere scattered among the things I did not see in the room—the lamp on the table, the kettle on the stove, the books on the shelf, the blankets she'd folded the night before, taken fresh off the line by the door—a stool must have been cast aside.

A decision takes time to reach; I have seen girls still as statues, watching their reflections, before deciding how they want to wear their hair. Even a dog will circle his bed before he sleeps. How long does it take? Is it considered over years or decided late at night or in the hours after breakfast, the length of a church service?

From a beam that held up the roof, from the end of a very long rope, my mother died.

I don't know how long my father was in the house before she was in his arms. He held her. He pulled at the cord, but it held her harder. He reached to her face, moved her tongue in her mouth, pushed air in her lips and her nose.

After a while, I realized my father was talking. He was saying things to my mother, but then he turned and he was saying things to me. I know because he said my name—"Mara." Like that. He said my name.

I couldn't look at him. I was looking at her. I was thinking of birds.

Suddenly he grabbed me so hard my knees buckled, and he slapped me. "Don't look," he said in the loud voice.

He turned me away from her, but I ducked his arm and looked at her again. My mother, who was leaving us by the minute. Who was at the very end of leaving us.

"Go to your room. Both of you, go to your room."

"Mara," my sister said. My sister looked frightened and I had never seen her afraid. "To our room," she said. "Let's go to our room."

Da was digging in a drawer. He pulled out a knife and saw me standing there, still. "Cover your eyes, damn you," was the thing he said. He climbed on a table and put one arm around her and began sawing at the rope with the other. He said, "Moira," and that was my mother's name. He pulled at the knife, while she was there at the end of the rope.

I saw something then. A bird, just the very top of a bird's

head. In her mouth. It was just looking out of her mouth. I cried out then, and Aileen came to my side. "Look," I said. "There's a bird in her mouth. They're inside her. The birds all went inside her."

"It's her tongue," said Aileen. "It's not a bird, it's her tongue."

"It *is* a bird." I could see now the flicker of feathers behind her eyes that would not look at anything. Their dark shadow was all over her. "We have to let them out," I said. I said, "Slice her open, Da." I said, "Let them out."

My father dropped the knife and came toward me. He fell to his knees before me. "Mara," he said. And then he said, "How can she let you see this. Your child eyes."

I began to speak to explain to him about the birds, but he covered my mouth, and then he picked me up in his arms and carried me beside my mother. He raised the knife and I thought I would end there, beside my mother. His eyes were not his own. And then he took the knife to my Sunday dress. He tore open the seam and sawed a long, wide ribbon from the end, and then he tied it around my eyes, so tightly I could feel my heart beat in my scalp. And then he pulled me to him. "You mustn't look," he said. "I'll keep you safe. You'll be all right, I'll keep you all right."

I stumbled and fell. My hands went out into the air around me as I fell, and I felt the hem of my mother's dress brush against me as I tumbled to the floor. I could see the light from the window but no shapes at all. Like this, I reached the other side of seeing. I left a world of colours and lights and figures and shapes, and woke into a dark world that was strange and unknown.

"Aileen," I whispered. I lay on the floor and didn't move. I could hear a sound so familiar that it was a part of me and knew Aileen was crying. I could hear Da moving about, his heavy feet on the floor, and Aileen's ragged breathing. I heard the knife tear her dress and then stillness, and then the sound of Da's knife against the rope again.

"Mara," my sister called me, and I found her. She was only steps away and our arms opened around each other. I knew that for the first time in our lives, she was more frightened than I was. I felt calm in a way I didn't recognize. This dark world we'd come into was safe in a way I'd never known or felt before. I knew that outside the bandage around my eyes, the world had come to pieces. I knew my mother was still hanging there or perhaps in my father's arms now. I knew that Da had never touched us like that before. That until today, he never would have, and that with this day began a new kind of Da. But in the dark world, I felt my sister's hand in mine and I was not afraid.

Hours later, after Da had put us in bed, though it must have still been afternoon, Aileen and I lay beside each other (she found her way over to my bed), and we listened to Da moving in the other room. I don't know what he was doing. Sometimes we would hear him speaking, but we couldn't make out the words. I was restless and cold and my head hurt. Before putting us to bed, Da had wrapped still more strips of fabric around my eyes, so that now I couldn't see even where the light was coming from. He'd patted my hair and whispered my name as he did it, but he tied the fabric tight, and now my head ached.

"She's dead," Aileen said. "You know that means forever."

"She won't come back," I said.

"No."

"Like when Da does the funerals for people. They go in the ground and it's forever."

"I don't know how she died like that."

"It was the rope."

"But how did it happen?"

"It must have got tied around her and it choked her. Like the Boston Strangler, like Aunt Una told us about."

"But who tied it there?"

"It could have been an accident," I said. I knew it was important that I not tell my sister about the birds who'd taken our mother's shadow and so I didn't, but I knew that at the end of the rope were those birds. I knew that they killed my mother.

"What was she trying to do with the rope, I wonder."

"I don't know. Oh it hurts, this thing around my eyes."

"Let's take them off."

"He might come back."

"We can put them back on if he does. He won't know we've done it."

"No. He looked so angry."

"Do you think he'll take it off us tomorrow? Why do we have to sleep with it on?"

"I don't know."

"Is your ribbon tight?"

"Yes."

"Mine too."

"What can you see?"

"Nothing. What can you see?"

"Nothing."

~

The next day, I didn't wake until Da shook me.

"Get up," he said. "We're burying your mother."

I sat up and nearly fell, I was so close to the edge of the bed, but Da caught me.

"Da, can I take it off now?"

"No. Get up. Mara. Aileen. Get up now."

He led me by the hand from bed, and then Aileen took my other hand. We followed him like that, through the door, which he held open for me. Into the kitchen, I could feel the tiles on my bare feet. Out the door, which whined as he pulled it. I stumbled on the steps and felt Aileen against my shoulder. He pulled me on.

"Da? Why do we have to wear this? Da, please take it off me?"

He didn't answer, but led us down the hill. I had to walk fast not to fall.

"Wait here," he said. He left us, and we sat down on the ground. We could hear the whisper and buzz of insects around us. The sun was warm on my shoulders though the air was still cool and I knew it must be early still. The grass was wet. In the distance, I could hear the water moving. Beside me, Aileen was crying.

My father came back, and I could hear something behind him in the grass. Then he began to dig and I understood that my mother was there on the ground, somewhere near us. It was a long time we were there. And then he put her in the ground. We got to our feet and he said, "I can't do the service. It's not a funeral. She's not with God. Your mother will stay here, you understand? Don't say anything and don't pray. It's a sin to pray. But this is the end of her. You must know that. She's in the ground. She's not with us and she's not with God. She's down there with the bugs and the dirt. She'll stay there."

Then he led us back to the house and to the kitchen table, where we sat in chairs and were fed breakfast, bread and apples.

I felt my father's hand on my shoulder.

"I'm going to tell you what it's going to be like," he said. "It's us three now. We'll be alone now. You won't go to school again. There was not a thing they taught you there I can't teach you better myself, you hear. So we'll do lessons at home and I'll teach you what's important. I'll teach you to know God, and I'll teach you your sums and things too. But there won't be any reading. And no writing. It wouldn't do you any good to read anyway, nothing but the Bible, and I can read you that."

He said, "Your mother committed a sin, do you understand that. The worst sin of all: despair. She left this world by her own hand, and it's God himself who forbade that. You know of Jesus, who died on Good Friday, you know all what happened there. You know how on the cross, he, even our saviour, despaired. He called out to God his father, 'Why hast thou forsaken me,' he said. Do you know what this word means? Does it mean something to you, *forsake*? Well, it's the same as your mother did here. She left you and will not care for you anymore. But it was a sin for Jesus to think this of his father, because his father was there all the time. He did not leave him and his care was infinite. And so, even Jesus who was divine despaired. But your mother's sin was the greatest despair of all. She left God's world. She held the great gift of God, this life, in her hand and threw it from her like a fistful of sand."

He said, "But it is not just her sin. She inherited this sin from her people and ours, yours. They took it with them from back in Scotland and they brought it here. It's in the blood, but most of all it's in the earth. Places, too, can be

19

damned by God. It's in the sea we fish from and the land we live on. Men here waste their lives not leaving. Because the land has a hold upon them. They get to loving the water and the soil. They get so they can't let go of it. There's miners that near commit the same sin as your mother going down in the pit every morning, knowing it will be their own grave they'll ride that cart to one day. And if they left here they could find their way to better work—there's places with good jobs that pay good money, but they'll never go there, because this land won't let go of them."

He said, "I won't see that happen to you. I've put that thing around your eyes, and I won't take it off. I'm going to save every penny I can, and we're going to leave this place just as soon as we've saved enough to get good and far away. I'll take the cover off your eyes then but not a day before. I'll keep you innocent. I'll keep you safe. This part of the world is a fist that takes you in it, and I won't let it teach you to love it or fear to leave it. This land is full of beauty and anger, and it's that your mother lived with and looked on, and I won't have you look on it and know it and despair."

After that he let us go outside, but we sat there and did not know what to do. We didn't know yet how to play without eyes to see. It felt strange even to talk to each other in the dark, so we sat close and held each other's hands and were quiet for a long, long time. Finally Aileen said, "I don't want to leave here, like he said."

"Where would we go?"

"I don't want to leave Mother if she's staying here."

"I want to go to school."

"Me too. We were going to learn to make curly letters, all hooked together, like grown-ups."

"Well, Da will still teach us some things, won't he. Like he said. Just not the writing bit."

"He's inside now, isn't he," said Aileen. "Couldn't we take it off, while he's in there? We can put it back on if he comes out."

"But we mightn't be able to do it in time."

"We'd watch for him. We can take it off just when he's not around. He won't know."

"We can't. Please, Aileen, we can't. We have to do what he says."

She was quiet for a while. I lay on my back on the grass. She asked, "What do you see?"

I could feel the sun on my face, but I could hardly even make out the difference in light when I turned my face toward where I knew it to be and when I turned away. "Nothing," I said. I reached out my hand for hers. "What do you see?"

She said, "Nothing."

There were two worlds, and my sister and I walked through a door between them. On one side, my mother stood with us and it was full of *things,* it was plump, bulging, fat with rooms and the things in rooms, the chairs and papers and spoons and pillows and dolls and dishes and coats and desks and other things people put in rooms, and beyond the rooms, the sky and clouds and stars and trees and crows and fleas, and colours, yellow red blue black brown gold white grey. On that side, there were people—the neighbours far down the road and the people we saw at church and the children in school. It was so busy and we were always being taken from one thing to do, one place to go, to the next. The telephone would ring or there would be a knock on the door. We would go for a swim or have our hair cut on the lawn. On the other side, it was just Aileen and me. There were voices—mostly my father's and sometimes we'd hear a voice from another room when Da would send us to our bedroom while a neighbour came by. But it was my sister I would feel beside me, always. We held hands almost all the time so we could know each other was near. And there were so many sounds in the new world. I could hear everything and know where I was in a room by the sound of a step on the floor on the other side of the house. The new world was loud but it was full of still-ness. Time was distributed unevenly in the old world—hand-fuls of it would be thrown out and wasted all the time, a day by the shore would pass in a matter of minutes, and a day at school would sometimes last till you were old. The new world released time on a spool that was steady, and the time it released was taut and long. We were safe in the new world. My sister was always beside me, her hand in mine, and I was only afraid of my father. We only left the house to play out-side and we never, ever went to the beach again. There was no church and no school and no other houses. We never had to talk to other children or shake hands with grown-ups. The new world was beautiful.

"Remember how it was before Mother died," Aileen said sometimes. "It was so pretty when Mother was alive. And exciting." Aileen missed school and cried often. I'd hold her hand when she did. Sometimes she'd get angry and push me aside. She was always the first to release my hand. Sometimes when we were outside, she'd go off on her own while I called her name. Sometimes she wouldn't come back for hours, and I would wander the hill and not find her.

I was always patient with her. She liked to list the things we used to see when Mother was alive. "Remember," she'd sigh, "the fire in the stove at winter. Remember the trees in autumn, they'd let go of all their leaves and they'd fall to the ground, but they were all different colours."

I'd tell her she was remembering wrong, that she was making it up. "They were, they were all colours," she'd say. "Orange and yellow and blue."

The more I told her she was mistaken, the more strange her memories became.

"Remember the birds," she'd say, "how pretty they were, their huge wings, the size of houses. They made that sound, *wump wump wump*. And they'd fight so hard with those other animals with wings, the ones with teeth."

The seasons turned and we felt them on our faces and we heard them. Summer was a long, warm dream that awoke to the clattering of leaves dead in the trees and their wheezing sink to the ground. Winter chilled us and we were cold even in our beds. In snowstorms, we went outside in our snow pants and coats and mittens and boots and lifted our faces up to the icy touch of each flake. I always thought I could hear the snow. At first it would seem everything became quiet, and then you would realize the world was not quiet but overwhelmed by another sound; the sky had opened its mouth and released its call to the winter below it. And the winter answered, and between them, they howled and murmured and roared into the quickening night. And then spring again, with its own sounds, that nasty insistent pressing of things out of the ground, the crack of roots emerging from split seeds, and there would be grass beneath our hands when we lay outside and let the sun burn our skin. This cycle went round and round, three, four times before it was done. And always my sister would ask me, when we were alone, "What do you see?" And I would say, "Nothing." And I would say, "What do you see?" And she would say, "Nothing."

My father taught us as he'd told us he would. In the morning for four hours and in the afternoon for two, he'd sit with us at the kitchen table and teach us sums and Latin and chemistry. But mostly he'd read to us from the Bible. We knew the Old Testament almost by heart at the end, and he'd ask us to recite passages.

But it shall come to pass, if thou wilt not hearken unto the voice of the Lord thy God, to observe to do all his commandments and his statutes which I command thee this day; that all these curses shall come upon thee, and overtake thee—

It would seem, I think, to some, a great sin that my father committed against us.

So that thou shalt be mad for the sight of thine eyes which thou shalt see—

When they arrived at last, one day, their hard fists on the door, men there to take my father, and women to gather us up in their sad, sorry voices and fat, busy arms; they told us a man would be jailed for doing to us such, a man that was meant to serve God.

Because thou servedst not the Lord thy God with joyfulness, and with gladness of heart, for the abundance of all things—

It was his sermons that had begun to frighten them. Their weak ears refused his warnings, and their eyes saw only madness in the hellfire he conjured from the pulpit. And it was then they came for us. But had they asked, before they forced him to resign his job, where his daughters were? What could he have answered?

And thou shalt eat the fruit of thine own body, the flesh of thy sons and of thy daughters, which the Lord thy God hath given thee, in the siege, and in the straitness, wherewith thine enemies shall distress thee—

The women sobbed and held us as they peeled the bandages from our eyes. I reached for Aileen's hand and couldn't find it. The sweaty hand of one of the women clasped mine instead.

And toward her young one that cometh out from between her feet, and toward her children which she shall bear: for she shall eat them for want of all things secretly in the siege and straitness, wherewith thine enemy shall distress thee in thy gates—

I heard my sister crying then. I heard her far from me. "Mara," she said. "Mara, I can see you. I can see you."

And the Lord shall scatter thee among all people, from the one end of the earth even unto the other; and there thou shalt serve other gods, which neither thou nor thy fathers have known, even wood and stone—

I was confused. I felt I would fall over. "Aileen," I said. "What do you see?"

"I see you. I see these women—oh Mara, it's Greta from the choir. And Da, they're taking Da away. Where are they taking him? I see the house—oh it's different. I forgot, I forgot the colours . . ."

And among these nations shalt thou find no ease, neither shall the sole of thy foot have rest: but the Lord shall give thee there a trembling heart, and failing of eyes, and sorrow of mind—

". . . You're so old now, you look like a teenager almost. Your hair is darker—is mine darker too?"

And thy life shall hang in doubt before thee; and thou shalt fear day and night, and shalt have none assurance of thy life—

". . . Everything is soft, it's not hard and sharp like I remembered. But it's so beautiful, isn't it beautiful?"

In the morning thou shalt say, Would God it were even! and at even thou shalt say, Would God it were morning! for the fear of thine heart wherewith thou shalt fear, and for the sight of thine eyes which thou shalt see.

". . . Mara? Mara, what can you see?"

And the Lord shall bring thee into Egypt again with ships, by the way whereof I spake unto thee, Thou shalt see it no more again.

"Nothing."

It never came back, seeing. Shapes, here and there. Something like what I remembered as colour, but only two. Black. White. Shadows. Glimpses of motion. Nothing more. There were doctors, and then they were gone. My sister was taken to the city. I was taken out West. I went to a special school. I married. The man took me back to his home, up north. I had a son.

I died.

Aileen

~

early June 1996

TWO

I'D FELT IT COME into the room when he stopped loving me.
Like it was something sitting between us. Like it was eating
with us at the table. Touching me in bed at night. His not loving me. It felt like something we'd overlooked when we reno-
vated the house. A ghost we'd just discovered.

First it was something that belonged to the house, that
hung around the furniture. I'd open a drawer and find it rolling around with the plastic forks, the twine, the clatter of pills
in their bottles, the saved stubs of emergency candles that one
night had burned for hours, the keys to the locked doors of
homes and cars we no longer owned. And then, after a while, I
could no longer shake the feeling that when I put dinner on the
table there were two of them there raising a fork. Stephan and
this shadow. The ghost, I thought, maybe, of us as we'd been
before. Unable to depart from the thing we'd become.

Because there was nothing to be done, I did nothing. But at
night, I complained to the thing that was happening to us like
it had ears to hear me. The thin skin below my left eye started
twitching. I had loved him since even that thin skin around my
eyes was smooth and perfect.

He looked at me like I was a threat to him.

When I was a child, there was a couple down the road who'd come across the border when the war began. They were young and wore weird, bright clothes. The husband built boats. I loved sitting beside him when he worked, smelling the wood smell of the shop. Sometimes he'd let me sand the boards with the last, finest piece of sandpaper, when the wood had become, after several stages of him bent over it, pushing and drawing different grains of sandpaper back and forth, like velvet. Soft as skin. When Stephan first took work as a carpenter, it was like love had a floor and it had opened up and I'd fallen down a whole other storey in love. He brought that smell, of built and mended things of wood, into our home. We lived in the North End of Halifax then, and together we tore out walls, replaced windows, hammered together a breakfast nook and built-in shelves. Some mornings, I'd get up before him when the sun was still low and pad around the dim house, turning the lights on in every room, pretending to be a stranger looking at our life, and feeling so lucky it frightened me.

He'd never done roofing before. He was helping out a friend.

He was supposed to build walls. He was meant to build floors. Foundations. Frames.

It was a simple thing to happen with a complicated end. The way it's easy to lose your footing and difficult to step from a roof out into air. The way falling is easy and landing is considerably more complex.

Sometimes I think of what he must have looked like on the ground. He could have been anybody, just someone else's husband or friend, broken. I picture myself standing there with him at my feet and I say, "Is that supposed to be surprising, am

I meant to look at this *body* and think, Who'd have thought a person could become garbage so easy and so fast?" If I'd been there, I'd have been able to stop loving him. Ha. I'd have said, "You think I wasn't expecting this?" And I'd sleep at night because there'd be nothing but dark around me and not him, falling, hitting the ground again and again.

They thought he'd die—they told me, "Be ready for him to die," and I said, "Be ready for my lawyer." But he didn't die. He didn't die, and if something like that happens, you start to think maybe you were wrong about everything. You think something awfully damn good has reached down and put its big ole finger on your head and said, "Go on, get out of here, I spare you."

He got better.

And then he got headaches.

And then he got moods like he wasn't even in that broken head of his anymore. He was defensive. He was distant. He went somewhere far, far away. And he just never came back.

I went to the doctor and I said, "When I touch him he flinches." The doctor said sometimes alterations like that happen with brain injuries. That was his word, *alteration,* so I started to see Stephan in my head like a pair of slacks some tailor had opened up a seam in. The doctor said it might change. And he said, "Then again it might not."

So I ate a year of dinners with that thing between us at the table. The day Stephan said he was tired of Halifax, that he'd taken a job in Toronto without a word to me, I said, "Okay." I came with him to a city where I knew no one. At the end of the phone calls I had with my father before he died 2,500 kilometres away, I'd go in the pantry of our new apartment to cry so Stephan wouldn't hear.

When he finally left, it was as sudden as if it had already happened. There was no conversation. Just the things he said. And the door behind him.

I'd been on the bus almost two days when the flat, dry plains gave way to bright yellow fields. "What is it?" I asked the old man across the aisle. "What's that growing there?"

"Canola," he said.

"What's it made of?" I asked.

"Well, it's itself," he said. "It's canola. Like the oil."

"Is it a GMO?"

"A who now?"

"It doesn't look natural. It looks like people made it. Look at the colour of it. It looks like it's all wrong because people made it." The words came out of my mouth too fast and too many at a time, as if they'd been shoved in there, too many to fit, waiting to escape.

The man frowned and got the sort of hard look on his face that I'd seen back home in Nova Scotia on other faces. He said slowly, "I don't know, I guess."

"Like mules," I said. "Or burros? Which one is it that's a cross between a horse and a donkey? Or a donkey and a mule?"

"I don't know what you're getting at there—"

"They can't reproduce."

"What do you mean?"

"You'd think people might take some kind of lesson from that. You'd think we might wonder why we can't even put a mule together without sterilizing it. Maybe every single thing we do is screwed up like that in some way we didn't intend." I hadn't spoken to anyone since I'd got on the bus. Now I realized it had been a mistake to start. I willed my hands to relax and set them in my lap in a loose, casual way, like they had just landed there on their own.

The old man leaned forward so I could see the way the lower lids of his eyes didn't quite make it all the way up anymore. They gaped at the bottom, revealing the wet pinkness beneath them. He said, "You want a Ringolo?"

"No, thank you."

He sat back. "Okay," he said, "but I'll leave the bag here." He set it on the seat beside the aisle and moved over to the window.

As fast as I'd made up my mind, I'd begun to regret it. Dumb, dumb, dumb, to cross a country for scarcely more than a rumour from a dying man. The words had started circling around in my brain the second I stepped on the bus, an unending chorus to my stupidity. What am I doing, what am I doing, what am I doing, I had heard when it rained the first afternoon and the wipers slapped back and forth across the windshield. But I had no answer, and then at last, just as the second night fell and we crossed the border into Alberta, I knew why I didn't: it wasn't the right question.

Just before dawn on the third day, we stopped in Calgary and the empty seats in the bus all got filled. A dark-haired girl with dreadlocks sat down beside me. "You mind if I turn the light on?" she asked. She had wide brown eyes with silver sparkles painted on the lids that made her eyes look enormous and startled.

"That's fine."

"I've got to read all this book before we get to Vancouver. You read this?"

I looked at the cover. The type was big but written in tilted, script letters. As I moved the book a little closer to my face, I was able to read the title. *The First Time Around*. I shook my head.

"It's all about how you're supposed to live your life like you have another one later. It's supposed to help you not get all stressed out about making mistakes. Like this is a practice run."

"Oh."

"It's pretty dumb. My dad is always sending me stuff like this to read. Really it's his way of telling me he thinks I'm making mistakes. He sent me this one months ago, and I lied and said I read it when he asked. So I've got to finish it before he picks me up in Vancouver. He's that kind of guy, he'll test me. Like, before we leave the parking lot."

I remembered being her age. I remembered how easily sneers settled on soft, pretty faces. I thought of something to say. "I used to want to write a book," I said. And it was true, though I hadn't thought of it in years. At the university where I'd taught composition before we left Halifax, they'd given me a grant to hire readers. I had large-print versions of most of the books I taught from, but I needed the readers to help me mark my students' papers. It was a laborious process as I dictated punctuation changes and grammatical corrections, but one or two of the readers got good at the work as the years went on. And the university had been kind to me, giving me smaller classes than the other instructors, though it meant those instructors made snide comments about their workloads when we crossed paths in the hall. And the department head, who'd known me as a student there, once said to me, "You know, you could dictate your own work to those readers. If you ever wanted to write something of your own. I still remember your essays." But I would have felt ashamed to ask another person to witness me fail at something so preposterous, and in any case, as I told him, I had a special typewriter and managed just fine on my own.

"No kidding," the dark-haired girl said. "Anyway, I'll turn the light off once the sun's a little higher, but it's bad for you to read when it's dim. You should be careful not to do that."

"I don't see so great," I said. I lifted my hands up off my lap but then, unsure where to put them, I let them rest back down. She was still looking at me. "I can't read that small print," I said. "Too late for me, I guess." I laughed and then fell silent.

"That's shitty. What's your name?"

"Aileen."

"I'm Rochelle. Nice to meet you." She smiled again and then started reading. I watched her, and how easy it was for her. Her eyes moved back and forth so quick, like little fish in two tiny bowls.

"I'm going to be forty in two weeks." It wasn't the right thing to say. I knew it. I waited for the sneer of her mean, young face.

Rochelle closed the book, leaving her index finger between the leaves. "Happy birthday," she said.

"Thank you. What I meant was, I don't see how many mistakes your father could think you've made at your age. You're . . . you're just starting." When he'd left, the door made a certain sound against the wood floor. A scraping sound that I had not been able to stop hearing. It was getting louder.

"I'll be twenty-three in February. I'm a Pisces. So you're a Gemini?"

"Rochelle." I whispered it, because I was worried the words might get away from me. "He fell off a roof."

"Who?"

"My husband."

"Is he okay?"

"He left me."

"I don't get it." Girls that age, they were so heartless. Understood nothing. Felt nothing.

"It damaged his brain. He just stopped. He just stopped loving me."

"No kidding. I never heard of that happening to somebody." She blinked so slowly, there was a moment you could pause and see her eyes closed, and then open again so wide the full circle of brown was revealed against the white, and it was strange how we got made like that, perfect, our eyes precise circles the way you could never draw them, not if you tried to copy what an eye looked like a hundred times on the page—it would never be symmetrical and perfect like her eyes were, staring at me and blinking so slowly that half the time I was just looking at the silver of her lids and trying to understand how to talk to someone who put sparkles on her face before getting on a long-distance bus.

I shook my head. "I just can't get my head around it. Can it be something that stupid that ruins your life? Can your husband fall from a roof and knock his love for you out of his head? Are other people living lives like this?"

"Well, if he doesn't love you anymore, you're better off—"

"He was the kindest man I knew. When we were at people's houses for dinner, he would ask if he could use their washroom, like a little kid asking the teacher for permission. He was raised to be nice to women. He loved his mother. Like I said, my vision isn't so great, but I could see him smiling from across a crowd. I was grateful every time he came into a room."

"You're going to just have to grieve, you know. This is something you have to do. It's going to hurt."

"I gave up my job for him. I moved to a city where I knew no one, just so he could leave me there. I never once said, '*Could we wait to move until my father finishes fucking dying?*'"

The woman in the seat in front of me whipped around and unnested her glasses from her perm, lowering them to the end of her nose so she could see me properly as she hissed, "*I have a child with me.*" Whispering was safer.

"You've got a lot of anger. You'll have to talk to this guy, work these feelings out. Are you going to see him now?"

"I'm going to my sister."

"I hope you guys get along better than me and my sister." Rochelle patted me on the knee. She said, "Sounds like you're going through a lot right now. Thanks for sharing it with me. I'm going to have to get back to this book, but if there's anything in here I think might be of use to you, I'll let you know."

Rochelle snapped open her book and began reading. I looked down at the smear of text on the page and then across the aisle at the mountains that were getting closer. Getting bigger. The Ringolos man waved his finger at me.

The right question was the one that never left me. The right question was important because it was the question she would ask me. I didn't need to wonder what I was doing. I needed to answer why I hadn't done it sooner. We were only children when I lost her, when she went, alone, out of the world we knew. Why did it take me three quarters of my life to go after her?

Rochelle was asleep when we hit it. Outside the window the sky had a thin yellow stripe of field beneath it, that was all. I was watching what looked like a storm go rolling across the sky, maybe an hour or a day away, who knew out here. And then the bus braked.

We were thrown forward with the hideous sensation of impact, our momentum colliding with something unmoving. It felt, briefly, as if the bus beneath us had been set free from the road.

We came to a stop at the side of the highway. From nine rows back, I heard the driver curse beneath his breath, it was that quiet. He stood up and looked out the windshield for a long moment, and then he pressed the button to open the door and climbed down. The lucky ones on the right of the bus leaned over to peer at him down there and report back to the left side of the bus.

"What is it?" asked the permed woman in front of me. "Is it a person? Oh my god, is it a child?"

Someone at the front of the bus called, "He's got a cellular phone. He's calling someone."

"Oh my god," said the woman with the perm.

I suddenly felt a sort of peace come over me. It was like sliding into a very deep tub of warm water. It was something I was inside.

"I'm going to see what's going on," a man at the front of

the bus said. He was wearing a dark suit and a black fedora, like he'd left some other time to take a seat on this bus.

"Me too," said a young woman beside him, and suddenly, half the passengers were on their feet and pushing their way through the aisle and down the steps to the ground outside.

"Rochelle," I said softly, and then louder. I even touched her, just a little on her shoulder. She still slept, the book against her chest and her face turned to the side in such a way that her neck looked like it was broken. Girls her age didn't think about their necks. Or what might be under the wheels of the bus they were on. "*Rochelle.*"

Her eyes flickered for a moment, and I told her to move over so I could get past. "Hurry," I said.

I was among the last to leave the bus. Outside, we waited ten feet back from the driver, who knelt to peer into the ditch.

"It's an animal," said someone, and I heard the disappointment in his voice.

"It's a bear," said the driver.

"Is it alive?" I heard myself ask. "Did we kill it?"

The driver stood up. He was a short, delicately built man. I could see in the way he carried himself what disdain he had for us. "I called it in," he said. "They'll see that the people who need to know are told. It's not our business. They'll send someone out here to clean up. And shoot the animal if need be."

I felt myself wander forward with the other passengers until we were just behind the driver, like we felt safer with him in front of us.

"Look," a child's voice said, "it's moving."

It looked like a wet heap of brown fur, its face turned away from us, except for its paws, which were turned so that we could see the dark pads beneath them against the grass. Its rear paws moved slowly, slightly, as if they were paddling in water. Viewed like that, with the underside exposed, they had the shape of human feet.

A few people lit up cigarettes and the driver watched them for a moment, and I thought he would tell them to get back on the bus, but instead he reached into his pocket and withdrew one of his own. He lit it and began walking down the highway, away from us, as if he'd leave us there.

I watched a man position his wife and daughter at the side of the road and crouch to photograph them with the bear behind them. The wife buried her face in her daughter's curled, dark hair. She was laughing and holding her daughter as tightly as she could.

It was the best I'd felt in months. As things had gotten worse and worse with Stephan, I'd felt myself learn how to be in a room and leave it at the same time. His sharp words, his irritation, and then his silences made a balloon out of me. I felt myself go floating up and away, from a string that grew longer and longer. I'd feel afraid and then I'd find myself thinking of something else. Like things came very, very close to me but never quite arrived.

There was a stink in the air, and we all smelled it and knew it was coming from the bear. A constellation of flies was circling above him, waiting.

Once when I urged him to see the psychologist his neurologist recommended, Stephan had crumpled up the paper with her number and thrown it at me. "Which of us needs help here?" he asked me. And for a moment, I was a woman who wasn't sure. And then I was a balloon, far, far away. But when he left, I figured out pretty fast the difference between me and a balloon. I hit the ground like a VCR. And I knew then that he'd been right. And I was crazy.

Except that, at this moment, I could see the bear and could hold the thought of the bear in my mind for minutes at a time and not think of anything else. Of how I was standing or of who was behind me or even of Stephan. Even of Stephan. But I could turn my back on the bear and begin walking back to the bus and stop thinking of the bear. I was going to be all right. I was saner than anyone on the bus.

Even of Stephan.

Climbing the steps, I heard a cry behind me. "It's moving!" a woman shouted. "It's trying to get up!"

The driver began herding the passengers back to the bus. I looked out the windshield and tried to see back down in the ditch, but the bear looked motionless. "Stupid bitch," I whispered to the bear. "She doesn't know a thing. Not even a dead bear."

Because when my father told me where she was, I hardly knew even how to find it on a map and it was too far for me to imagine a way across that kind of distance or what I'd find when I had crossed it. Because when he said her name, it was the first time either of us had spoken it in decades and I realized I had all these years imagined she was long gone from any map, that I had somehow understood the world to have removed her in some permanent way, like death removes someone. But even death leaves a mark, the place where the person was, the things they left behind, and when she was gone, my life closed up around her and there was nothing left except my own reflection in the mirror, which would sometimes startle me for how much it looked like her. I never thought of looking for her because it never occurred to me that she had gone somewhere where I could follow after.

My father was dying for a long time before he was dead. He must have told me to visit her a hundred times before, at the end, I found out where she was. I hadn't seen her since we were children and she was put in the custody of a second cousin in Alberta, while I was sent to a great-aunt in Halifax, who said she couldn't care for two children, let alone one of them stone blind. (It was only what she called Christian charity that kept her paying my tuition at the boarding school I was sent to after it was discovered that one could not go to school with boys and girls who could distinguish each letter on the page if one could not do the same. That if one was legally blind, it was, in the end, not so much more helpful than being blind the way stones apparently were.) At my father's funeral, the second cousin's daughter came down from Ottawa. She told me the name of the town where my sister had moved years ago. Somewhere in the northern territories, farther away from my home than anyone I knew had ever gone. Long before Stephan left me, I had meant to find a way across the map to look for her. But there was always a reason not to go.

I hardly knew I'd slept except that when I opened my eyes, the seat beside me was empty. A man with a dark, beautiful face was sitting across the aisle now.

"Excuse me," I said. "Excuse me. Do you know where we are?"

"Well, you just missed the coffee stop in Fort Nelson, didn't you."

"How far is that from the Yukon?" I asked the beautiful-faced man.

"I guess we're going to cross the border before dinner, that's what I would say."

"Oh." I stared out the window, where hills were climbing higher into the streaked sky and disappearing behind us. "I guess that's the last stop. I guess we'll all have to get out then."

"Mm-hmm."

I took a deep breath as he turned his face toward the window. "The thing is," I said, "the thing is, I just realized that I'm not sure where I'm going."

"Bus is a good place for someone in that situation."

"My sister's in Dawson City. It's up there above Whitehorse, the Greyhound attendant said."

"Sure."

"The Greyhound attendant said there's no bus to Dawson City. He said I could get a plane, but . . . I don't like to fly. And I don't drive." I flinched at the wheedling tone in my voice. I heard what I was, a middle-aged woman, all but lost, clutching at the mercy of strangers. Stephan had once said, irritated and trying to hide it in a joke, that I would be needy if I had any social skills. He told me it was only my congenital churlish streak that drove people away before I had a chance to cling to them. "He said I'd have to buy a ticket for a tour bus, but I don't even know how to find one. I don't know anyone in Whitehorse. I . . . I don't even have a winter coat."

"You can always wear all your clothes together. Just layer them up."

"I didn't bring much . . ."

A woman's voice from the seat behind me said, "He's teasing you, honey."

I turned around to see a brown-haired woman who was either young-looking for her age or old before her time—there was some war being fought on her face but it was unclear who was winning.

"You don't need a winter coat in Dawson in June," the woman said. "We got plenty of winter when it's winter, but we sure as hell get summer. I left three weeks ago and it was already getting warm."

"Oh," I said.

"I got a load to pick up in Whitehorse, before I head up to Dawson, but you can ride beside me if you want. I'll be driving all night, so if you can stand another six hours on the road, I'll get you there first thing in the morning. Annie."

I was confused for a moment before I realized the woman had reached a slim hand around the back of the seat. I took the hand. "I'm Aileen."

"So, you like to dance, Aileen?" asked the beautiful-faced man.

"Oh, I love to dance," Annie said.

"Aileen here looks like a dancer."

"That long neck," said Annie.

"I don't dance, no," I said quickly.

"I saw this movie once," said the man. "Or was it a dream? *Pomegranate,* it said at the beginning, like in this old-fashioned writing. Must have been a black and white movie."

"Oh, I saw this one," said Annie.

"Starts out, there's this pencil making a line down a page. It's all quiet, so you just hear the scrape of the pencil on the paper. And then the line bends a little and it's drawing the side of a face, you realize. Just one line to stand for the side of someone's face."

Annie nodded, as if she were helping him along. For a moment, all I could hear was the man's low, gentle voice and not anything else. Not even the sound of our front door, closing again and again.

"There's a voice, but you can't see who's talking. He says, 'I draw no one but her. I draw her always.' And then you see a woman dancing, and she's young and beautiful. Oh she's so young. She's a ballerina. She's dancing and dancing in this studio and all the light gets in from the windows. And there's this man, he's a different sort of dancer. But he gets in there and he's dancing with her, in this different sort of way. It's beautiful, the two of them together. They go on and on, they dance everywhere, all over the room, for days and years. There are things going on around and behind them, because they go so many places and such a long time goes by, but I don't know what those things are. Then one day he looks for her there and she's gone. The room is full of little girls dancing, children in skirts spinning around and around, but none of them is her. Even though he knows that, he grabs one of the girls, so he can see her child face and look at it up close, and he says again and again, pressing his cheek to her little-girl face, his voice so sad you know his heart is broken because it isn't her, but he doesn't even know that, he wants it to be her so bad, 'Pomegranate . . .'

"And then you see a bus making its way down this skinny little road around this big hill. Coming down the hill. And the sides of the bus, it's all covered in ads like they are. But the ads are drawings of the dancer's face. All over the bus. And at the back of the bus she's sitting, with the road just sort of disappearing in the glass behind her. With her ballerina hair and her ballerina face and her ballerina eyes that could be anyone's eyes. Just looking. All finished something. And you hear the voice from the beginning, and he says, 'It is not so very hard to draw a woman who was happy.'"

"What a great movie," said Annie. "I love that one."

"I think it was a dream," said the man with the beautiful face.

"It reminds me of something," I said. I tried to remember what it reminded me of and then I realized. "One time my husband was driving and we saw this man just lying in the snow, it was winter, he was just lying in the snow beside the sidewalk across the street. So my husband stopped the car. He pulled over. All this traffic, people walking by, but my husband stopped and ran across the street—it must have been thirty below, and the man was out there with no coat or gloves or anything. I watched him from the window. My husband pulled him up to his feet. And then he started to go over again, taking my husband with him. But Stephan caught him and put him on his feet. And then he gave him something, money or something, and talked to him for a minute. I was getting angry because I was waiting. But he came back in the car and just started driving, without saying a word. I looked back just in time to see the man fall, slowly, slowly, slowly, like someone had a hold of him, all the way to the ground. He hit the snow and just lay there. My husband didn't see. I just never knew a person who would do something like that before. Who would go pick up a man on the sidewalk." I covered my face with my hands. "Oh, I'm sorry. I don't know why your story reminded me of that."

"It's about beauty," said the beautiful-faced man.

"And there's the falling part," said Annie. "That's sort of like dancing. A lot of those dancers, they jump in the air so high, and I just think, oh boy, she is going to really hurt herself when she comes down! I got a sister that used to do ballet. Her kids do it too. But they don't hurt themselves. They land like snow does, soft like that, like they've got their own invisible parachutes. But right up till that last second, sure looks an awful lot like falling."

"I think I might have just gotten distracted," I said. "I think I forgot what I was going to say. I'm not myself right now. Ever since he slipped on the roof—"

"Not to worry, honey. Hardly anybody in Dawson's themselves," Annie said, and then she took out a pink satin eye mask that said *dormir* on it and went to sleep. The man with a beautiful face and I sat in silence while British Columbia disappeared.

Because only once I'd been inside an airplane, and it was only a two-hour trip to see Stephan's sister in Toronto, but I shook the whole time, because there was nothing, not one thing, holding up that plane. Because when I put my hand out for Stephan's, he said, "You're being ridiculous—look at everyone around us. People fly every day and nobody but you thinks that the plane is going to fall out of the sky just because you're on it." And I looked around and it was true; everyone had their plastic cups of soda or their coffees and their papers, and they looked tired or cranky or they were asleep, but not one of them looked afraid. And so I knew there was something wrong with me. And that thing wrong with me was another reason that there was never a day I woke up and thought, *Now.* Now it's time to go and find her.

~

Whitehorse was a clean, small city stretched out beside a river. A man named Jim met Annie at the bus, and she introduced me to him. "Is he your husband?" I whispered, as we walked toward the truck.

"Hell, no, Jim? No, not that he doesn't take that kind of liberties sometimes. Me and Jim go way back. He's the only man I've known as long as I've known him and I can still stand. He's a fool though, and an asshole. They all are. But he's a good man as fools go."

As she backed us out onto the road, Annie explained she drove rigs all over Western Canada, and sometimes farther, too. "And I love it," she said. "Some folks just suffer through, because the money's good. But I've never minded it. Feels like you own the highway, and that's something. Some folks never get to know what that's like." Annie had her hair pulled through above the plastic strap at the back of her hat, and she looked almost like a kid. I hadn't realized how tiny she was until we'd stood up from our bus seats, and I saw that her shoulders hardly cleared the back of the seat. And then Jim, sitting on the other side of me, was maybe the biggest man I'd ever seen. When he hugged Annie at the bus station, he picked her up so high that you could see what a fluid movement it would be for her to keep flying over his head, for him to just heave her up into the air.

"You ever been in one of these?" Annie asked.

"No," I said. I'd had no idea how high truck drivers rode. It didn't feel like driving. It was like we were sailing along above the traffic, just minding the lanes.

"Oh, it's a trip," said Annie.

"So, Aileen," said Jim. "This here's your first time going to Dawson?"

I nodded. I'd never been anywhere. Toronto was the farthest from home I'd ever gone. Jim looked at me with interest, while Annie was busy watching the road, which was paved but rough.

"Oh honey, you're going to love it," Jim said.

"Jim was born there," said Annie. "He thinks nothing's got scratch on Dawson. You could be in New York City, and he'd be standing there saying, 'What's the big deal?'"

"In gold rush days, they called it the Paris of the North. You know that, Aileen?"

I didn't.

"So why are you coming here?" Jim asked. "You looking for work?"

"No," I said. I hesitated. I didn't like how friendly he was, how he was leaning to look me right in the face, even though I kept my eyes fixed on the road. I didn't like his hand on the seat-back behind me. I said, "I'm not looking for work."

"Oh," said Jim. "Aileen's got secrets." He said my name like *Eileen*.

"Plenty of people in Dawson have secrets. Jim, you ought to be used to people not liking to be asked too many questions," Annie said, but she took her eyes off the road to give me a deep, hard look.

"It's bright out," I said. "This is what they call the midnight sun?"

"Oh this is nothing," said Jim. "Just you wait. Right now, back south, you'd be seeing the sun start to drop, right? In another hour or two, it'd be gone. But you watch. By the time we drop you off in five hours, it'll still be so bright you could do your needlework outside."

"Where are we dropping you off anyway?" Annie asked. "You said you got a sister or something here? She expecting you?"

"No," I said. "She doesn't know I'm coming."

Annie gave me another look. She said, "Most folks let someone know when they're coming to stay."

"I don't actually know where she lives. We haven't talked in a long time."

"I got a sister like that," said Jim. "She got out so fast we hardly knew her. Like she was just waiting to go since my mother birthed her. She moved to Arizona, of all places. I haven't talked to her in years. Don't need to either. I got no love in me for that country, or the people there." He reached behind him and pulled out a can of beer, which he cracked open. I looked back to see a two-four. He offered me his can, and I shook my head.

"Well, if you're drinking, I'm smoking and that's that," Annie said. She lit up a cigarette, and Jim wheeled down his window. She said, "Jim doesn't like me smoking, but it's none of his damn business."

"I never had a cigarette in my life," said Jim. "My mother smokes, my sisters smoke, my brother smokes. But I hate the shit."

"He just likes sitting there like a bastard judging people."

"You smoke?" Jim asked me, and I shook my head again. He said, "Me, I've got to protect my singing voice. You sing?"

"No," I said.

"Jim, don't you start. Half the time, he sings the whole way. Not normal singing either. Opera shit. If there's something worse than being stuck in a cab with someone singing in Italian, I don't know what it is."

"I love Verdi," said Jim. "But Wagner's my favourite. You like him?"

"I don't really know opera," I said.

"Some folks don't like him because they say he was a Nazi. I don't go in for that. I've got no problem with Jews. I've got no problem with anybody. Except Americans. And the French. You French?"

"No," I said.

"Just as well. We get a lot of French up here. But I figure, I don't got to like the guy, I just like his music. Right?"

"I guess so," I said.

Jim tossed the can in the back and opened another.

"You keep drinking at that pace, Jim," said Annie, "and I'm going to have to toss you out by Carmacks."

But he did keep drinking, and Annie kept driving, and I looked out longingly at the scattered houses of Carmacks as we passed by without anyone tossing anyone out of anything.

Because there was Stephan, there was always Stephan. And because not one day was I ever sure that if I were to leave, he'd still be there when I came back.

It was around midnight that we passed the Dawson airport.

"We gotta take Aileen up to the Dome," said Jim. "Come on, Annie. It's the first time she's seen Dawson."

"Jim, I'm warning you. I'm tired as hell and I've got no patience. We're not going anywhere but home."

"Come on, Aileen. Tell her. The first time you see Dawson you gotta see it from the Dome."

"What's the Dome," I said.

"It's the big hill by Dawson. You can see the rivers and the city from there. It's just a view. Nothing special," Annie said, lighting a new cigarette with the still-burning end of the one before.

"Annie, you'd tell God and his angels they're nothing special. It's the prettiest thing I've ever seen. Woman, you take us up the Dome."

"Don't you call me *Woman.*"

"Woman, I'll call you whatever I want if you don't take us up the Dome. Aileen wants to see the Dome."

"I don't really care," I said.

"You think your shit smells real sweet, don't you," said Annie. She'd put away a few cans during the last few hours of the drive, and her face had taken on a suspicious look. "Care about precious little from the look of you. Jim wants to show you his town. We gave you a ride all this way, and he wants to show you his hometown. Show some manners."

She turned a hard right, and the truck began to edge its way around an enormous hill. She had animal eyes. Glittering animal eyes. She said, "Don't know that I should really have this rig on this road. Give me another beer, Jim."

Jim passed her one and reached across my lap to pat her knee. "You're my girl," he said.

"Shut your mouth, you drunk."

Jim shut it in a big smile, and beamed at us both and at the road all the way to the top. We jackknifed into the parking lot, where two other cars were stopped, empty. Jim stumbled a little unsteadily from the truck door and offered me a dirty hand. I clambered out Annie's door instead.

We were at the edge of a hill that plunged down into the sprawl of a town at the base, where two rivers met.

"The brown river's the Klondike and the clear one's the

Yukon. You can see them still separated there, between the dirty half and the clean half," said Jim.

"I thought it was a city," I said.

"Used to be," said Jim. "In gold rush days, it was booming. Now I don't suppose there's much more than a couple thousand of us left, even in summer.

"Check it out." He pointed. "That's Annie's place, way up there in the corner, and I'm just down the road a ways. Best bar in town's The Pit, you can just about see it down there. They'll still be drinking hard there. We should hit it for a couple more drinks. Annie, I can give you a spin on the dance floor."

"Piss off," said Annie, opening another can.

"Come on, Annie. Annie's a beautiful dancer, aren't you, hon." Jim grabbed her from behind and put his arms around her. Annie fought him, her face nasty and pinched.

"I said piss off, you fool."

I wondered if I should intervene. Jim had his arms around Annie as lovingly as if she had asked for it. And suddenly, her face softened into a thrill of a smile.

"Come on, Annie," said Jim. He hummed something that sounded more like country than opera, and the two of them danced like that on the hill. I felt uncomfortable and trudged down the hill a little way. I had fifty dollars on me and a credit card. My bank card. I hadn't worked out money with Stephan before he left. I had no idea if he was still drawing on my account or adding to it. I wished I could hike from here down to the town and get a hotel without needing to say anything else to these people. I looked back and they were still dancing. He had a deep smile on his face, pressed against Annie's hair and the side of her face. She'd taken her hat off, or it had fallen off. She was so tiny, he was bent in two over her, but he looked

53

like there was no other way to dance. He moved like a different kind of man. Like a gentle man. Like a man who would
ask permission to use someone's bathroom.

"I'm going to go down now," I said. "I've got to find a
hotel room. Can I just follow this road down?"

Annie turned to me, her face still smiling like she was a
little girl at Christmastime. "You do what you want, honey.
But it's a long road down and no hotels to be had this time of
night. Be careful of the bears."

"You're not walking down," said Jim, letting go of Annie.
"We'll drive you. You can crash with me tonight. I got lots of
space."

"The hell you do," said Annie. "She's staying at my place.
You got a tent?"

"No," I said. "Just that suitcase, that's all I brought."

"You'll have to get one tomorrow if you don't find your
sister. You can crash on my couch tonight. Let's get out of here."

We drove into town, in the strange blue light of near dark
that never quite became dark. When we dropped Jim off,
Annie got out of the truck and hugged him for a long time. He
opened his arms to me, but I stayed in the truck.

"You have a nice visit," said Jim. "I bet that sister of
yours'll be real glad to see you. It was nice to meet you and I
hope to have the pleasure again."

"You're such a cornball when you've been drinking," said
Annie.

"Hey, Aileen, you know I've got a boat. I could take you
out on the water—you like fishing?"

"No," I said. Annie looked at the ground and Jim turned
sad, blurry eyes to me. "I don't really want to go fishing," I
said.

"Okey-dokey," said Jim. "Well, I'll be seeing you, Annie."

"You take care of yourself," she said.

Because until Stephan left me, I had always been just this side of being alone. But never all the way. Until he left, I never had a whole week of nights in the dark remembering how three years of my life long ago had been lived in the dark and how there had always been another out in that darkness, a hand waiting if I reached mine out . . .

We drove to Annie's house in quiet. It was a small, white wood-frame house. Annie piled a blanket and a pillow on a couch. "There you go," she said. "There's coffee by the fridge, but I'll ask you not to wake me in the morning."

"Thank you," I said. "Thank you for the ride and letting me stay here. I don't know what I would have done."

Annie had the hard, shining eyes of someone who's had too much to drink, but her voice was sober. "You got a mean streak in you, don't you," she said softly. "You shouldn't have treated Jim like that. He's a good man. There's no cause for treating people that way."

Before I could say anything, she turned around and switched off the light. "Good to meet you, Aileen," she said, and headed up the stairs.

I stretched out on the couch, leaving the blanket on a chair beside me. The night was warm. I closed my eyes, but already the blue light was getting brighter and whiter, filling the room. I lay awake for hours in the quiet of someone else's house.

Mara

THREE

AND THAT WAS HOW I would answer him when he asked. Again and again he asked me to tell him the story of what happened, and again and again it was the same story I told. Until my answer became his.

But there were the things he never asked. He worried one question like the ocean worries a stone until all that was left of the question was the answer I gave, which got harder and surer as the question itself dissolved. Eventually I could have said to him, "You are the story I am telling you," because that was what he was and all he was and he was the only thing that was, that I had ever had for my own. "Tell me what happened to you," he said, since he was only a child, and long after he knew every word I would answer. And he meant, "Tell me why you can't see," and so I told him what answered that, but what he came to mean later, and only I knew it then, was, "Tell me what the difference is between what happened to you and what you are." And what he didn't know to ask was what I never told him. How a story, like an answer, is a net made out of holes, and it's in the holes that he should have gone looking.

Aileen

❧

early June 1996

FOUR

I DREAMT OF OUTER SPACE. I dreamt I was a child, paddling the darkness as I swam in a vast ocean of stars.

And then my dream collided with a sun-glared living room I didn't recognize. I peeled my face from a rough wool blanket beneath me, squeezed my eyes shut again, and thought for several moments before I remembered where I was. *Dawson,* I thought at last. Oh hell. Then I opened my eyes and looked around.

It was a fussy, mismatched sort of room. All the furniture had flower patterns on it—the overstuffed cotton sofa beneath me, the sectional couch that faced it, and an armchair by the door—but none of the patterns matched, and the curtains were made of white eyelet lace that did not look entirely clean. I heard a floorboard squeak above me and stood up. She had told me I was cruel.

I knew the kind of look she'd given me. She was like people back home in Halifax, where people's friendliness was a measure of how big a fool they thought you were. They liked the look of themselves doing favours and thought you might fall for thinking that was kindness. Annie's eyes had said what she thought of her and what she thought of me. So I found my suitcase where I'd set it down by the door and I left Annie's house.

It was even hotter outside. The sun was so bright that, for a moment, as the door closed behind me, I couldn't see anything at all. Then, when I squinted, I saw a street that seemed to have been peeled out of the Wild West. Elderly couples clung to each other and strolled down board sidewalks lining an unpaved road that shook brown dust into the air every time a car went past. The storefronts that faced me had signs painted in the sort of typeface usually reserved for phrases like "Wanted: Dead or Alive." It was as if the entire town had at some point conceded that it would no longer be an actual town. Instead it had become a myth of itself: a museum harbouring its own memory of having once been a real place.

I followed the sidewalk I was on until its end, and then I got a glimpse of the river several blocks away and realized there was little more to the town than I had just walked and the distance between where I stood and the riverbank. Somehow it had looked bigger from far above.

I cut down to the next street below and saw a hotel sign. I pushed open the door underneath it and approached the desk inside, where a boy stood staring at something in his hands. He had hair combed over his eyes in stringy points and shoulders that poked through his T-shirt like sticks. "I need a room," I told the boy.

"How many nights?" he asked, without looking at me.

"I don't know." I thought. "Maybe a while," I said.

He shook his head. "No rooms," he said, and I stepped

closer till I could see he had one of those little electronic games in his hand, and it was that he was staring at.

I put down my suitcase. "Where can I get a room?"

He shrugged. "Nobody's open before June 14. Any place open now is booked."

"But *you're* open." I wanted to snatch the game from his hand. He had a slack, sullen face, and I knew that behind his lowered lids, his eyes would have that dull, empty look all kids' eyes seemed to have these days. I felt my heart rate become faster till I could hear the pressure of blood in my ears and throat.

"But we're booked."

"Booked until when? Can I get a room tomorrow?"

He shrugged again. "Don't know. I'm just watching the desk for Ivan. Ivan said no rooms."

"What do I do?" I asked. He hadn't looked at me yet and my voice sounded too high, too thin.

"Lady," he said. "Lady, lady, lady."

"I'm looking for my sister," I said softly, my voice anemic, my voice a bony hand reaching.

"So stay with her," he said.

I didn't mean to start crying. I never cried in public. But I did and it was then he put down his game and looked at me. At first I thought he was disgusted, embarrassed because I was old and a woman and maybe I reminded him of his mother, but he just stared at me and I stared back. He had long, dark, wet-looking eyelashes around his pale eyes, the eyes of a startled, lovely girl.

"Ivan will be back soon," he said at last. "You wait there." And there was no chair where he pointed, only a flight of stairs, so I nodded and wiped my face and stood by the stairs to wait for Ivan.

An hour passed while I stood by the stairs. Not one person came in or went out the front doors, and the boy didn't raise his eyes from the game in his hands. Eventually I sat down on the bottom step, and the boy said nothing. The room was so dim that I struggled to keep my eyes open. It was warm and airless and lit only by a narrow barred window facing the street and a piano lamp on the glossy desk shielding the boy. I couldn't tell if the wallpaper was pink or brown, but a headache had begun pounding behind my eyes, and I slowly came to feel as if the walls were the colour of the inside of my head and its pain. Finally I stood up.

"Listen, kid," I said to the boy, "are you from this town?"

He set the game down on the desk and it made a series of tinny sounds. "No," he said, "but Ivan is."

"I can't wait for Ivan," I said. "I've got to find my sister. Listen, kid, I have to tell you something and you may not be ready to hear it."

"I don't know," he said.

"I have to tell you that it is rude to play with that thing when someone is talking to you. You've got a job here, do you understand that? It might not seem very important to you, and it isn't really a very important job. It's kind of a stupid job. But when somebody is here for a reason that is important, like if somebody is here to find their sister, you've got to do better than this."

He blinked and then the door swung open. "That's Ivan," he said, glancing at the door.

Before I turned, I leaned over the desk and said, "The whole point is to look at people and listen to them. The whole point of the whole thing is to not be staring at some goddamn video game."

"Like life, you mean?"

I wondered if he put gel in his hair to make it into those little points, if he was so stupid he thought that was the kind of thing he should spend his time on, or if he was just so dirty, his hair found its own way to looking stupid.

"Like life," I said and looked at Ivan, who crossed the room with a sigh. He was a dark-haired, heavy-set man whose features seemed to have retreated from his wide cheeks and jaw to crowd the centre of his face. His eyes were so close together they almost crossed as they stared at me.

"You need a room?" Ivan asked.

"Yes," I said.

Ivan unhooked a key from a line of nails behind the desk and handed it to me. "Taz, get her credit card. It's a no-smoking room. No pets either."

Then Ivan climbed the stairs, and only after he had disappeared did I remember that I hadn't asked him if he knew my sister. By the time I turned back around, Taz was handing me back my card. "All done. Enjoy your stay."

I slept until past dinnertime. When I woke, I was shocked to realize I had fallen asleep right on top of the plaid bedspread. "You think they wash these for every guest?" I'd always told Stephan when we stayed at the motel by his sister's place.

My headache had somehow gotten worse while I slept. Rubbing my temples, I stood and looked out the window at the town below. It was so small and yet I hadn't a clue how to find her in it. I would have to ask someone—who knew how many people—till I found someone who could tell me where she was.

Exhausted at the thought, I sat back down on the bed. No one knew I was here. There wasn't anyone to know, not really. With Stephan gone, and the only people we'd met in Toronto friends of his from work. I'd had a few friends left from the university I'd taught at in Halifax, and when we lived there we'd have dinner with them once in a while. But they weren't the kind of friends you kept in touch with once you were gone from a place. So there was no one but Stephan to tell that he had left me.

It was thinking that that made me realize I could just as easily leave this place as stay. No one would miss me if I left. My sister, wherever she was, would have long ago stopped wondering when I'd come for her, if she ever wondered at all. The few people I'd met would be glad enough not to see me again—Annie and that boy at the desk. If I could just get a ride somehow back to Whitehorse, I could sleep away the four-day drive home and it would be as if all this had been a dream. There'd be nobody I'd even need to confess how stupid I'd been to—it would be as if I'd never come and I could resume my life as if I'd never left it.

But at the thought of turning the key in the lock of the front door of our house, I felt a chill. What life, after all, would I be resuming? I had only a part-time job teaching rudimentary grammar to Korean immigrants, and nothing to spend my days on except thinking about a long trip I'd taken to find no one and then come home again to no one.

I couldn't stand being in the hotel room. I noticed a faint stain on the quilt by my hand or maybe just a worn spot, something that reminded me of the hundred other bodies that had slept on it, fucked on it, sat at the bottom of the worst of their godforsaken lives on it and tried to weasel out of the one thing they'd meant to do. I had to leave.

I grabbed my purse from the bedside table and hurried out the door and down the stairs. Taz didn't look up as I passed him, and I slammed the front door behind me as I stumbled down the steps onto the street.

The sun was still high and bright overhead, and I squinted as I made my way along the sidewalk with the idea of the river in my head. I got as far as I'd gone earlier in the day, and then I turned down toward the water and kept walking. Down by the shore I could see a couple dozen people gathered, and I could hear a woman singing.

As I got closer, I could hear her voice rise and fall in the air. A guitar rang out. She hit a high note that seemed unlikely, even impossible, her voice flickering so easily all the way up there and down again.

It was music like the folk songs of my childhood. Earnest, not tired like most music I heard these days. It was some kind of love song she was playing. I could tell that from just the sound of it. How it made me think for a moment again how easy it would be to go home. How I might go about finding him, how I might ask one more time for him to stay . . . the other words I might use to convince him.

I crossed the last street before the river and climbed down the hill to where people were gathered in front of the woman with the guitar. She was just finishing her song when I took a seat on the grass not too far from her. I realized she was scarcely a woman at all; her face was still round and girlish and almost too large for her slightly plump but delicate frame. And then I realized that some of the words she sang weren't English. She had light brown skin and black hair. Maybe she was Native Canadian. Or were they Inuit here?

An old man seated beside me put two fingers in his mouth and whistled when the song ended. The singer said she would take a short break. I heard again the scrape of our front door against the floorboards as he closed it behind him. The sound, still in my ears, was getting louder.

I suddenly realized that Stephan didn't know where I was. If he were to try to reach me. I pictured my kitchen, yellow in the afternoon light. I pictured the phone on the wall, ringing.

"Mara?"

A young woman, maybe ten years younger than me, stood before me. She had a broad face and long black hair. An Indian woman—no, *Inuit*, I thought. The woman stared at me, and I stared back.

"You aren't Mara," said the woman slowly.

I was confused, and then I understood.

"Who the hell are you?"

"Mara's my sister," I said. "She's my sister. You know her? You know where she is?"

There was no need for the woman to look at me with such mistrust. Like she thought I was a liar or dangerous. The woman stepped back and looked over at the singer, who was holding her guitar by the neck and leaning against the gazebo, talking to a dark-haired man. The woman reached into her pocket and pulled out a cigarette and lit it with her face down.

"Okay," she said. "How come I've never seen you before?"

"I haven't seen Mara since we were children. I came here to find her. Is she here? Can you tell me where to find her?"

The woman exhaled smoke in two columns through her nostrils. "Okay," she said again. "I think you better talk to Jason."

I felt myself get angry. "Who's Jason? Where's Mara?"

The woman narrowed her eyes and said, "Jason's her son. You stay here and I'll get him. You stay here."

As the woman walked away, turning once to look back at me, I was suspicious. My father had not said anything about Mara having a son. Why should I have to speak to this child instead of to my sister? I was tempted to leave. Then I wondered, And go where? I thought again of my kitchen.

The singer was staring at me. The woman who'd spoken to me approached her, and I saw the singer put her hand over her sweet, pretty mouth and nod.

"Who are you," said a man's voice.

I turned around and saw the man who'd been talking to the singer. He was maybe in his twenties. He had dark, narrow eyes. His face was angry, but as I looked at him something loosened in his mouth and eyes.

"You aren't her son," I said. He was too old. He did not look like her. He was a liar.

"Ma," he said. "Who are you. Who the hell are you," He looked younger now than I'd thought. Maybe just twenty or even a teenager. He stepped toward me and then he was in my arms. I didn't know who opened whose arms first.

"I told you she looked just like her," said the first woman to the singer, who now stood beside us.

As fast as he was in my arms, he was out of them. "What are you doing here," he said. "Why'd you come here."

"I wanted to see Mara. I wanted to see my sister."

"I told you," said the woman. "But older, right? And those yellowy streaks in her hair. Mara never dyed her hair."

I spoke to the boy. "Can you take me to—"

"She's dead," he said and turned his back to me. "Which one of you wants to buy me a beer."

The sweet-faced singer answered quietly, "I will. Let's go, Jason."

The air was hot and dry, and the sun was burning the back of my neck and the part of my hair.

"You're a liar," I said softly.

The boy didn't turn around, but the woman who had brought him there watched me. "He's telling you the truth," she said.

"What's his name?" I asked. "What did you say his name was?"

"It's Jason," said the woman. "I'm Minnie, and that's Angel"—she pointed to the singer—"and you'd better tell us your name."

I told them my name. Angel turned and looked up at me from the corners of her eyes and then turned her face down again. She fiddled with her hands and touched Jason's sleeve, but he didn't move.

"What happened to my sister?"

Minnie looked sharply at Jason.

"When did she die?"

"Don't you get too excited. It's been a long time now. Maybe five years she's been gone now," said Minnie.

"Six."

Even Minnie flinched. She nodded at Jason, who stared fiercely at the ground, as if he'd said nothing.

"It was sudden," Minnie said. "She didn't have any pain."

Jason stood up.

Suddenly his hand was in my face. I drew back, but he held his hand close, his thumb tucked into his palm, so that I could hardly see. "How many fingers am I holding up," he said. "How many fingers."

"Get away from me," I said. "You're not her son. She was so gentle."

"How many fingers."

"Four," I said. "Get away from me."

He took his hand away and looked hard at me. He was much taller than I. "How come you can see," he said. "How come she was blind and said it was something that happened to both of you."

I felt a hand at my waist and realized Angel was there beside me. She looked up at Jason, and he took his eyes off me to look back.

He was breathing deep and hard. "Who is she," he said.

"It's Mara's sister," said Angel. "You know she had a sister."

"Why didn't she come before."

"I don't know," she said softly. "I wish she'd come sooner."

Jason began to walk away from us.

"Jason . . ." called Angel.

He had this energy about him like he might suddenly stop walking and reach out and throw someone to the ground. I was trying to figure out how to leave. I was dizzy and tired. Far, far away, light was leaving my kitchen.

"I have to go," I said. I left them standing there, and I found my way back to the hotel. I climbed upstairs to my room, which exhaled faintly sour-smelling, warm air as I opened the door. It must have been late. It must have been nighttime by then. The sun was high in the sky, and I slept in its suffocating heat.

～

I woke from a dream of Stephan. Immediately I was unable to remember what he'd been telling me. I knew if I moved, the dream would be lost forever, so I kept my head still on the pillow and closed my eyes, digging deep into the dark there. Reaching back for my dream. Then I heard my name again.

"Aileen?"

I hadn't realized until I heard it again that it was the sound of my name that had woken me. And then a knock on the door.

"Aileen, are you in there?"

I stood up slowly and went to the door. Through the peephole, I saw a face I didn't recognize looking back at me. Then I remembered her name. "What do you want, Angel?" I said through the door.

She apologized for waking me, but said Jason wanted to meet me at a bar in an hour. I didn't answer, and she knocked again. Her face was anxious and I was tired.

"How'd you know where I was staying."

She turned her face down. "I asked Ivan about you. There aren't very many places open now."

I slipped the chain lock off and turned the knob, peering at her through a crack just wide enough to rest my face between. "I don't have a real good reason to believe that roughneck kid that can hardly string together a sentence is my sister's son. But what I know for sure is that you aren't anything to me."

Her eyes watched mine for a moment and then she bobbed her head, like she'd understood something. "I'm sorry," she said. "I lied to you. I didn't ask Ivan. I followed Jason." The sides of her mouth turned up, but she wasn't smiling. "*He* followed you here." Then she turned away and headed down the stairs. I listened to the creaking of the steps under her feet and then I heard the front door close.

~

I tried to sleep again but felt smothered by the hot, airless room. "Are we that far north that it would be too many god-damn miles to drag a goddamn air conditioner?" I said out loud. The walls were so thin I thought maybe down at the front desk they would hear me.

At last, I threw on the lightest shirt I had and the only jeans I'd brought and left the hotel. I stopped at a restaurant on the way, but it was even warmer inside, so I took my sandwich to go and headed down to the river again. I passed where Angel and the others had gathered hours before, but they were gone now. The bank settled into rock and then to river. It was not such a steep walk down to the blue moving water. It looked so cool and fresh. I slipped my shoes off and stepped carefully down the rocks. I reached a foot into the river.

I'd never felt anything so cold in my life. It burned through me and I burst out laughing. I could hardly feel my foot and would not have been surprised to see it bobbing out to sea. I felt awake.

It was astonishing how swiftly my whole body was cooled by a moment's submersion of one part of it in the chill water. Now I felt more sure that the sun was lower than it had been and that the air was loosening its hold on the day's heat. I crouched down onto the rock and then spread both legs out and plunged each foot into the water.

Again I laughed.

And then I reached my hands into the water, so that I nearly fell in.

I was no longer young. I was, I supposed, middle-aged.

And I'd been an only child for six years and had not known it. And now I knew.

My hands burned and my feet burned and I thought my heart would stop. Stepping out of the water, I rubbed my hands and feet till the blood flow returned to them. Then I put on my shoes and walked back up the hill. Mara was so frightened of water. In that moment I could remember as closely as if my sister's damp, relentless hand was still in mine, how she had cried when our father taught us to swim.

I wasn't surprised when I saw Angel sitting there, beside the road, watching me and playing her guitar.

"You followed me again?" I asked.

"It was Jason who—"

"I know," I said, and she went back to her song. I couldn't figure out how I hadn't been able to hear her singing all the time, her voice was so clear now. I told her I was sorry and she nodded.

"We're late," she said, putting her guitar away and it made a soft thrum of sound, knocking against the case.

The bar was called The Pit and it was a good name. It was a good name for a place that felt like a basement but wasn't. It was the sort of bar I would have avoided back in Nova Scotia.

Angel and I took a place at a table along the back wall. I wondered why bars like this were compelled to line their walls with rusted bits of trash and kitsch. Why did they want this refuse to speak of the kind of place this was and what was kept in it?

The waitress was pretty and young and all wrong in this place. She was polite enough and brought us two pints that Angel ordered. It was the type of bad draft beer that tastes too sweet and then leaves its sour fingerprints in your mouth for hours afterwards. I drank it fast so I wouldn't taste it. I didn't see Jason anywhere.

"Maybe he didn't believe me that you would come," Angel said quietly.

"Maybe," I said, "he just didn't give a shit."

Angel turned her chair so she could see the door, and she watched it like a dog with its eye on a bone. I was grateful she didn't want to attempt some sham of a conversation, but it made me nervous to watch her in profile, staring steadily ahead and hardly blinking.

The waitress came and asked me what I wanted. I looked down and saw my glass was empty. "Another," I said. "Something in a bottle."

He hadn't left a phone number for me. I didn't know where he was staying, if he was even still in Toronto. He'd only been gone a few weeks. Was it stupid to leave, when the only way we could reach each other would be for him to find me in that house? He knew where I was if I stayed there. If he doubted. If he hesitated.

"We're like an old married couple," he used to say if I was naked in front of him unceremoniously. Cutting my toenails into the trash or dressing in a hurry in the morning. "We *are* an old married couple," I'd said to him. Again and again, he said that, I said that. I'd thought there'd be things like that we'd go on saying all our lives.

It could have become the kind of thing we'd look back on later, together. Not an ending, but a strange time that we got through, together. Maybe he was at my door the day after I left. Maybe he was at a bar somewhere right now, thinking of me, growing tipsy and dizzy with thinking of me.

"I'm going to find Minnie," Angel said, getting out of her chair so fast I gasped in surprise. "Maybe Minnie will know where he is."

I nodded. She walked away, and the eyes of the dirty men with their backs against the bar took the long measure of her and the way she walked across a room and out a door.

Stephan would get halfway to one place and then turn around and go back the way he'd come. He reached decision like steel reaches flint—a snap of thought and a glint in the air and then all was certain, but fitfully so. A question or a glimpse of something in the distance and everything could be changed. I'd seen it before, how I'd say something dull or too cloying and he'd become hard and far from me, defensive and even cruel. I'd feel him leave the room from across the table. There would be no way to bring him back into it. I could only wait until he saw a woman be kind to a dog, or a warm wind pushing the curtains apart and entering the house before a storm, and something would alter in him again and he'd be mine. He had the caprice of something horribly light in the air. A falling leaf that is lost to you at the last possible moment, that is taken by a wind so slight you only know it by the sudden, surprised emptiness of your open hand. I saw him at my door. It was yesterday, it was seven o'clock last night, it was exactly right now. That moment, whenever it was, would keep all of his secrets. His back at my door, his hand on the bell, peering through the window for light inside—what he looked like, what he thought of as he stood there before my empty house. His return to me would be forever bound to that moment, in conspiracy with a regret or hesitation I would never know of. Because I hadn't been home when he came back to me.

"Another," I said.

A bluegrass band was playing at the other side of the room. I hadn't noticed that they'd stopped tuning up and started playing real songs, but now the hands of some nicotine-faced man were fluttering up and down the neck of his guitar, and an ancient-looking singer was baying.

A plywood door swung open beside the bar and slapped against the wall like it was hardly worth the effort to stay on its hinges. Jason walked through the door and leaned against the bar and a beer slid in front of him. He picked it up without paying and began to drink. The old men at the bar were speaking to him, but he kept his eyes on the band and his mouth shut around the neck of his beer.

There was nothing of my sister in him. By now, I supposed, my sister would have looked old like me, but I remembered her soft, pink face and corn-coloured hair. His eyes were a dark slice across a hard brown face. There was no gentleness to him. There was swing in his walk, in his weight against the bar, but it was a violent sort of swing. Like there was something in him so fretful and charged, he was full of the mysteriousness of it. Like he was the wonder of something that might soon happen. You'd watch him, close to you, like you'd watch an animal that had been raised without kindness.

So then it was a man from here who had been the father of my sister's child. How did Mara find her way here? How funny that Mara, sightless, had made it so far, when I had hardly left the Atlantic.

I watched a girl approach Jason and get maybe half his attention for her trouble. He drank and watched the band while she looked up at him, laughing. Finally, the girl turned away, bored, and watched a piece of hair wind between her fingers. Jason looked up then and saw me.

Where was Angel and who the hell was she to have left me alone like this? She seemed sweet as pie, but I could tell there was steel in her someplace down deep. Maybe she'd planned this whole thing. To leave me here, drunk, with an empty glass and no way to go to the bar without speaking to him, and no way to leave the bar without speaking to him.

"You know you look like her," said a man's voice behind me.

I turned around and saw a hippie-looking fellow in a loose-brimmed green hat with shaggy grey hair around a shaggy grey face. "Mara? You know Mara?"

"I heard her sister came up here. I heard her sister didn't even know she was passed on. That true?"

I pushed back my chair. "I don't see how it's at all your business."

The man's face lost its earthy geniality. I saw it slip off a face as hard as Jason's. I turned my back while he was still putting his backcountry charm back together, and took my empty bottle to the bar.

"One of these," I said. I tapped the bottle with my finger. "The ones with the horse on them."

I grabbed the beer from the bartender's hand and looked at Jason over the bottle as I swung it up in my fist, like I used to drink as a teenager at the harbour. After I'd got switched over to the regular high school, the only kids who hadn't minded me hanging around were greasy-haired punks who'd dare me to dump bottle after bottle of whatever booze we could get our hands on down my throat. It made them like me, how I said yes to everything they could come up with. "You'll do anything," they said, and I wasn't stupid enough even then to think it was admiration in their voices, but what it was was close enough. They thought I was fearless.

"Where's Angel," Jason said.

"Went looking for Minnie. Or you. I don't know. So where's your father?" I settled my back against the bar, beside him.

"Dead."

The band was playing some reeling country song, and the bar folks were loving it. A crowd of girls and women were kicking their heels up and spinning each other around in time with the clinging, ringing snap of banjo strings.

"None of those girls were here two days ago," Jason said, flat.

"This band just touring up here?" I asked him.

"No, they all the time play here. Just not usually for a bunch of tarty southern city girls."

I looked at his hands, loose at the end of his bent arms, which rested against the bar. I looked at the way the fingers were long and thin and ever so slightly squared at the tips. I looked at my hands.

"Maybe you should go get Angel," I said.

"She'll find her way back," Jason said. He took his eyes off the band and I felt the angle of his face turn toward me, though he looked down at the floor. "When'd you get here," he said.

"Just yesterday. I didn't know how I would find her."

"You drive here," he asked.

"I took the bus, and then . . . I got a ride with someone," I said. The top of my head was perfectly aligned with the top of his shoulder. I was precisely the height of his shoulder.

"Uh-huh," he said. He shifted his body and looked at me straight. "So what are you doing here."

I told him.

I started with when we were small. Not when we were

together, but after we weren't anymore. After Aunt Una took me in to her south-end townhouse. I told him about how I was pulled out of the school she first sent me to because I couldn't seem to learn the letters and finally someone noticed it was my eyes and not my brain that couldn't figure out the difference between an *f* and a *p*. I told him about the school for the blind I was sent to, where we were taught to read with our fingertips. How after several years, I began to notice that I could make out larger print—street names on signs, children's books, the titles on book covers—the words that once were smeared shadows emerging into something like clarity. Until one day the commission gave me a special typewriter and told me I'd recovered as much of my vision as I ever would and was being transferred to the regular high school, where a special reader was being assigned to read me any books that weren't available in large type.

I told him I fell in love. And Stephan was the first thing I had ever been able to see clearly.

I finished my beer and took another from the bartender, but left it on the bar beside me, untouched. I told him how my aunt used to take me to see my father in the hospital once a year. How while I was at university I started to go more often, on my own. It would confuse things to say that I loved him, because I hated him a little, hated how even at the end of his life and the end of the beginning of mine, he was so mind-blowingly inadequate. How he was the smallest possible scrap of a family, but he was mine and I couldn't stop myself from seeing him. He was feeble and thin and looked like a paper man—I'd look at him and think of what he'd done to me and how I could take a deep breath and fill my lungs with what he took from me and blow it out and sweep away this paper man who was not even a paper father. Who was less even than that.

Angel came in the door and leaned against the wall beside us, listening for a moment. Then her eyes met mine, and she stepped away into the crowd of people stamping their feet and clapping at the whirling, winding, whorling thing the band was playing now.

I told him the doctors had asked me not to talk to my father about when Mara and I were young. They said it would only upset and confuse him, and that he wouldn't remember it anyway. So we never talked of another daughter, another sister. I'd tried as a child to find Mara. A teacher had helped me write to the family of a second cousin in northern Alberta who'd agreed to take in the fully blind child Aunt Una had felt incapable of caring for. But they had given Mara up after just a few months. She had been taken in by a Catholic charity home for the blind, which shocked me then but made me laugh inside my head years later by my father's bedside, because it would have killed him years before his heart did to know the papists had a hold of his own blood. The second cousin said she was better off there and never wrote again. The older I grew, the less I thought of my sister as a person who still lived in the world. When I was mistreated at school, I'd remembered this person who once was as close as my skin, but as if she was someone irretrievably gone.

The day I went to tell my father I would be leaving Halifax and would not be able to visit anymore, he asked if I was going to see Mara. He told me he had got a letter once from the cousin in Alberta. That she'd married and moved to some far-flung corner of the Yukon Territory. After I arrived in Toronto, when I phoned, he spoke more and more often and urgently about Mara. He often asked when I would visit her. Eventually I began to answer, "Soon."

"I didn't know until he died if it was true," I told Jason. "At the funeral, the daughter of the cousin in Alberta came. She told me it was true, and said Mara was living in Dawson last she heard. I swear I meant from then to come. But it was so far away, and I didn't know what kind of place this was, how you'd find someone here.

"Two weeks ago, Stephan left me. I waited for twelve days for him to come home. He didn't." I said, "I had nowhere to go."

Jason was turned so far from me I could almost see his back. I looked up at his face. His eyes. He was watching the dancers.

In front of the band, the long, swing-haired girls in their loose jeans and shiny lips were tiring. They were drunker, sexier. They wanted to be taken home. The boys watched from chairs and were too tired or too sad to take them home. A couple older women laughed to themselves and danced in a clumsy way, apart. In the dark, behind the other dancers, near the door, Angel held her hands above her like a child and moved her body ever so slightly, like a steel string plucked and ringing. Her black hair had light in it.

We tipped our bottles to our mouths and watched.

Mara

FIVE

WHEN YOU HAVE A CHILD, it's like all you are and everything that happened to you is just one story, and that is the story of how you got there, how you arrived to being the start of another person's life. Every story I told him was essentially that one, because that was the story he wanted, and after a while, that was the only story I had to tell. So I'd tell him the story of how I left the place where I started, but somehow that story always ended before it got to the place where I finished. Somehow we never came to speak of what had happened in between, about all the mornings and nights I lay awake alone in a bed far, far from the place I'd once thought to be the world, and how as I lay there I had not one idea of how my life would end. I never told him about the doctors who made me hold still so they could press their instruments against my eyes and sigh, so that I could imagine them shaking their heads at the woman who had brought me there.

All the things that got lost in the story I told him, all that happened in between, began with her, the woman who had brought me there. If I were to tell him now what I could not then, I would start by telling him about Nellie.

Nellie was a distant cousin of my mother and would often

heave sighs of her own and repeat to herself, as if reminding herself it was true, that her own mother would have wished it so. At last she told me the doctors had done all they could do for me and there was nothing left but to take me home with her. I didn't dare to ask her the question that was as much a part of me as the bones beneath my flesh, because I feared her answer.

She took me in her car with her to a hotel that she told me was near the airport, so we could get an early start. She took my hand to the surface of the bed so I could find my way along the mattress to take the other side beside her. I lay awake and listened to the sound of her turning pages beside me and knew the answer to the question I hadn't asked and that it would be only us two who'd take a plane into the sky tomorrow.

Minnie

~

late June 1996

SIX

I KNEW THE SECOND I saw her what I was looking at. There's trouble in pants, I thought to myself, and I went right up to it like someone who didn't know that the things that ruin people's lives can show up with dyed blond hair and a suitcase. I knew better, but I couldn't stop myself. Maybe, just for a second, I wondered what if he'd been telling the truth all this time. But I should have known better. He came out of his mother lying, and there wasn't anybody who could show up out of nowhere and make his lies true.

And of course, after that, there wasn't anything else to be done. I had maybe a moment when I could have pretended I didn't see her there, and maybe that would have been that. I looked hard at her the first time I saw her, when I was still trying to figure out what I was looking at, and I saw all of her. She was sharp and soft at the same time, bony hands and knees and elbows on arms and legs that looked like they had no muscle to them at all. Her face would have been good-looking once, like Mara's, but it was more worn out than Mara's ever got, with worried lines back and forth on her forehead and around her pale, watchful eyes. If I said this, nobody would know what I meant, because his were dark and much narrower, but they were Jason's eyes in her head. Her mouth was the only thing I liked about her. Her mouth looked like it could laugh good and hard, or tell a dirty joke. But I would have rathered I never heard one word come out of that mouth. And maybe if I'd just left her standing there by the river, looking like she'd been dropped there from the moon and didn't have the sense God put in a peanut, maybe then she'd have gone back wherever it was she came from. But there's no sense to that, to even wondering about that, because it isn't what happened, and after I'd let her say who she was, it was over for Jason and I knew I just had to wait for him to figure out what I'd known from the first second I saw her.

She didn't leave. She was moved into that hotel and had started calling it home. And I didn't buy it, because she came here from somewhere and that was where she'd go back to, sooner or later, and home was the place you were headed, not where you'd holed up for a while. But Jason did. "I've got to go home," she'd say at the end of a night and peel herself out of her chair, and I'd see his eyes shining when she said the word, because to him, I knew, she was saying, "I'm here." Or "I'll stay." Or something like that.

At first, she'd just sit at the bar beside him, mouthing the neck of a beer, and some nights hardly a word would pass between them. Or she'd listen while he talked to someone else. Or she wouldn't listen, just sit there glassy-eyed and looking like her mind had gone back to where she'd come from and left the rest of her there in the chair. It took nearly two weeks before she started to ask questions.

∼

That night, he had his back turned against her, though he wasn't talking to anybody else. I was watching the two of them, because I had it in my mind to keep an eye on her and because I could feel the stare of Glenn Stuckey on my back like it was his hot, stinking breath on me. I'd heard Glenn called a mean drunk, but he wasn't any nicer sober. "That kid should be with his father," he'd hissed at me when I sat down. "Some mother you are. Out at the bar till all hours with a kid at home. I pity that boy." He had the palest eyes I'd ever seen, and back when we were in school a lot of girls were taken with those eyes. There were a lot of kids without fathers in this town, and people figured at least a few of them were his. But it was the only mercy I'd seen him show that he never laid claim to them. So I kept my mouth shut and turned my eyes to where Aileen was twisting on her stool like she had something to say.

I thought she'd just sit quiet like she usually did and wait till he let on he knew she was there, but then out of nowhere she said, "So your father's dead."

He turned his face and gave a little nod but didn't look at her.

It was like she was testing whether he'd answer the way she was expecting. "Before Mara?"

"No."

She was braced like she thought he might hit her. "How?" she asked.

"Well," Jason said slowly, getting more interested, "for weeks, hunters had been returning from the woods, saying there was a grizzly out there bigger than any they'd ever seen before. Some said it wasn't even a grizzly but some new creature, like a grizzly had come across something else, one dark day in the woods, and the two animals had lain together and

93

created this new beast. My father didn't believe the stories, and so one day—"

I lost patience listening to this. "Just a wreck," I told her, and she looked up in surprise, startled to see me there, two seats down the bar from Jason. I looked right back until she lowered her gaze. "He wrecked his truck. It was bad weather and he lost control of his truck. It happens," I said, and I looked at Jason. "And that's *all* that happened."

"I'm sorry," she said to Jason after looking back and forth between us for a moment, and then she watched as he lit another cigarette and put it down beside the one already burning in the ashtray. She reminded me of someone. If I ignored her eyes. If I looked only at her mouth.

"I've been drinking too much," she said to Jason, more quietly, but I could hear her fine.

"You know what they say about Dawson," he replied. "What we've got here is a drinking town with a mining problem."

She laughed, relieved, like she hadn't thought he could tell a joke. She'd asked Angie what he did for a living the second day she was here. That's how you could spot a southerner two steps into a conversation. What do you do, they always wanted to know. Like the most interesting thing about you was what someone paid you for. She acted like she thought Angie was joking. "A *gold miner*," she kept saying.

Now she said, sort of casually but there was something intent in her, "Will you take me there sometime?"

"To the claim?" he asked.

She nodded.

"Yeah. Okay." I saw him think about the idea and start to like it. It was things like that that let me know what he was starting to feel about her. "I'll tell you one day when and we'll go."

"Okay," she said and a smile started on her face and then went all the way across, but slowly. There was something about her sometimes, like she wasn't all the way grown up. Like she hadn't earned the wrinkles on her face. She was all kinds of trouble. "Okay, you tell me when."

"I'll take you fishing too," he said. "We'll go down by where the old nets used to be and take my boat out. I've got a boat, you know."

She shook her head, and her dull eyes widened and then she dropped her face. I wondered again who she reminded me of. "I don't go in boats."

"Not ever?"

She shook her head again.

"Neither did she," he said.

And I saw that Aileen didn't have to ask who he meant, so she wasn't stupid and she knew what it was they were all the time really talking about. And maybe she was behind the whole conversation, already knowing how it would go, because the next thing she said was, "Jason, how did she die?"

It had come out rushed and stiff in a way that made it clear she'd practised it, and I could tell Jason noticed that too. He opened his mouth and I had no idea what he was going to say, so I said, "It didn't happen here in town."

"Where did it happen?" Aileen asked, looking from Jason to me, like she wasn't sure which one she was talking to.

"It was—" I began.

Jason was looking straight at me when he said, "You weren't there." Then he turned back to Aileen and said again, "She wasn't there."

"But Jason . . ." Aileen stopped herself, seeming to see how he was doing his thing of leaving the room from the seat beside her, going back somewhere deep into himself. More gently, she asked, "Can you tell me what happened? She was my sister. I don't have anybody else."

Jason was thinking hard. I saw his hands in fists in his lap.

"There's nothing to tell," I said. "It was just a—"

Jason cut me off again. "Aileen, you like stories?"

"What?"

I was so pissed then I almost left them to it. If there was a way to circle around a thing instead of getting to it, he would find it.

"Aileen, I'll tell you a story, okay."

Joey Innis was sitting at the table across from us, same place he sat every time he came down to the bar, doing the thing he did most times he sat at that table, with his hand tucked down his pants, and the tears just running down his sorry cheeks. He didn't make a sound, but somehow Aileen had noticed him there. She was staring at him. Good, I thought, let her be a little afraid of this place. Let her think there's something a little wrong with people here. Then Aileen looked up at me as if she knew what I was thinking. I grinned back at her. "You're going to tell me a story?" she asked Jason. She hesitated. "Like a . . . First Nations story?" She looked like she wasn't sure what he would think of those words, or as if she'd just learned them. "I mean, it is, a Tr'ond . . ." Her voice faded away.

"Tr'ondëk Hwëch'in," I said. It didn't surprise me she hardly knew the word, because it was the one we gave ourselves. She wouldn't have hesitated to say her own people's word, when it was still our name, even a year ago.

She had the sense to look ashamed. "I didn't know. I thought you were . . . I thought everybody up here was Inuit. But a man at the hotel told me—"

"Sure," said Jason. "Sure, I'll tell you a Han story. That's not just our people, that's a whole bunch of First Nations around here. But sure, I'll tell you one of our stories. My mother used to tell me stories she learned from my father's mother. I can tell you how the world began, if you want."

She was looking at Joey again. There was something pitiful about her. Something I almost liked and something I hated, something weak. I remembered that Jason had said she came here because her man had left her. She was that kind. Went and fell in love with someone that didn't want her. Weak and hard at the same time. So I couldn't even all the way feel sorry for her. "Okay," she said softly.

"Well," said Jason, "things began with a man and a woman."

Old Man always was. There was not a time when Old Man was not. Long ago, there was only water, and Old Man travelled the water in a boat, looking for land. After he had travelled a ways, he sent down a duck to swim beneath the water and see if he could find land below it. But the duck came to the surface and had found no land. Then, after some time, Old Man sent down an otter. But the otter came to the surface and had found no land. Then the Old Man sent down a badger. But when the badger came to the surface, he, too, had found no land.

At last, Old Man sent down a muskrat. But the muskrat did not return. The muskrat was gone so long that Old Man said to the other animals in the boat, Duck, Otter, Badger, Muskrat has drowned. And as he was preparing to paddle away, Muskrat appeared at the surface. He was exhausted and nearly drowned. In his claws was a ball of mud.

Old Man took the ball of mud from Muskrat and rolled it between his hands. Then he blew on it and it became the world. In the world, he made mountains and rivers. He made oceans and lakes. He made fishes and birds, berries and flowers. Then, with a bit of clay he had, he made a wife.

Together, Old Man and his wife, Old Woman, decided how things would be in the world. Together, they made people. Old Man said he must have first say about how things would be made. Old Woman said, All right, but I will have final say.

Old Man said, Let people have eyes and a mouth, set up and down on their faces.

Old Woman said, Yes, they shall have eyes and a mouth. But let them be set crosswise on their faces.

Old Man said, Let people have ten fingers, five on each hand.

Old Woman said, Ten are too many. They will have eight fingers and two thumbs. Four fingers and one thumb on each hand.

And so people were made.

Then Old Man and Old Woman argued. Should people live forever, like gods, or must they die, like animals?

Old Man said, I will throw this buffalo chip in the water. If it floats, people will die for four days and then live again. If it sinks, they will die forever.

He threw the buffalo chip in the water and it floated.

Old Woman said, No, no, no. I will throw this stone in the water. If it floats, people will die for four days and then live again. If it sinks, they will die forever.

She threw the stone in the water and it sank.

Old Woman said, Then people shall die forever.

And so people die forever.

But Old Man was angry with Old Woman. He thought he should have got to decide about the world. So when Old Woman went to cook some fish for dinner, Old Man said that women would have to bear children. He said that out of the suffering and humiliation of their mothers' bodies, children should be born. And they would carry with them their debts. Their debts would be like secrets in their hearts that made them dark and quiet. They would sometimes hurt each other and would not know why. After their children were born, mothers would grow old, and their children would find them ugly. But because they had debts in their hearts, children would become men who would find wives who looked like their mothers. And their wives would love them. As their mothers had. And the love of men for their wives and mothers would be a kind of murder.

When Old Man sat down to eat fish with his wife, he found it was cooked in fat and delicious and hot in his mouth, and he ate up his share and hers. Although it burned his hands, he did not wait for it to cool. He saw the way she looked at him and knew she was sorry for what she had done, but he would not forgive her.

When he fell silent and looked at us, my mouth was still open. Not much surprised me, but I never thought he'd make a lie of something like that. Those stories were ours. I never remembered half of them, though my father had liked to tell them to my sister and me. His stories were not the same as my mother's or the Elders', and he never told them the same way twice. But somehow they were always the same. And the stories were about the way they'd always been told by other families before us, and not about twisting them to tell someone something you didn't have the guts to say.

I remembered him and his mother and how they'd tell those stories back and forth to each other. Mara loved them. They weren't her own people's stories, but she took them like they were and would tell them to Jason over and over. They both were like that, though, and would sooner give you a coloured-up tale than a simple answer to whatever question you asked them. When we were all still kids, my sister used to bring me by Mara's house most nights in the winter, and we'd sit there round the stove while she told Jason a story to put him to sleep. The house always had a smell about it like old rotted leaves, like the forest in fall, when everything is waiting for winter. But it was warm round the stove, and Violet and I weren't the only ones to come sit there to listen. When Jason was not even school-age yet, the stories were mostly from the Bible, or that's what Mara said, but they were different from the ones we heard at St. Paul's on Sundays and maybe had the mark of her on them too. For somebody blind, she could make you see every solitary thing she spoke of. I remember in that stale-smelling house half-buried in snow knowing just how a grain of sand shone under a Jerusalem sun. And then when Jason got older, the stories weren't about God or St. John anymore, but about Raven or Bear, and Mara made them her own too. And even as Jason got older, she kept telling him those stories, one a night, and sometimes he would even tell her a story back, and it was the way they talked to each other and told each other things, because I heard few words pass between them other times. Remembering the stories Mara told him, I got up and took a seat beside Aileen, to watch her.

And it was then I realized who she reminded me of. Though it had been almost ten years since I'd seen that wide-mouth smile. And though Lopita's eyes were black and bright and had never looked unsure or caught like Aileen's always did. But when she showed her teeth, when her mouth stretched around a grin that seemed to catch her by surprise, it made me think of that other smile. And even now, with just the glint of a question in her eyes, I thought of Lopita.

She seemed to be trying to think what to do next, and I knew from her face the story made her like him better, made her want to ask him more questions, made her want to stay here longer. And I knew before I opened my mouth that she wouldn't believe me. She would be the kind to prefer a well-told lie to the truth. And there'd be nothing I could do to convince her. Not now, when what I'd tell her was true. And not later, when it would be a lie.

Mara

SEVEN

WHEN WE ARRIVED at her house, Nellie told me that her own daughters would be home from school soon and I would have to be very nice to them, as I'd be sharing a room with her oldest daughter, Megan, and it would be a surprise to them both to find another little girl living in their home. She took me by the hand and put my suitcase in the other, and then she led me up a flight of stairs.

"Here," she said, pulling me through a door. "This is where you'll sleep. Alexander put a mattress on the floor for you, see?" She grabbed my hand and pushed it onto the mattress. I stumbled, startled, and dropped my suitcase. She cried out, and I understood that it had landed on her foot. "You have to be more careful," she said. "Being the way you are, you won't be able to go to school. But you can't be underfoot all the time. You'll have to learn to be resourceful. The blind are very resourceful."

She hesitated, and I felt for the mattress behind me and sat down on it. Then I heard her take light, quick steps across the room. "Well, I'll turn the light off. This room doesn't get much light, but I don't suppose you'll need the lamp like Megan does. See that you check it's off. The switch should be down, like this. Come feel. No need to waste money lighting up the room if . . ." She stopped again, and I withdrew my hand from the switch, which I'd slid my fingers along like she asked. "This will be an adjustment for everyone," she said at last. "I'll leave you to get settled."

After I heard her steps go down the stairs, I lay down on the mattress. I thought about getting up to feel my way around the room, so I'd know where things were and be able to be careful, like she'd asked. But in the end I fell asleep there, and didn't wake until I heard their voices at the door.

Aileen

~

late June 1996

EIGHT

"THAT IS NOT THE END of the story," said Minnie.

I turned my head to find she was now sitting beside me at the bar. Something about her made me nervous, and I had a feeling she didn't mind that. She seemed always to be watching me and Jason, always nearer than I thought she was. But I was glad for something to say beyond wondering what Jason's strange story meant and why he told it to me, or if he only wanted to distract me from the question I had asked him. "What do you mean?" I asked.

"I heard that story plenty of times, and that's not how it ends. He made that ending up."

Jason had his head down, lighting a cigarette.

"It ends with Old Man and Old Woman agreeing that the people will die forever. There isn't any more," said Minnie. She had a flat, expressionless face. From her eyes and mouth I couldn't have told how sharp her words were.

Jason sucked on his cigarette hard and didn't look at either of us.

"Maybe there are different versions of the story," I said quietly.

Minnie barely glanced at me. "That end sounds more like something from the Bible or something his mother would say than anything that ever came out of our Elders' mouths. I've never heard it that way. Never."

Jason said, "Minnie."

Minnie looked closely at me then. "He's a liar, you know. Oh yes he is. You are."

Jason said, "I don't have to take shit from you."

Minnie said, "You ask anyone here. Everyone knows he's a liar. Isn't he," she asked the bartender. "Isn't he. Don't you believe anything he says. Nobody does."

Jason raised his bottle and slammed it down on the bar. Hard. We both jumped. The bottle did not break. As beer foamed and spilled over onto the pitted wood of the bar, Jason shoved back his chair and walked to a table at the other side of the room.

"Jason," called Angel, whom I now noticed sitting at a table near enough that maybe she'd heard everything. The two of them were like gulls circling a meal. More and more, I felt like the meal. "Come sit down with me."

But Jason didn't answer and took a seat without sending a word or a look her way.

I turned back to Minnie. "Why did you say that. Why did you say that to him in front of everyone."

Minnie said, "He's got no right to change the stories. He can make up whatever stories he wants about himself. I don't say anything when he does that. He's got no right to change the stories."

Across from us, Angel stood up. Minnie and I watched her cross the room and then lean over the table to where Jason's head was bent down, studying the table as steadily as I'd seen him do anything. We couldn't hear what he said, but we saw Angel straighten from the back, her spine drawing up. We saw how quickly she walked out the door after that.

Minnie said to me, "What are you doing here anyway. What made you come here now?"

I said, "I had nowhere else to go."

Minnie watched me for a moment and I looked away. "That's how most folks come here," she said.

I thought I could understand why Jason would say whatever he said to Angel. He made a kind of sense to me. For some reason, I thought suddenly of a time in my twenties, loving Stephan. Of course it was something else with him—it was sex and it was how he looked at me and all kinds of other things besides. But there was that way in me, how I felt like I could look at this man and know him. And because I knew him, I loved him. And because I loved him, I forgave him. You could forgive anything.

I walked to the door and looked out across the street and then pressed my face to the glass to peer down along the road. I couldn't see Angel anywhere. The sky had a quality of blue in it, a near darkness that I hadn't seen since I'd got here. I'd heard by August the leaves would begin to change colour. This strange brightness and these dry, hot days were already written over with their end.

Opening the door and letting it close behind me, I imagined the road buried in snow. How high would it rise? How cold would it be?

There was a sound and I saw, around the side of the building, a girl crouched on the ground. A cigarette burned down in her hand.

"Angel?" I said.

Angel threw the cigarette behind the building and stood up.

I didn't like to see women cry. I caught a glimpse of her tiny, pointed teeth like pearls before she covered her mouth with her hand. There was a bloodless look about her pale brown face, and she wiped her eyes with the back of her hand and turned away from me.

She said, "He kissed me."

"He kissed you?" I looked at her. I knew she wasn't lying.

"And then, inside, he said . . . I just wanted to know if he was all right. I liked the story he told you."

I watched her closely. I was thinking that maybe she wasn't all that bright. I asked her, "What did he say to you?"

She began to speak and then shook her head. Not stupid though. She wasn't stupid. "It doesn't matter," she said.

"He's not like you, is he," I said.

I heard her breathing slow. She stood up. "I'm going home," she said.

"I wouldn't think you'd have trouble finding someone else to kiss in this town," I said. I knew my voice had changed. Gone hard. I said, "You go where you need to, but I don't know why you'd go home. He'll be waiting for you inside."

She said, "You think you know him?"

I said, "All I meant was I don't think he'd be an easy person to love." She looked in the window of the bar. Ha. There were some women who could only love men who scared them a little. "I'm going inside," I said. "You do whatever you want."

She looked at me and then walked away, down the street, in that slow way she had. Her face and figure were soft, despite the sharpness of her features, but from behind, she looked so thin. From behind, she could have been a child shuffling home.

Inside, Jason was back at the bar again, and Minnie was talking to someone at another table.

"You dare me?" Jason was demanding at the bartender,

who looked bored. She shrugged her shoulders. "You dare me?" he said again.

I came up beside him and opened my mouth to speak, but he turned away, grabbing a pack of matches from the bowl on the bar. He whipped it open and bent the top match back, and in one fluid movement, like a snap of his fingers, he flicked it against the striker and then lit the entire pack on fire. Then he raised the burning matchbook in his right hand and held his outspread left palm above it. "You count for me," he told the bartender. "I'll hold it as long as you say."

The bartender looked faintly interested then. She tipped her head to one side, letting her honey brown curls fall over her shoulder. She had the eyes of a cat, and they narrowed as she gazed at him, unblinking. "One," she said.

He held his palm so it was less than an inch above the flame and kept his eyes glued to the bartender's.

"Two," she said.

The other men at the bar had started to pay attention. I could tell from the way Jason settled into his seat then, a cocky languor easing over him, that he enjoyed their eyes on him. His hand was steady as the flames crept down the matches.

"Jason," I said sharply. "Stop that. Stop it right now."

"Three," said the bartender, an insolent smile sliding across her face. She lowered her elbows onto the bar and leaned over them, so her face was as close to Jason's outstretched hand as his.

"You're going to burn a hole clean through your hand, Jason you fool," said one of the men, but the others shushed him.

"I don't feel a thing," Jason said coolly. "You know those guys that teach themselves to eat poison, a little at a time? I've been training myself so I don't burn. One time I lit my whole hand on fire. It just burned itself out. As far as fire goes, I'm goddamned invincible."

"Four." The bartender took her eyes off Jason's at last to stare with the rest of us at what was left of the matchbook in his hand. The paper matches were burned to the base and all that remained was the thin piece of cardboard that had held them all together, burning between his fingers. I smelled a sweetness in the smoke and thought it was the seared flesh of his palm and fingertips.

"*Jesus Christ,*" I hissed and watched as my hand flew out and clumsily knocked the matchbook from his hand. It scuttled across the bar and the bartender whipped a glass out from the shelf below and caught the last burning scrap as it slid over the edge. Then she turned and dumped it down the sink, without another word.

As if nothing had happened, Jason pulled out a cigarette and lit it with a new matchbook from the bowl. I tried to catch a glimpse of his left hand, to see how badly it was burned, but he clenched it in a fist and tucked it under his other arm.

I sat down beside him. He didn't look up, but took three swallows of beer in a row.

"She went home," I said at last.

He took another swallow of beer.

"You want a shot?" I said. He shrugged and I ordered two shots of whiskey. When we drank those, I ordered two more.

"So did you talk to her, or what," Jason said.

"Just for a minute. She was out there smoking."

"Angel doesn't smoke."

"I don't know what to tell you. She was out there smoking."

Jason took a drag on his own cigarette and thought about that.

"She told me you kissed her," I said after a moment.

"Who'd he kiss?" said Minnie. I hadn't realized she was behind me.

Jason looked at Minnie and then pushed a cloud of smoke out between his parted lips without taking his eyes from her.

"I'm sorry, Jason," she said. "You hear me, I'm sorry."

He turned back to the bar but said nothing.

"Oh Jesus fuck, Jason. Screw you." She turned and I thought she would leave, but then she leaned in to Jason and whispered, "You think this woman is your friend? You want to call her your family? I'd like to know who you think is going to be here to take your shit when she's gone. You want to tell her all your secrets, you go right ahead. And then you watch her go. What are you going to do, follow her?"

She turned to me then. She said, "You know he's left this town three times already. Once he went to Edmonton, to get some oil job there. He was maybe sixteen years old. Dropped out of school for this job. Said goodbye to everyone. Not three months later he was back. He said it was just a contract job, but when he left, he was all like he was never going to see one of us again. Then he said he was going to school. Someplace down in Prince George. Was gone nearly six months that time. Came back and said it rained too much. Said there was nothing they could teach him there. Last time he went to Whitehorse—Whitehorse! Didn't even cross the border. Said he had some government job lined up there. I don't believe there ever was a job. Most people don't. Thought it was just more of Jason's stories. And what was the reason that time, Jason? Why'd you come back?"

I didn't look at Jason. But Minnie did. She pulled a stool

up in front of Jason so she had her back to me. "Jason," she said. "I don't blame you for coming back. You know I don't. But I wish to fuck you'd stop going around like you were too good for us here. Every time you come back here you're madder and harder to take. You treat Angel like shit. And what's it for? They no more want you in the south than this woman here will give another thought to you come August."

"You should go," I said.

"Angel's worth ten of him," Minnie said. "If he'd just get over wanting what doesn't want him, maybe he'd see that. Maybe he'd stop going around with that attitude like he's better than us, or that look like a beat dog."

"Fuck you, Jason," she said. And she pushed the stool into the bar so hard it toppled to the ground. She left the bar without speaking to anyone.

"Will you get me another shot," Jason said.

"Sure," I said, "sure." I ordered two.

Into the silence and the drinks between us, I said, "I turned forty last week."

"Oh," said Jason. "I didn't know."

"Should have," I said. "Her birthday too."

"Oh," said Jason. "I forgot. I guess I forgot."

"That's okay," I said. My tongue slipped a little on the *s*. I was not used to drinking, and now I had drunk too much, too much. "I did too, almost. But all I'm saying is, you're awfully old to be the son of a forty-year-old. How old are you anyway?"

"Twenty-four."

"Oh," I said. I pushed away what remained of the whiskey. No more drinks. "Oh Jesus. Jesus, Mara. Sixteen."

"She told me she was glad to have me," said Jason. "She

said my father wouldn't have married her if it hadn't been for that, and if he hadn't married her, she couldn't have left the school."

"It was bad there?" I asked.

Jason shrugged. "It wasn't good," he said.

"I know," I said. "I know, I know." I looked at the boy, who looked younger when he drank, when his face went all soft around the eyes and mouth like it was now. I could tell his eyes weren't focusing as easy as they should, and I thought mine might be the same way. "He was from here, your dad?" I asked.

"Yep," said Jason. A man paid for his beer beside us at the bar and, without a word, slid one over to Jason. Jason took it with a nod, and peeled the label off the glass in one solid piece. "She was in school in Alberta," he said. "My dad was working there on a job, and he got in a fight that had him in jail for a spell. She was with this Christian group that would go there and read to them from the Bible. Except of course, she didn't read. She could just talk it at you. She had the whole Bible in Braille, but most of the time she'd just talk it at you."

Think of the little girl with yellow hair and that voice like mine but not mine, that other that was always and in all things like me but not me. That small hand in my own small hand.

I said, "She was blind? She was always blind?"

Jason said, "She could tell if there was light or dark. She could see if something moved around her."

Remember that it was not a little girl who got pregnant with the child of a man who did "spells" in jail. It was another Mara. A tall one, grown older, like me. Grown tired, too, and a little ruined.

I said, "Was she happy?" My voice was so quiet and it was almost the voice of a yellow-haired child.

Jason said, "Sometimes my father beat her. Not very many times. Only once I ever saw him hit her with his hand closed. But she always seemed relieved afterwards. Happier. Once, he knocked her jaw so hard I heard it move in its place, and I was behind him with a plate in my hand, with it over his head about to come down, when I saw her look up from the dishes and there was a peace on her face I never saw before."

There was something wrong with my heart or lungs or something. There was a thing that was wrong that was why I couldn't breathe. I thought I would say his name, Jason, and tell him he had to stop talking so he could call the hospital. I thought, was there a hospital in this place? What kind of place was it where you couldn't breathe and someone wouldn't stop saying these things to you and there wasn't a hospital?

Jason said, "I don't know why it would be that she would be glad then. I don't have half an idea. But it makes me think that no, she wasn't happy."

"Jason," I said. "Jason."

Jason said, "It's true what Minnie said. I tried to leave. I kept trying to leave. I don't know why I can't." He ordered another drink from the bartender and pushed it toward me. I took it though I didn't want it.

I said, "Jason. I don't have anything to go back for. I'll stay here as long as you let me. I won't go like she said."

Jason said, "She loved him though, you know. I mean, she really, really did."

I said, "Or say you'll come back with me. My husband can get you a job at his company. He works in construction. We could go now if you wanted."

118

Jason said, "And I'll tell you something. He worshipped her."

"I couldn't have known about this, Jason," I said. I shook his arm. "I couldn't. How could I know about this?"

Jason said, "I didn't say you could. I didn't say shit to you."

There was that little girl with her hair still like pale honey and her face that would trust anybody. There was the way you could know the body of another—in the dark you could, sightless, know another person by the touch of them, by the way their hands met your own, in the air, their hands closed around your own, as if they'd been reaching at the very moment you knew that you needed, wanted to put your hand out into the dark and hope and hope—

"I'm sorry," I said, "I've been so sorry. I was going to tell her. I came here because he left me and I came here because I loved her, I did. But I came here, too, because I was going to tell her, I was going to say I'm sorry, and she isn't here and I can't tell her, so I have to tell you."

He said, "I've got some money coming to me, you know. You don't have to give me a job. I've got money coming. They've been in talks for years now, and they say word's going to come any day now. Any day now. We're all going to get money from the government. For what they did here. I'll be a rich man then. I'll be able to go anywhere."

"Jason," I begged him. I said to him, "Jason. Let me tell you I'm sorry. Let me tell you what happened." I said again and again until he listened to me, "Let me tell you what happened."

Mara

NINE

I HEARD THEM AND LAY STILL, afraid to move. It had been so many years since I had heard another child speak, and if I listened hard enough their voices sounded like hers.

"She's sleeping," whispered one. "Megan, we shouldn't wake her."

The other voice was more like the one I longed for, soft as wind and sharp as the end of a saw. "It's the *daytime*." I felt the mattress beneath me buckle and thought, That is her foot kicking the mattress underneath me. "Wake up," she said. "*Wake up*. Open your eyes."

The other girl whispered, "Maybe her eyes are closed because she's blind."

"Don't be stupid, Elizabeth," said the one named Megan. "She's lazy. She's lazy and blind. I never heard of us having a lazy, blind cousin. Why should I have to share a room with her. And she's ugly too. Look at the colour of her hair, it's like no colour at all. It's like the tail on the end of corn."

"Corn silk," I said. "Da said it was like corn silk. Mother's was like that too. He said she must have grown out of a field of corn and some farmer came and picked her like a piece of corn, and she was so beautiful he let her go, while all the other corn had to go to the mill and get cut into little bits for all the chickens and animals to eat." I didn't hear either of them say anything after that, so I kept my eyes shut and said, "And that's why he fell in love with her. Because no other ladies had hair like corn silk or got picked from the field by a farmer, and so there was only one like her and that made Da love her. But now she's dead, nobody loves her at all."

"Jesus loves her," said Megan, but she didn't sound sure.

"I'm sorry you don't have a mother," said Elizabeth. "Mom said—"

I sat up and said to Megan, "*Know ye not that ye are the temple of God, and that the spirit of God dwelleth in you? If any man defile the temple of God, him shall God destroy; for the temple of God is holy, which temple ye are.* Jesus did not love Mother. Jesus despised her as God did. As Da did. She died like Judas died, falling headlong, burst asunder in the midst. Our bodies are the members of Christ."

It was quiet all around, and then Megan said, "I don't want you here. I don't want you in my bedroom." I heard the door open again and then heard footsteps down the stairs and Megan calling for her mother. I thought I was all alone in the room, and then I felt a soft, warm hand take my own. It could have been *her* hand, and I held onto it like the ocean holds the sand.

Angel

~

late June 1996

TEN

So I followed him sometimes. Could have felt shame about that, yes, could have. Could have felt it like my mother and how she'd look at me sometimes and say, "Aren't you ashamed of yourself, Angie. Weren't you raised to be better than you are?"

But I never was, oh no, I never was. Not ashamed of that. And if there were things I thought when I was in my own bed, things I wouldn't have told even June there, on the other side of that small window between us, that was not the same as shame. That was something different. If I let my hand go down beneath the sheet, looking for myself, if after, I lay with my hand still wet under the sheet, and felt it in me deeply, was made to cry after that and feel the salt drops without sound fall on the pillow and still feel as sweet and alone as a person could feel—it wasn't shame that made me cry.

She told me to watch after him. Before the thing that happened to her had happened, when I thought it was only for lack of proper working eyes that she couldn't watch her son herself. I'd come over to see him, was still young then, maybe only ten, eleven years old, and stood there in the doorway, knotting and unknotting some bit of cotton in my hand, a

scarf or a thing like that. She was just sitting at the table, peeling potatoes, and I wondered if it was safe for her to do that,
how she'd know so she could not cut herself or get blood in
the potatoes, and so I watched close and sharp as a knife to see
if there was red there in the potatoes. She said, "Angel, didn't
you come by yesterday, too, looking for him?"

And I said yes, I did, and the day before that too. I said
he'd been busy or something, I guessed. I said he'd forgot to
wait for me after school was done.

She cut the potatoes still and didn't stop doing that all the
time she talked to me. She looked at me as she did it, but I
knew she didn't see me or anything. She said, "Angel, your
mother and your father, have they ever been anywhere but
here?"

I said Papa went sometimes to the whale camp and once he
even let Charlie and Jude go with him, but not me and June.
I said June said it wasn't fair because she was the same age
as Jude and anyway they didn't like to do things different or
apart, but Jude gave her a look and she shut up fast.

And she said, "Did your mother ever go away from here?
Down south, I mean?"

And I said no, I didn't think so. And she asked me if I
wanted to go away somewhere when I was grown, and I said
Jude and June were going to get an apartment, they already
had it decided, and June said Jude was going to let her deco-
rate it and she already knew what it was going to look like.
They said it might be in Whitehorse or maybe in Memphis,
because of Jude liking Elvis so much. But they said even if it
were in Memphis they'd let me come be there with them. But
I told her that I didn't want to go to Memphis or Whitehorse
neither.

"Why not?" she asked me, and I said because I hadn't been there so I didn't know if they might have the things there that I liked, like the shining beads we were learning to stitch together at culture camp and a sledding hill like up the Dome or my father. And she nodded and said Jason would stay too. Then she asked me if I would watch after him. And I said yes, but then I said, "What am I to watch?"

And she didn't answer but she said she would like me to stay in Dawson there with him if I could and not go to Memphis or Whitehorse, and then she said I should not be sorry if he did not wait for me after school was done. She said, "Later he'll come looking for you, and it'd be a good thing for you to do if you'd look out for him then."

So I said yes, and even after she died and after he didn't go to school anymore, I still looked for him like she told me. And it didn't matter anyway, what she'd said, because June never went to Memphis. Not even Jude did, he just went to Calgary and didn't come home anymore. And June just stayed beside me in my room and didn't talk about Jude or about Whitehorse either. Sometimes she said she knew now how I must feel, not to have anybody who looked like me or had once been a baby with me in our mother's belly, how lonesome I must feel, and I said yes, and got in bed with her and let her hold me like she did when I was little and muss my hair with her hand until she fell asleep. And all the time, I kept watching Jason and what he did and said, so I'd know when he came looking for me.

"Did that feel like love to you?" he'd said to me, back at The Pit. All I'd wanted was to know what it meant to him to tell

Mara's sister what he did, and to change the Old Man story like he did. I wasn't sure what he'd been getting at by saying it to her, if it was a way of starting to tell her something that he'd better not. I knew it would make trouble for him with Minnie and knew, too, he didn't often tell his mother's stories anymore, so he must have his reasons. I was wishing he would show them to me, his reasons. I felt that I knew him and why he was the way he was, but sometimes I needed him to show me his reasons.

I knew there was a way I could look at him so he didn't get rough with me when I asked him questions, like he did with other people. I'd thought I could be the one, the only one, he'd make confessions to. Sometimes when I followed him, I imagined him turning around and seeing me there, and I would know in that second that he'd always known how I'd followed him, and we'd finally got to the place he'd been taking me all along, and then I'd say, "Confess to me," and he'd tell me everything.

But instead, after he told her his story about Old Man, he went to a table by himself, and I went after him and in a soft voice that would make him not afraid or rough, I said, "Are you all right?" and he said, "Why would you come over here like something of me is yours. What we did by the river, did that feel like love to you?"

We'd gone to the river after that first night we saw her. I knew what it meant to Jason to see her show up here. Minnie maybe knew a little, but I knew the most what it meant. So I went with him to the woods by the river, and we didn't say much at all, and then he put his hand in my hair so it hurt and he was pulling me toward him. And now I, who'd wanted to keep all his secrets for him, had told Aileen we kissed.

I'd got as far as the steps of our house, and now I sat down and tipped my head so I could see the deep blue centre of the sky, which the sun had circled away from, as if it wanted to escape to the earth but the sky kept pulling it back.

We didn't just kiss.

When we were done, he had let me lie there in the curve of his arm for a little while, and then I felt him restless again and could hear the thoughts turning between his ears.

"It's nice she came for you," I told him.

"She didn't come for me," he answered.

"It's you who'll keep her here. She'll want to know you," I said.

"No," he said. "She won't."

We didn't go to the river again, and after that he never laid a hand on me or looked at me like he knew a thing about my body that my clothes didn't show. But he went there with her. Just a few nights before, I'd followed her there to him and seen them sit not far from where he had done it to me, with their heads together like it was secrets they were sharing, like he was telling her everything.

It wasn't her I'd been following that night but him, and I knew she would be going to him, I knew as soon as I saw her that first day after I was done singing that she'd get to following him too like I did, and I knew he'd make it easy for her to follow after. The sky was grey as stone when she went down to meet him there at the river, and I had to stay so far back that I thought I'd lost her until I heard them speaking together and I followed the quiet sound of their voices to where they were. I could hear what he said to her, but not always what she said back. He was talking all boastful like he would get, like he wanted her to think something was special about him. But then he said to her that sometimes he thought he went looking for a reason to be angry, because the feeling that was a feeling in his body of being angry for no reason was unbearable. I couldn't see her face then, and I wanted to know if she looked scared or if she was sorry for him or thought it was like the stories he'd tell of himself, just him trying to get listened to. I wondered if he'd have been able to tell, if he'd told me that, that I knew he was saying something true.

Then he told her a story about one time when he was something like fourteen years old. He said he and his ma had had a goat and he tied it up behind the house, way far back in the yard. He put down a bowl of food real close to it, but not close enough that the goat could reach it. He didn't change the food all week and it got so it stank, but the stink of it was nothing on the sound that goat made. He said his mother would holler at him to fix what was wrong with the goat, and he'd pretend to go and see it, but he'd only stand outside the house looking at it, listening to the sound it was making. Then he'd go inside and tell her he thought it had took sick and that he'd get some medicine for it, but he didn't get anything at all for it. And after a week that goat died, and then he thought that maybe it wasn't even for want of the food but for water that it died, because he'd thought it would be another week before he'd have to move the food closer. He hadn't thought of the water. And he said he told his mother that the goat had died of its sickness, and when he said that, the woman Aileen asked, "Why did you do this thing?" And he said, like he had himself all figured out, "Because of how it felt to listen to that goat. Because of wanting to keep feeling like that and know why."

And then I got a notion that he was lying now. You had to listen so careful to Jason. He'd tell you things about himself no one else ever would. And sometimes he wouldn't tell you anything at all. And sometimes he'd tell you a lie that you were sure was a lie and then you'd figure out that it was the truest thing he'd told you. But I couldn't remember him having any goats. His mother had rabbits for a while, I remembered, and then she didn't anymore. But I didn't remember a goat.

And then again, I thought, since his mother's sister had come to town, he had fallen into telling the truth more often than he told lies. I wondered why it was. To his own mother, lies had come from his mouth like birds. But to her sister, he was different. I watched how he was, the danger and the slyness gone from him. I saw the lies leave his mouth. I'd thought I knew him best, and then I saw how much there was I didn't know at all.

I didn't know if she believed his story about the little goat he did not feed. After he was done with talking, she began to talk about her husband and I heard her crying and I listened, though I couldn't hear a word, until he took her home.

This night was dark enough to remind me of nights in winter. Blue. Steady. I was sorry I had left the bar. I was sorry for the way it would feel shameful to go back again when I did, and I knew that I would. I knew if I went back now while he had drink in him, he would let me sit beside him and maybe he would even say he was sorry or do something so that I'd know that he was, like ask me how June had been doing or make a show of blowing his cigarette smoke out to the side so it didn't go in my face. If I waited a day or more, he would be so ashamed of himself it would make him mean with me, and it would be weeks till he'd come talk to me again. Weeks when he wouldn't say *"Angie,"* or look at me sideways and just about almost smile.

So I knew I had to go back and knew I would, but I let myself look at the sky for a little longer. I decided to let myself have a count to a hundred before I had to go. I lay back till my head was on the boards of the porch beneath me, and I counted all the way, and then it was time to go back.

I took the longer way there. I went down almost as far as the river, and then as I cut up past the bank, I heard a sound. It was a woman crying sound, I knew it. I looked and there, by the pay telephone, there was a woman crying into the phone. And I knew the woman. It was his mother's sister.

I called her name, but she wasn't looking at me. She was just staring like that at the phone box, her ear all crushed against the phone. She didn't answer me. And so I waited.

And then, after a while, I saw that she wasn't listening to anybody say anything and so I took the receiver from her hand. She let it go and sat on the ground, while I put the receiver to my ear and listened to the sound of a ringing, unanswered phone, and then I hung it up.

"You go home now," I said to her. She was slumped like dirty laundry on the ground against the phone booth.

"I drank too much," she told me. "And then he told me, he said . . ." She stopped speaking.

"Do you know how to get home?" I asked her.

She gave a nod and looked up.

"You want some help to get home?" I asked her. I reached

for her hand, but she snatched it away and then she got herself up. And I waited for her. And when she stumbled for a moment, I was there beside her and I caught her. And then we walked like that, her weight on me, all the way till we got to the hotel, and I remembered my father and how he'd be in my arms like that the nights he got paid, until the night he died and I didn't have to go get him and take him home anymore.

I let her sit on the steps of the hotel while I went inside and told Ivan I was going to need some help to get her up the stairs. Ivan made a sound like all the air had got sucked right out of his mouth and said it was no good at all for the guests to see people drunk like this. He said it gave the tourists the wrong idea about the town.

"But she is a tourist," I said. He just shook his head and said he didn't want anything to do with it and I'd have to get her upstairs myself.

So I went back outside and I got hold of her as best I could, though she didn't want me touching her, and I took her through the door to the stairs, while Ivan went outside to smoke a cigarette. Again and again I put her hand on the railing, and then when she took it off, I put it on again, and so finally we got to the top of the stairs. When I closed her door and came back downstairs, Ivan was behind the desk again and didn't look up as I left.

Hardly anybody was left on the street now, and the sun leaned over town, pushing its way up. But when I opened the door to The Pit, nothing was much changed except the glasses that were emptier and the ashtrays that were filled. I walked to the bar where Jason sat next to Papa's old friend John and I took a seat beside them. I felt Jason's whole body notice me, but he didn't look at me, didn't let me have even just that second of knowing something about him and what he thought of me.

And I sat there with my elbows on the yellow wood of the bar, without a thought in my head of what was going to happen between us. And then a thing happened that made me not think about him anymore or how even though Mara's sister was gone home now, he was as full of her as if you'd have to put him through the sluice to mine her from him.

And all that happened were four words and the touch of a hand. And after, John sat with his long legs stretched out to the floor beside me, him with his eyes soft and black, and me thinking how, how, how gentle a man could be. And who'd have thought a man you'd known all your life could one day look at you with soft, black eyes and there you'd be and not feeling like you were different than you had been when you sat down on that stool beside him, when you reached in your pocket for the money to pay and he caught your hand and said, "No, no, let me," and you were left with the feel of his hand on your wrist and not looking any different than you had before, but everything now changed.

And I thought of that and could no more look at him than Jason could look at me, and I thought of everything I knew about him and wondered if he touched my arm again if I'd feel what I had again.

Then John stood up and said he had to go talk to Eloise about something. "Hold on," I began saying and then had nothing more to finish it with. He looked at me and even Jason turned his face so he was watching the bar in front of me though even then he wouldn't look at me. "We're going to have a practice at my house tomorrow. June and me. And

Lando. You could come by if you wanted. After lunch, you could come by."

"I heard you were going to sing at that festival," John said. "That's something special, isn't it. Lou would be proud as a rooster to have his little girl sing in front of all those people."

"You could come by," I said again, and John smiled at me.

"I'll be seeing you," he said.

I looked down to see Jason's hand that he had laid there between us. I wondered what he meant for me to do with it and then thought for a moment of how it made me tired to wonder about another person and never be sure.

"You can't talk to me like you did," I said to him.

He shook his head, and I thought he would apologize, but instead he said this, he said, "Aileen betrayed my mother."

I didn't want to hear about Aileen, so I stood up, but Jason said, "Angie, Angie, sit down, while I tell this," and so I sat down again.

And then he put his hands to his head and talked to the bar like it was listening to him. He said that when Mara and Aileen were little girls together, their mother hanged herself. Their father went crazy then and blindfolded the girls to keep them from seeing their mother. And later he refused to take the blindfolds away. And after that, the girls didn't see anything anymore.

Except.

He said, "Except that Aileen did. After the first year, she says she started to take off her blindfold when her father wasn't around. She was surprised by everything she saw. Nothing was the way she remembered it. She didn't tell Ma what she was doing. She says she thought Ma must be doing the same thing. Aileen would test her, always asking her what she could see, waiting to catch her in a lie. But she always said she couldn't see anything at all. Then Aileen got to be angry with her for not betraying her. She started to leave Ma alone whenever she could. Sometimes, she'd be gone for hours. She found some hippies two miles down the road who were fixing an old farmhouse. The husband taught her how to help him with the boats he built in his barn, and the wife would bring them hot tea and bread while they worked."

That was the second I saw it happen. He wasn't talking to me anymore. He was making a story out of it, talking to the story itself, like it was happening before him, becoming what had happened in the air between us. Like the words themselves were what it was built of.

"And then one day," he said, "Aileen was coming back from their house, and as she climbed the hill toward home, she saw Ma on the hill, snapping the heads off of dandelions with her thumb and singing to herself. The ground was all uneven, so she couldn't walk quite right, like over and over the ground itself would rise up and catch her by surprise, so she almost fell but never quite did. She looked alone in a way that made Aileen feel sick. And when Aileen put her blindfold on and went to her, Ma started singing. This is the song she sang: '*Aileen smells like wood, Aileen smells like wood when she comes back, where does Aileen go and what is Aileen made of.*'

"And then Aileen noticed her hands were rough with sawdust, and she sniffed her fingers and thought she smelt nothing but wasn't sure.

"And after that she didn't take the blindfold off anymore. She didn't visit the hippies again, even though whenever she was bored she'd get to thinking of the way the wood had felt against her hand. Almost two years passed before she saw again, and when she did, she couldn't get her eyes to focus right, to see like she used to. Somehow the world had got blurred while she wasn't looking at it.

"The doctors said it was not enough to have two eyes and a brain, the right parts in all the right places. The brain and the eye have to learn how to talk to each other, so the eye can tell the brain what it sees. But Ma's eyes never had anything to say to her brain, so after a while her brain stopped listening for good.

"But Aileen's eyes hadn't gone so long without seeing anything at all, and so for her the world was like a light bulb that had gone dim. And slowly her brain started listening again to what her eyes had to tell it. After a few years, she could see enough to know what looks people had on their faces and how far away her hand was from the things it reached for. She couldn't read or drive, but she could live like a normal person. She could have a normal life.

"But my mother hadn't seen a thing for almost four years. For her, the light bulb went out altogether and it never went back on.

"Aileen told me that. And then she asked me to forgive her."

"For keeping the secret from Mara?" I asked.

"For blinding my mother," Jason said.

But I didn't see how it was Aileen's fault. It was wrong that she could see and her sister couldn't. But, too, it was wrong that she was alive and her sister wasn't. And I couldn't see how either thing was her fault, not even though she'd lied. I told this to Jason, and he looked at me like I understood nothing.

"That's not the point," he said.

"What is the point?" I asked.

He didn't answer and we were quiet for a long while until he put money on the counter and said to me, "Come home with me tonight."

I got up before he was awake, like I knew he'd want me to. His face was turned down, so I couldn't see what he looked like. I would have liked to see his face before I left.

I decided I could have a count to fifty. I let my mouth say the numbers while I watched his back. I was afraid to stay. *Forty-nine*, I thought as his hand opened and closed on the pillow and then reached for the sheet, pulled it tighter around him. *Fifty.* I held my breath. And then . . . *One.* A count to twenty, I thought, and then I'd be gone.

Already I had the idea that I wouldn't see him sleep again, and after this day had happened I wouldn't think anymore of what it had been to be this close to him and see the shape of him in the sheets beside me. To be close enough to touch him. To be the only person in the world in the room with him, near him, waiting for him to wake.

Twenty, I thought, and then I was gone.

Momma's truck was missing in the driveway when I got home. I was glad to not have to see her or tell where I had spent the night. Whenever I used to bring my father home from the bar or a girl in town caught a disease from some white boy staying at one of the hotels, she would tell me the worst harms to our people always started with opening our legs or a bottle of booze.

I lay in my own bed till lunchtime, but I wasn't sleeping.

I could hear June in the hall, her fingers clicking the keys on the computer she'd won at school and set up in what used to be the linen closet. She was smart that way and had fixed the computer twice by herself. Now she used it to write to Jude. She said he never would write back, but she knew he liked to hear from her and it would help him remember to practise using the computer so he could get a raise at work.

"June," I whispered.

"Yeah," she said and the sound of the computer keys didn't stop.

I stood up and went to the door. I leaned against it and watched her. She was wearing an old pair of Momma's jeans and they were too short for her long, skinny legs. "I could fix them," I said.

"What?"

"Those jeans. I could take out the hem for you."

She stopped typing and pulled her glasses off. "What is it, kiddo?"

I looked at her. She'd done the perm herself, but it looked as good as if it had grown that way. Everybody said she was the best-looking girl in town.

She sighed. "Something you want to tell me?"

I didn't want to tell her. Almost, but didn't. She half knew already, I could tell. And if I told her all the way, she would make me feel, not ashamed, but something else. Like I'd taken something good and dirtied it. Taken something out that couldn't get put back. "Maybe we could have practice outside today. Might be nice."

She made two lines of her eyes. "That's it?" Then she pressed a button and everything on the computer disappeared. "Well, let's do it then."

141

Outside, I laid my head back on the steps and stared up at the clouds while I tuned my guitar. Behind me, June was trying to reach an extension cord from the kitchen so she could plug in the electronic piano she'd bought two months ago. I liked it better when she played the regular piano, but it took her almost a year to save up the money, so I told her I thought the sound was good, more interesting than a real piano. "More modern," she'd said and looked pleased.

I was thinking about lying on that porch the night before and how strange it was to be in one moment and not another, and for those two moments not to talk to each other, like Mara's brain not able to listen to her eyes, or only one to talk to the other, so you could know what had happened but not ever know what would. And then I heard him say my name.

"Angel," John said again and I lifted my head so I could see him, standing there in front of me on the road, wiping the shine of sweat from his face. "Angel, do you remember you asked me? Is it okay that I came?"

His face was full of worry, and his long, tall body was stooped over. I knew if I asked him to, he'd turn and go home again and think it was his fault. "I'm glad you did," I said. "June's in there. Lando should be here any minute. We thought we'd play outside today."

"That's a good idea," John said and his face filled with a smile. "Why play music inside the house. Plenty of time for that in winter."

"John." June climbed down the steps and cupped her hand over her eyes to stare up at him. He was taller than even June, who was so tall. "Isn't this a nice surprise." She hooked her finger under the collar of my T-shirt and gave a pull. "You want to help me set up, Angie?" she asked. She nodded at John. "We'll only be a minute."

I followed her in and she closed the door behind us. "Angie, what's John doing coming over here?"

I whispered to her, "I asked him to."

She made her lips tight like Momma's. "Now why'd you do that."

"He was Papa's friend," I said, still whispering.

"Angie, he's seen fifty come and go." I knew June wasn't as mad as she wanted to seem. But she thought she was meant to be like Momma when Momma wasn't there.

"Last night he touched my hand," I said. "I never had a feeling before like when he touched my hand then."

"Angie, is that where you . . ." She took my face in her hands, and I let my eyes tell her nothing.

At last she said quietly, "Well, Papa always liked him." She pushed open the door and said, "Maybe you'll get free trips down to Vancouver now."

John and Lando, our cousin who was only fifteen but a mean good drummer, were waiting on the steps, looking up at us as we stood there in the door. I'd not been to Vancouver ever.

"Hey, Lando. So, John," said June in the voice she talked to boys with, "how's it flying?"

"Pretty good," he said shyly. "Pretty good."

"How long are you in town for? It's an awful treat to have you stay a while."

He looked at me first before he said, "I don't know yet. I bid for a vacation leave till August. Thought I might take a holiday here for a spell." He was a pilot and that meant he was richer than a trucker and wouldn't have to leave you for weeks at a time if he didn't want to.

143

I looked up at her and with my eyes let her see that I needed her to say yes when I asked her, "You all ready then, June?"

He jumped up when she nodded, and asked how he could help. And I liked how serious he was, letting June boss him around and carrying chairs from the porch to the yard. I liked how he checked that the ones he'd set up for us were on the most flat part of the grass so they wouldn't lean one way or the other, and how he took the chair with the broken arm for himself, and how I could still remember him in the basement, tipped back on Papa's green chair that we weren't allowed to sit on, while Papa poured into his glass until it looked like it was full of gold and said something to make him laugh, and me watching from the door, not yet ten years old, and John seeing me there and saying, "Not in front of the girl, Lou," or how it made me happy to think that while I was just a child, he was already a man and being made to laugh by my father.

And when everything was set up, I sat on the chair John had carried there for me, and I couldn't stop smiling. He took off his jacket and laid it on the back of his chair before he sat down. He was whistling "We Just Couldn't Say Goodbye," and when he noticed me looking at him, he stopped and then smiled a big, slow smile back at me.

"You start us off, Ang," Lando said. "Tell us what you want to start with."

Our mother said she named me Angel so I'd always be thinking of heaven. She said, "You won't get in any trouble if you just keep thinking about heaven." Papa said that while she was pregnant with me, for a time she'd got to going to church with our neighbour Sissy Grant, and she thought it would be nice to raise us kids like Christians, but then the mood passed. That was her way of saying it, which Papa said sounded stuck-up. But I knew he liked that she was a proud lady and that when she changed her mind, and she always did, she would toss her hand as if it were something she'd set free and say, "The mood has passed."

Momma's moods were clouds slipping away across the sky, but mine were heavy stones and I still liked to think about heaven. I never went to church or read the Bible, so I didn't think about whatever Mara or Sissy Grant had thought about when they put their minds on heaven. But I thought about what might happen to a dead person there that could stop them from wanting to stay in the world, that would peel their fingers from the living. When I was a kid, heaven looked like the river when it froze, and we could sail away on our skates forever but never be anywhere else, and I could see my brothers up ahead and they never got farther away. And now that I was older, it was the basement and my father still there in his chair. Or a long sleep in a black, quiet place. Whenever I sang, I let myself think about heaven.

That day, I looked at John watching me and started singing, and I didn't think about heaven.

When I finished the last song, I looked over at June and saw she was watching someone coming up the driveway.

"I guess we're late," Jason said. He didn't say it to us but to Aileen, who was beside him looking like we'd caught her in the middle of something she shouldn't be doing. Jason lifted his legs over the fence and then unhooked the latch for her. He looked up at me then, frowning. "You said you were having a practice today. I thought we'd swing by."

"Jason said you're playing at . . . some kind of a music festival?" Aileen asked uncertainly.

"It's a real honour," John told her. "Maybe a thousand or

more people come up for it. It's something special to get asked to play."

"So," Jason said, "did we miss the show or what? Are we going to have to buy a ticket to see you now?"

I lifted my shoulders. "We can do one more," I said. "There's a couple more chairs in the basement."

"Don't need chairs," Jason said and grinned, but watching me closely like he still wasn't sure what I was thinking. He sat down on the grass and after a second, Aileen sat down beside him.

"Angie," June said. "What's next?"

I sang about a story one of the Elders, Patty, had told me. It was about Raven stealing the sun back from Bear. I was proud of my voice lifting out of me. It was sweet and deep and when I got to the highest notes, it stopped being part of me and became part of the sky and the sticky, sweet shining sun. Down low, I made my voice like a whisper, like a grown-up, dark, rough thing being said, like someone who'd wanted you, someone who'd had you—someone who still remembered what it was to want you and then have you—would speak to you.

When I finished, Aileen was staring at something far away down the road. "Aileen," said Jason, and I saw his hand touch her back and it was light and brief, but his hand was there for a moment and for a moment I felt that touch as if in the crook of my own back. I drew a breath into me and saw his eyes, that quick look he showed to Aileen's face—that question in them about her and whether she was okay. And sometimes I had these moments watching him when just for a second I'd know the things he gave a shit about. And there were some other moments when I'd look at him and my breath would be cold in my throat. And I'd see how his eyes and the bones of his face were as sharp as something you could cut yourself on.

But this time I let my eyes go from him and see John stretched out on his broken chair, comfortable the way a big man or a middle-aged man usually isn't, and his clean, round face was something I thought I'd like to see again and again. And I saw in his eyes how he'd liked the song I sang him.

And then he came over to me and said softly, "That was a good song you sang. I liked that story about Raven." He stood there humming what I'd sung, and I sat down in the grass then and made a sign so he'd know I wanted him to sit beside me.

I saw June watching us and then she stood up and waved to Lando. "Come on inside, Lando," she said. "I want to show you something."

Aileen slid her hand across her forehead. She and Jason were as close as two pages of a book but not touching at all. She looked like she had something to say but hadn't said it yet.

"Did you like that story?" Jason asked her.

She looked startled. She turned her head back and forth, slowly, and then made like a shrug with her shoulders.

Jason said, real fast, "It was about Raven. You want to know where Raven came from?" She started to say something, but he said, "And the sun and the moon." He looked at John. "I know how everything in the sky got there. Do you know a story like that?"

John said he didn't, and Jason looked at Aileen again and said, "I know a lot of stories. Ma used to tell me one every night. If I asked her a question, she'd always answer with a story. You asked me a question last night. I can tell you the answer. I can tell you what happened to her."

"To Mara?" I didn't know what the look on her face meant when she looked at him then.

"It will take time, okay. It will take till the end of the summer. Then you'll know what happened, when the summer is over, and you'll know if you want to stay here." His face looked worried. "You said you were going to stay here."

She smiled but didn't say anything back.

I thought, from the look on his face, that he would stop talking then, but he didn't. After a moment, he said, "Okay, then there are eight weeks until the summer is done, and I will tell you seven more stories. Eight is the right number in our stories. You must try things four or eight times before you succeed. Because we have two arms and two legs and two bones in each one. So I will tell you eight stories, because that is the right number for something that you want to happen. After the eighth story, you won't want to go."

"You want me to stay?" she asked, and we all looked at Jason to see what he would tell her.

He said, "You won't want to go."

Then he said, "Now I'll tell you the second story." He reminded her, "There will be six more."

Old Man did not forgive Old Woman for what she had done to him. He did not forgive her, but one day, he found her looking at herself in the river while she braided her hair and she didn't know that he was watching her. She wound the hair around itself, and her hands moved so fast that Old Man could hardly see what she was doing, but the thing she made of her hair with her hands was perfect.

Then he thought of how she had looked at him, before

*there was a world and when they were young and new. He
thought of the way she had loved him then, how she would
smile so all the white points of her teeth showed whenever he
touched her. And when she brought him food, she would let
him eat first and she would watch him as he ate as if it fed her,
too, his eating. And she would gather her hair into braids to
make herself pretty for him. And when she spoke to him, her
voice was so soft and sweet that he thought he could taste it
in his mouth. And when she took off her clothes for him, he
wept.*

*He thought of these things and remembered how, once, he
had loved her so much that he made her a ring of gold and a
ring of silver, so that she could wear one on each hand and not
forget that even as the ring was round and complete, so was
his love for her. And he gave her each ring and she said, What
lovely gifts you've made for me, but she did not touch them.
And he begged her to put them on her hands, but she shook
her head and said, If I put them on my hands to remember
your love for me, what would happen if I forgot one day to
look at my hands and then forgot the way you've loved me.
What if I trailed my hands in the river to cool them one hot
afternoon and then the rings were lost in the water and I forgot that you were the man who first unfastened my hair and
called me beautiful. What if an animal with many teeth should
set upon me one night while I slept and tear my feet from my
legs and my arms from my body, and later I should wonder if
I had ever been loved and not know.*

*No, she said and shook her head. Let the sky keep them for
me, so they will never be lost and I will never forget this time
before time, this world between us that is before the world,
when we have loved each other as a man and woman are able*

to love. And then she took the rings in her hand and threw them into the sky, where they stayed forever, even long after the two lovers had become cruel to each other and the rising of the moon behind the sun became a thing that mocked them.

And as Old Man watched Old Woman, he remembered all this, and he felt something happen inside him as he watched her play with the birds at her feet that were beloved to her of all things. They crept around her in the grass and followed her wherever she went. Her favourite was the largest and the blackest of all birds and she called him Raven. Old Man saw that the birds' love for her was no less than his and that they would do anything for her.

That night, as Old Woman slept, Old Man took the birds that huddled around her and gathered them into his arms. Every bird in the world was there, and as Old Woman turned over in her sleep, Old Man threw the birds into the sky. They made a terrible sound of squawking and Old Woman woke suddenly and turned to him.

What have you done? she cried.

Old Man was confused. I have put the birds into the sky with your two rings, that you may always look at them and know how much I love you, he said tenderly.

She leapt to her feet and called to the birds, but they had forgotten her now. They were in love with their own wings and the pull of the sky upon them. They soared higher and higher, and though they sometimes came to the ground for a moment or two, or granted her a glimpse of their shining feathers when they paused for a moment on a branch or bathed themselves in the river, they were never hers again.

She sobbed bitterly and cursed him. You have taken everything from me, she said. You have taken everything.

As he watched her, he felt his face grow hard and cold. She turned her back on him and as she covered herself in blankets and let her tears soak the pillow, he said to her that he hated, You never loved me enough.

When Jason was silent, I looked down and saw that John's hand was in my own.

Mara

ELEVEN

FOR ALMOST THREE MONTHS, Nellie put me to bed every night, saying that everybody there was trying and it was incumbent on me to try too. I never was brave enough to ask her what *incumbent* meant. "We're all sorry for what's happened to you," she said, "but we've brought you into our home and that's Christian charity and you must learn to show your gratitude as a guest in this house."

During the day, I tried hard to understand what she wanted from me, but failed more hopelessly with each day that passed. She wanted me out of her way, but she would heave sighs that seemed to shake the walls each time she found me gathering moss, as she called it if I sat with my hand against the glass of the window or the wood of the floor so that I could feel the cold or warmth hidden deep inside and think of how once the floor was a tree and the window was a seashore somewhere far away.

Alexander would stand silent in the doorway while Nellie braided my hair and told me what prayers to say. He would not argue when she told me the wrongs I'd done that day or instructed me to try harder the next. But he would linger when she hurried out the door, her frustration wafting behind her, and sometimes he'd touch my hair or my face and say, like I was his own daughter, that I wasn't a bad girl. "You've got to learn to be careful," he'd say before he left, if she had been especially angry that night.

But I couldn't seem to learn where things were in the house, as I had in our own home. Too many times I found a chair where I hadn't known there to be one, as I took a stack of plates from the table to the sink, or found Nellie's favourite vase had been on top of the turntable where I played the *Unicorn* record Alexander had given me over and over. I learned to walk slowly and afraid, to hesitate to move my arms or stretch them out before me, but I couldn't seem to learn to not try to catch myself when I fell and it was always that sudden, desperate reach of my hands that brought disaster. When I broke a glass bird that Nellie had loved, and stood there, bewildered, not even knowing where it had been or what it was that had caught me at the knees as I tried to make my way to the stairs, I heard Nellie cry that it was more than she could take and Alexander tried to quiet her, while Elizabeth whispered in my ear that it was not my fault. Later she told me she was almost certain Megan had left that stool in my path on purpose, and said she'd never known the bird to be on that low shelf where I'd knocked it as I tried to catch myself. "You must try not to make her angry," she whispered. "And you'll have to be more careful." And then she taught me how many steps it was from my bedroom to the bathroom, and from the kitchen table to the stove, and from the bottom of the stairs to the door, so I wouldn't have to bother her mother for help and make her cross. And she took me by the arm and showed me around the house where all the breakable things were, putting my hand up to touch the glasses we drank from, the smooth

156

glass of the frames over the piano, which she told me were full of photographs of the family but mostly Megan because she was born first, and especially, the heavy bowl at the top of the sideboard that Nellie's mother had carried on the steamer all the way from Oban. And it must have been then that something changed in me, because each plate and glass before, the bird even, had astonished me, but I was not at all surprised when some weeks later the bowl was left on the kitchen table, which had been moved a few inches from the door, enough for me to feel it strike my hip and send me grasping for a handhold and finding only the bowl, closer to the edge of the table than it ever should have been. And nor was I surprised when it was after that that Alexander came to my room and held my hand while he told me I'd be going to a special school where they'd be able to better help me with my defect. Downstairs, Nellie was still weeping, and outside the open door, I heard Megan breathing.

The next day, Nellie and Alexander took me to a school where a man I was told to call Father, though he sounded nothing like Da, told me to say the Lord's Prayer, and then gave me the Bible to hold in my hands and asked me to read what I could. "Can you see this?" he asked me softly, and there was suddenly a greater whiteness to the world, and I asked him, "Is that light?" He squeezed my hand and told me it was.

Nellie took my arm more gently than usual when she took me back to the car, and she told me that we would have to pack up my suitcase again and bring me back after the weekend. "We'll have a nice weekend together," she said. "And Fa—Mr. McGivney said that we can visit every Sunday if we like. You know how busy our weekends are, but—" Her voice changed as she opened the car door and helped me into the seat. "In heaven's name, a Catholic. But God will know I tried."

I heard Alexander take a seat in front of me and the click of his seat belt. He didn't say anything at all.

Aileen

~

late July 1996

TWELVE

I GOT USED TO DAWSON. I got so it seemed normal to sleep with the curtains pulled shut to keep the sun out. The long days stretched out and became long weeks, and every day I woke up and found I was still in Dawson.

Taking Stephan from my thoughts was a steady labour. I opened drawer after drawer in my heart, unfolded him, removed him. And what I found, as each night grew a little darker than the one before and he was all but gone from me, was that each drawer I emptied was now full with my sister. The not-being-there of her, the not-knowing of her. Her town, exhausted of her and yet gasping with her.

At first, I called our old home every night, though before I left my hotel room for the bar, I'd vow I wouldn't. At the bar, I'd turn down the drinks I was offered, because I knew they'd only cloud my head and fill it with Stephan again. But later, on my way home, I'd pass the pay phone box and for a moment, I'd see him, somewhere far from where I stood, older than I'd ever imagined being and alone. I'd see him unlocking the door to come home to me. I'd see his suitcase in the closet again where it always had been.

A minute later I would find myself standing with the phone

in my hand and that unanswered ringing in my ears that came
to haunt me, that crawled into my dreams at night to find me.
After a couple weeks of this, I called a lawyer in Whitehorse.
"I think I want a divorce," I said. "Can you find him for me?"
And then I gave the lawyer Stephan's sister's address and
waited.

During the day, I had nothing much to do with my time,
so I would sleep late like a teenager and then wander around
town, looking for something I hadn't seen yet. I tried to stay
out of the way of the locals. Maybe people knew I was Jason's
aunt, or maybe it was because the town was so full of tourists
that you didn't have to hang around long to stand out, but I'd
begun getting nods when I went places and I didn't want them.
I remembered a boy at the school for the blind I went to as a
child. The boy was older than the other kids on his floor, but
a bit slow or something. He'd get picked on even though he
was bigger than the rest of them. They'd move the furniture in
his room so he'd be disoriented. Once another girl and I were
invited to sneak into the boys' dorm and listen as the older
boy dropped things and tripped, trying to find his way around
his bedroom. I had the best vision of anyone at the school,
and I could see the shape of him clearly, moving around in
a room that had suddenly become a dark, formless antago-
nist. He became blind, again, in that room. I watched him trip
against the edge of his bed, hesitate and turn, backing up and
colliding with the wall in his confusion. After some time, the
boy began to shuffle around with a kind of savage mistrust of
the physical world. He would get pushed on the stairs. The
boys would pour water on his full dinner plate. He lost the
surprised look he'd had in the dorm that time. He came to
look expectant—injured and defiant at the same time. And I

heard that he had begun to sleep with a staple gun in his hand. The girl who told me snickered as she said it, and I knew I was meant to find it absurd, such an inadequate weapon against a persecution that was only confirmed inevitable by his weapon choice. But instead it frightened me. I knew what it meant to him. The kind of hurt he dreamed of. Remembering it years later, as I sometimes did, it made me depressed as hell to think about. Some people had zero chance, right from the start. And here, walking around in Dawson, passing locals who began to nod grudgingly when I went by, something in their expressions reminded me of that boy, and I had the feeling I was living among people who slept holding staple guns. I looked away from their whipped-dog faces.

Still, there was something about this strange place. Those mountains, endless, and the clouds that hung over them, the green and the dirt and the endless plains, the endlessness of the world here, the wildflowers of all colours, the aloneness of everything. And I thought maybe I was getting it. Slowly, I got how you could come to love a place like this. It wasn't a thing I could make sense of, but more like something I felt in me, somewhere so deep it was like climbing the stairs in the dark and you think there is one more step than there is and raise your foot, let it land where there's nothing upon which to land, and in the searing flash of a moment before your foot finds the ground again, everything in you falls; you feel what it is to have your whole body know something, to have your head and your kidneys in conversation about the importance of what is happening to you. That was what it would feel like, I thought, to love a place like this.

At the end of each day, when I couldn't bear the heat any longer, I'd go back to the hotel and nap until the sun had dropped from the centre of the sky. And then, after dinner downstairs at the hotel, I'd show up at The Pit, as if it was a surprise every time to find Jason there. As if either of us had somewhere else to go.

"It's growing on me," I told him one night, shaking my head at Eloise as Jason signalled to her to bring us another round. I hadn't finished my first drink and didn't intend to have more than two. In this place, I'd learned, not getting drunk was a persistent, exacting task.

"What is?" he asked.

"Here," I said. "This place."

He shrugged and I thought he was going to turn sullen, but then a grin broke out across his face. "Dawson City?" he said.

"Sure."

He tilted his head back and laughed, so sharp and loud the whole room took note. But the look on his face wasn't bitter but gleeful. "Dawson City. Shit." He took the beer Eloise slid toward him without a word. "What's it, the scenery?"

I wondered if it was the kind of thing I could talk to him about, what it was like to look at those mountains, or that river. The way they made me feel was like the way I'd felt at home, so many years ago it would make me tired to count them, and never again till now. "Up here, it feels like you're at the edge of something."

He watched me. "Edge of what?"

"Maybe the world." I swung my beer back into my mouth, reckless. "Like you might fall right off."

He looked like he couldn't decide if that made him mad or not. "People like you always say things like that. I'll tell you what it feels like. Feels like the goddamn middle of every-thing."

"What does that mean?" I asked.

"The middle is where you end up if you don't go anywhere. You have to do something to get away from the middle."

"You don't like it here?"

"What would it be to not like it here, when this is the only damn place I've ever been."

"Minnie said—"

"It was like she said. I tried to go other places, but I always end up back here. In the middle."

I thought about that. "I was in Toronto, and people there thought they were in the middle of everything."

"Those people." He grinned. "Those people are so far over the edge, they went right over to the other side. I think about that place, or New York, wherever, these places you hear about that think we're just a bunch of half-naked Indians run-ning around in the woods and don't know what century it is till one of them shows up to tell us, and I picture them and all those big, tall buildings hanging upside down from the other side of the world. If one of them were to show me where in a book it says the world is round, I'd say, 'Bullshit, I'd believe you if you weren't walking around on your head.' You don't believe me? They show up here in their buses or their big cars like buses, RVs with fucking bowling alleys in them, and they get out of their cars like this." He turned around and mimed like he was walking around on his hands.

I started laughing and tried to pull him back in his chair, but he went right over, launched his feet into the air and was walking on his hands for a few steps before he crashed to the ground.

"Fuck, Jason," said Eloise, squeezing past him with her tray held high to show how hard her job was. He just lay on the floor with his eyes closed, laughing wild as an animal.

"Come on," I said, smiling, reaching my hand down to him, "come on up, Jason."

He let me pull him up. "I swear to God. They get out of their cars like that. Fuck knows how they drive."

I waited till he was quiet again and then I said, "I'm glad I came up here, Jason."

He glanced up at me and then reached for his cigarettes. I didn't know how to say it to him or even if I should. I'd been thinking about the stories he was telling me, and I was sure now of what I'd only worried at first. I didn't know how to tell him that I knew how she had died. And because of my own mother, I knew how hard it would be for him to put words to it, to how he hadn't been enough to keep her in the world. What it felt like to know you weren't enough to live for. I started again. "If I'd known she wasn't here, that it was only you, I'd have come anyway."

He shrugged and turned his face away, making his mouth into an O and sending smoke rings in halos over our heads. And then I started thinking about Stephan. What was it about Jason that reminded me of him? I knew it was wrong, probably, to feel there was anything alike in my love for my husband and my sister's son, but there was something there that I couldn't put a name to. Something wrong with him that I was dying to forgive. "I don't have any other family," I said. "I guess you don't either. Stephan thought I was crazy . . . when we were angry at each other, he'd always tell me I was crazy . . . or make me feel I was, or be afraid that I might be. I never was like other people. I don't know what it is or was. My eyes, or what happened to our mother"—I looked at him then, but he wouldn't meet my eyes—"or our father, or the school I went to, or just something wrong with me. But I never fit with other people. I see other people laughing, talking so easily, and if I'm laughing or talking to them, I'm thinking, Can they tell that I'm not like them? What if they stop laughing first. Things like that, I'm thinking all the time. And that's just kid stuff, right? Like everybody thinks that in high school or at some time. But I just never got so I felt like I could talk to another person without being afraid."

"What about Stephan?"

"Stephan," I said. I smiled. "Don't you know what I mean?"

"I don't know," he said, but he was smiling too. "You sound pretty crazy to me."

"You know what I want?" I asked.

He shook his head.

"I want you to take me to the—what do you call it? Where you work."

"The claim," he said. "That's what we say."

"I want you to take me to your claim," I told him.

"Okay," he said. "Okay. I told you we'll go sometime, and we will. But what are we doing tonight?"

I knew he knew that it was Angel's concert tonight, the second-last show of the music festival that the locals had all done their best to avoid. I knew he was counting on me knowing it. He would wait for me to say we should go, he would make it something he was talked into. Maybe he would even skip it if I didn't insist. And for a moment I thought about it, and how we could spend the rest of the night here in this bar if I let it happen. And then I saw Angel's face, the way on her face hurt didn't look like surprise. It looked like a reminder. I thought of her face and how those calm, steady eyes of hers would look out from the stage and not be surprised to see he wasn't there.

"We should go to Angel's show," I said at last. And he gave a long, slow nod, as he raised his full glass, with something like relief.

Somehow we got there early, or the concert started late. We found ourselves waiting in the gallery over the back of the church where Angel was scheduled to sing, and I could feel Jason getting restless and wanting to leave, hating the commitment that waiting for something proved. He'd left a seat between us, put his feet over the back of the chair in front of him and tilted his head back, his cigarette almost falling out of his mouth.

"Well, look who it is." A tall man with thick grey eyebrows nested over bright blue eyes climbed into the gallery, taking the stairs two at a time and trailing a short, shrewd-looking woman. The man smiled at me, and I couldn't help but smile back; he had the kind of face that was altered all over by smiling, deep-set laugh lines vaulting from the corners of his eyes across his cheeks, meeting with the curve of his mouth in a crooked grin. "And I know who this is." He reached out a hand and clapped mine closed in it. "Glad to meet you, Aileen. Peter here. I'm sure Jason has told you all about me."

I could feel the energy in Jason shifting as he settled more comfortably into his chair. "Not a word."

"Get your feet off that chair, boy," Peter said, his tone teasing, but to my surprise Jason listened to him. "Jason works with me at my claim up the road."

"He's my boss."

"I've known Jason for years. Knew your sister too."

I nodded.

"I'm very sorry for your loss. A great loss."

"Well," I said and didn't know what more to say.

"I'm Pat," said the woman behind Peter. "Married to this one long enough to know I'll grow old waiting for him to introduce me. I was very sad to hear what happened to your sister. A sad story, that one. Some lives are burdens, aren't they. Maybe it's wrong for me to say, but I wondered if it wasn't a blessing that she passed. I don't mean because she was blind, don't misunderstand me. But she seemed picked out for unhappiness. It's like that for some folks, isn't it."

"I don't know," I said coldly. I felt swarmed by her unanswerable questions. I wasn't sure if I agreed with her and was embarrassed not to be. "I don't know what it's like for other people."

"Watch your mouth," Peter told his wife, but his tone was affectionate. "Not your place to talk about. It was a tragedy, no doubt about it." Then he told Jason to move down so he could sit next to him, while Pat gave me a sharp look and took a seat beside me.

I turned to listen to the story Peter had begun telling Jason, but immediately felt a tap on my shoulder.

"You know," Pat whispered, "we had a bear at the camp today."

"The camp?"

She nodded, her tight, dyed red curls unmoving, as if they were sculpted onto her head. "We have a little cabin by the claim—we're only here in the summer. Rest of the year, we have a house in Whitehorse. I was on my knees trying to

unclog the kitchen pipe today and then I stood up and what
do I see but a grizzly sniffing around, maybe four feet over on
the other side of the window."

She stared at me, expectant of some kind of reaction. Was
I meant to be impressed? Sympathetic? "Does that happen
often?" I asked at last.

She shrugged. "From time to time. But that's the closest I
saw one get. Didn't see it long though."

"What happened?"

"Duncan shot it." She smiled at me. "He works with Peter
there."

"Shot it dead?"

"Well, if he hadn't, it would have come back. That's the
thing. A bear that's lost its fear is a dangerous bear. Can't have
that around the camp."

I wondered where he had shot it and how it had died.
Would it have happened all at once or slowly. "I saw a bear,"
I said, remembering. "I think it was dying too."

But she didn't seem to hear me and I followed her gaze to
the stage, where the lights came up to illuminate Angel standing in front of a tower of scaffolding with her guitar. Behind
her, lit in blue, her sister sat at her keyboard and her cousin
was seated on a stool with his drum. But the first song, she
sang alone.

She didn't introduce herself or the other members of her
tiny band, which the festival program called Black Wing.
She didn't even take time to set down her guitar, and instead
wrapped her arms around it and held it like an infant as she
sang.

I had not noticed, that day by the river or that afternoon
in her yard, how big her voice was. It was so sweet and clear

170

that I'd lost track of it in the open air somehow. It had seemed to settle into the sky like birdsong does, a satellite of sound, beautiful and distant from life on earth. But now, within the walls of this church, it filled the room and seemed not to float toward us but to surround us.

I turned to whisper to Jason that she was doing great, and then fell silent at the sight of him.

He sat perfectly straight in his chair, his mouth half open as if her singing was something shared between them, and stared steadily at her with eyes that were wide and unguarded. He looked like a child. He was, I realized, in love with her.

The band joined her in the next songs, and they played for only an hour. When they finished, Angel bowed and turned her back to the audience to acknowledge her bandmates, and then they quietly left the stage. Though more than half of the audience stood up and the applause went on long after they'd gone, they did not come back for an encore.

For reasons I didn't understand, I felt moved by the performance. Or maybe it was Jason's face that stayed with me. But I didn't want to talk to Pat or her husband, and so I stood up quickly and snatched my bag from the floor. "It was nice to meet you," I said with a nod at the two of them. "Are you leaving, Jason?"

Jason turned slowly and looked at me as if he'd just realized I was in the room. "Maybe I'll stay," he said.

I nodded. "Yep. Good idea. She'll be glad to see you."

"No." He shook his head. "You stay too."

I sighed. "I'm tired, Jason."

He crossed his arms and grinned. "Well," he said. "Let's see if we can do something about that."

Jason led me downstairs to the bar set up at the back of

the church and ordered me a coffee. He leaned against the wall while I drank it, his eyes searching the room behind me.

"You don't see her?" I asked.

He shrugged. "Just checking who's here." Then his eyes met mine. "So you like Peter?"

"I didn't really talk to him."

"I should find him. You should talk. You'll like him. He's a big storyteller. When we're together, the two of us, people around town say even the dead are listening. One time, at a party, he got to telling this one story, and whenever he got tired, I'd jump in and keep going, and whenever I got tired, he'd jump in and keep going, so it just didn't stop. And everyone at the party stopped talking and just listened to us. Morning came, and we kept telling the story all that day and all that night, and then the next day, and the next night. For three days, we told that story, and nobody moved or said a word, they were listening so hard."

Before I could reply, Jason had pushed his way into the growing crowd, which was filling the church so tight I wondered if he'd ever find his way back. But he returned with his boss, both of them flushed with some kind of energy that seemed to crackle and move between them.

"So, Aileen, do you dye your hair?" Peter boomed.

I touched it, where it had begun to fall over my eyes, needing to be cut. "Well, I used to," I said. "I'm not sure if I'm going to anymore."

"You're as pretty as your sister," Peter said. "Natural blond, she was. I loved the colour of her hair. You know, I once dated a blond girl who looked a little like her, if you can believe it. This must have been twenty years ago now. That fall was my first year in these parts, and I came up with money in my pocket and bought that claim, and went digging around on it like a kid in a sandbox. Didn't have a clue. Found a skeleton of a dog. A tiny, little dog, must have been wild or belonged to some miner back in the day. Had a broken leg that hadn't healed right. I felt attached to that little skeleton and sorry as could be for digging it up. That little blond gal would come by in the evenings then in her little car. She lived in town and drove this 1968 VW thing, like a little tin can coming down the road, didn't make any sense in these parts. She was right creeped out by that skeleton, I'll tell you. I had it set up on the shelf over my bed. I don't know why, but it made me feel glad to keep it in there with me warm, and I felt good looking at it there. But she'd make me put a sheet over it whenever we got amorous. I couldn't blame her for it. Not that she had any right to complain, being the second cousin of a guy who kept his own foot in a jar. Remember him, Jason?"

And the two of them talked back and forth, their voices rising louder and louder to be heard over the crowd that was bigger and bigger and getting drunk waiting for the next show. Every story branched off into three more, and any time Peter paused, Jason would jump in, just like he'd said. Sometimes they'd correct each other, but the corrections were always embellishments. "His wife was hardly up to his elbow," Peter would say. "Your memory's got the slip of you, old man," Jason would interrupt. "If she were walking ahead of him and stopped too sudden, she'd've knocked her head on his belt buckle."

And then the lights, without warning, went out, and I gasped as if the dark were a sea I had plunged into. I heard laughter and shouts across the room, and suddenly felt conscious of the heat of the hundreds of bodies around me, pushing against one another. I felt unsafe.

173

"Jason?" I whispered. "Jason?"

And then I felt him grab my sleeve and pull me toward the wall. "Come on," he said in my ear. "Come on over here."

"I need to go home," I whispered back, but the words disappeared in the sudden swell of light and sound as the band emerged out of the darkness onstage, washed in violet light and already in the midst of a loud, throbbing chord as the drums kicked at the sound from underneath.

And then the volume dropped and a fiddler appeared in a white spotlight, planted on the highest platform of the scaffolding, elevated above and beside the band, like a dream rising up from the music it was making. She was playing a feverish riff, a twisting line of music that she pulled out of her fiddle, somewhere between rock and the Celtic music I'd grown up with, and beneath her, her feet danced.

Watching her, I felt the steps in my own feet. I'd long forgotten being taught them as a young girl who still could see the world perfectly, lined up with my sister and the other youngest children of our church in its basement, while the older ladies called out *step-shuffle-hop-tap-tap*. I had never danced them again after my mother died. But now, I felt how my feet wanted to join the fiddler in the crazed rhythm of her dance, speeding up as her playing did, the impossible countering of her feet to what her hands were doing to the fiddle they held.

"Jason," I whispered. "Jason, I . . ." But I had nothing to say and he couldn't hear me anyway. And I saw then that mine were not the only feet that had caught the rhythm of the steps from hers. All around me, I saw boys and girls half my age bobbing in the crowd, maybe themselves remembering whoever had first taught them how. Right in front of me a petite girl with dirty-looking pink hair bounced up and down, kicking out her feet at random, oblivious, apparently, to the sequence of the steps, unaware or uncaring that she didn't know how.

And then the crashing guitars and drums of the band swelled up behind the fiddler, and the music seemed to break apart in all directions, including everything and everyone in its dizzying swirl, coloured lights cycling around the room to illuminate not just the musicians but the church full of dancers that had been made out of the audience before them, and a cry went up across the crowd and suddenly it seemed everyone was shouting and dancing, a sea of loud and moving bodies set free.

A sudden weight fell against my back and I turned to see that people had filled in the space between me and the wall, and the young man who had, in his exuberance, crashed into me danced on with just a grin in my direction to acknowledge the collision. For a moment, I felt as if I were being swallowed up in this church. I felt myself begin to disappear.

But then something happened. Looking around me, I realized I was wrong. I was not disappearing, I was dissolving—into whatever it was that was happening in the room. And then I looked down and saw, to my surprise, that I was dancing.

The boy behind me, his elbows and hands careless and wild, knees pumping tirelessly beneath him, looked at me approvingly as I spun around and met his eyes. A smile broke out on my face. And then I turned an ankle and crashed to the ground.

"Here," said the boy, reaching his hand down, and instinctively I extended mine toward it, thinking he wanted to help me to my feet. But pinched between his fingers was a lit joint, and there, on the floor, I took it without question. It had been years since I smoked, and then only at a few disorienting wharf parties, where pot was another version of suffering the company of more normal young men and women. I had emerged from boarding school like a snapped elastic band, hurtling into the sighted world of youths who knew far more and dared far less than I did, I who had felt then that I had experienced everything. I had once smoked bowl after bowl by myself at the harbour, as the kids I'd come with found their way back to their cars to make out or follow weaving paths home. I'd passed out there and woken up staring at the shoes of a little girl standing over me. "What are you doing there?" she'd asked me, and I had no answer.

I drew deep on the joint, refusing to let my throat tighten into a cough, feeling the smoke bury its claws in my lungs. I held it for a minute and then let it out all at once, a sweet, musky cloud that I watched travel up into the air, joining a dim haze that now hung over the whole room, exhaled from a thousand lungs. I stood up. And then I took another draw. And another.

When I returned the joint, it occurred to me that I wasn't sure if I was still dancing or had stopped after my fall. Checked. Feet were still. And yet everything around me moved, and I moved too. I looked at the boy, head back, eyes closed, hauling on the last of the joint, and tapped him on the shoulder. "I danced like this when I was little," I told him, my voice incredibly loud, cutting through the music like a bell. He opened his eyes, smiled, nodded. "I'm from Nova Scotia," I explained.

He leaned in and shouted at my ear, "I'm from Conception Bay."

That made me smile. I leaned in to shout something back,

but hesitated. What was there to be said, really. "Oh," I told him. "Good!" And then I added, "It was like this. When I was little. Before my mother died. We were learning to dance, and it was like this. My childhood."

And then I thought happily about a time when it had been. A church even had been part of it, but of course not like this. Yet it had been the same. So full like this. A whole family at home, and people at the church and at school. The world we knew filled to bursting like this room was. I thought that and felt something like sadness, but even that I enjoyed in a deep, satisfied way. Everything was slowing around me, and I felt perfectly still, a point of silence and clarity at the centre of a spinning world. And then I noticed the music had changed to something slower, and that was good too. The room now swayed and rocked, dancing still but horizontally, the frantic bobbing heads tipping from side to side instead.

I wondered where Jason was. I remembered that he had been beside me earlier and saw that now he was not.

It took two songs to find him, standing by himself beside the bar. His eyes were bright and black under the flickering lights, fixed on something in the distance. I turned to see what he was looking at and saw a tall man dancing a very slow waltz with a woman at the end of the room, near the exit where the crowd thinned. He had his face bent down to rest against her shining hair, and all that was touching between them were their faces and their hands. All these people, this loud music, everything went on, while Angel and John circled each other in the corner of the church, like there was music we were deaf to that somehow they could hear.

I tried to think of something I could say to Jason that would make him look away from them. But then I noticed

177

something more important. The fiddler, who was now playing something slow and tender with closed eyes, looked like
she had pulled her fiddle to her out of love; her cheek rested
against it, drawing something crooning and beautiful out of it
with the stroke of her bow. But underneath her, the pedestal
of scaffolding she stood on seemed to be leaning away from
the stage, as if releasing her from the band into the arms of the
crowd before her.

"She's falling," I said, but no one turned or heard. So I
watched for a moment, more interested than worried. "After
all," I said to myself tenderly, "you are very high right now."

But then another song began, this one the heaviest and
loudest yet. The crowd roared with joy, and the sound
pounded out, beating against the walls of the church. It was
an angry sound, and I wanted it to stop now. The fiddler stood
on her perch, looking out over us all, her face unreadable as
the music played. And then suddenly the guitars and drums
sank into a downbeat and the tempo slowed and she raised her
fiddle to her shoulder again. I didn't think to be afraid for her
until a clangour of distorted chords and bass resumed, and she
began jumping in rhythm on her little pedestal, like the young
people throwing themselves against each other just in front
of the stage. "Oh my god," I said, and this time, the heads in
front of mine turned.

Inch by inch the scaffolding beneath her sank. Each time
she leapt and planted herself to the ground again, it wobbled
farther. She seemed not to know or care, perhaps disoriented
by her own music.

And then, suddenly, all at once she and everyone in the
room seemed to see what was happening to her. Only the band
was oblivious, thundering on through their song, while the

crowd stilled and waited for what now seemed inevitable. At first she held her fiddle in position though no longer playing, watching, wide-eyed, at us below. Then she lowered her fiddle and took a step backwards, but it was as if with that gesture, she gave a signal, and everything released.

In an instant, the scaffolding reached its tipping point and plunged to the floor in front of the stage. Someone, or everyone, screamed. And the fiddler disappeared.

At first they told us she was dead. Huddled outside the church, where we'd been ordered by the paramedics, we shared cigarettes and rumours. Then someone said that she had lived, but was in a coma and the six people she landed on were dead.

It was a deep blue night and the sun would soon give up and go back the other way again. I wandered the street, smoking a cigarette someone had given me and looking for Jason.

I thought that maybe he'd forgotten about me and felt sorry for myself. And then I thought of the fiddler and was ashamed. She'd looked so young. Maybe only twenty years old.

Suddenly I felt sick, and I threw my cigarette to the ground just as a hand clapped down on my shoulder, and I turned and Jason was there.

"Hello," he said, and I burst into tears.

He stared at me. "What the hell."

We stood with an arm's length between us for a moment, him looking at me like I came from the moon, and me crying, my chin lowered almost to my chest, my arms loose at my sides. Crying like it was draining out of me.

And I didn't know how to tell him that when that fiddler fell, it was like watching my own past come crashing to the floor. How this girl had fallen right in front of me and I was standing on the street grieving my childhood. How she might be injured or dead and might be only twenty years old, and what was wrong with me that, even knowing that, I could think only of myself, of Mara and me in the basement of that stupid church with no clue that everything about to happen would hurl us here.

"This fucking town," I said at last.

And with that, the worried, mildly annoyed expression rose up and left his face. "Yeah," he said cheerfully. "Fuck this town."

I wiped my eyes and looked around at everyone in the street, waiting for word from inside and trying, in their own ways, to comfort one another. And I thought for the second time that night that I understood why somebody would stay in a place like this.

"I was inside talking to a buddy of mine who's a ranger," Jason told me. "Girl's got a broken wrist and maybe a sprained ankle. She'll be fine. Violin's toast."

"She fell so far," I said in wonder.

"She had a soft landing. Right into the mosh pit. Some of them won't like waking up tomorrow, but nobody's hurt too bad."

"I want to go home," I said, realizing it.

"I'll walk you there."

I looked up at him. "Jason?"

"Sure."

"I can't stay there forever. At that hotel."

He frowned. "You want to go back to—"

"I want . . ." I cleared my throat. "I was wondering if I could stay with you. Just for a while."

"You want to stay at my house."

"Just until I get a job. I'm going to start looking this week. I'll find something, and then I can get an apartment. But till then I'd be a good roommate. I'm a good cook," I said. I was not a good cook.

"You want to stay with me."

I shrugged. It had been a bad idea. I wondered if he would avoid me now, punish me for trying to draw him too close. I looked back at the church, so as not to look at him. In the window I could see people clearing up. I could see a woman standing by the window, like she was searching for something outside. I stared at her and she stared back. The features of her face were made obscure by the light of the sun, already rising again, hitting the window. It made her look like a ghost, an outline of someone not entirely there. "I wonder who'll be blamed," I said, to say something. "Who built the set on the stage. Whose fault it was."

"My buddy said they never should have had a show like that at the church. Usually bands like that play the tent. But in the end nobody was hurt much. By next week, nobody'll care."

I wasn't listening. The woman was still watching me from inside the church. I thought for a moment I recognized her. Something in her pale gold hair, her white, stricken face. I moved toward her and saw her features take shape, becoming more surely the person she could not possibly be.

"Jason," I said softly. "Look at her."

"Who?"

I pushed my way through the crowd till I stood before the window, looking for her that I'd always been looking for. It was her face. There at the window, looking back at me.

There, as the sun lifted into the sky, I saw the shadowy forms of people working in the church disappear, till all I could see was my reflection in the glass. And I saw her face.

I turned back to look at her son, who had not followed me. He pulled out a cigarette and lit it, watching me, and I could see thoughts tumbling in his head, the push and pull of what he wanted or thought he did.

"Never mind," I said, walking back to him. "I thought I saw someone. I was wrong."

He didn't answer for a moment. And then he said, "You'll stay in her room."

After we left, we stopped at the hotel and I paid while Jason carried out my suitcase. We walked the rest of the way in silence.

The house was a small clapboard two-storey, with peeling yellow paint and green wooden windows. The steps up onto the narrow veranda creaked under my weight, and I looked back at Jason, bent over beneath the weight of my suitcase, which he'd hoisted on his back. "So this is your home," I said.

But as I opened the door and walked into a bright, open living room that connected to the kitchen, it hit me all at once that it wasn't his home I'd asked to stay in but hers. In only the clutter, the indiscriminate collapse of one thing here or another there—a plastic mesh hat on a pot hook over the stove, a calendar from the Yukon National Bank tacked over the wooden chair by the door where he sat to pull off his boots when he came in—was there any sign of him or of a man like him. The rest was all white-painted wooden furniture, the tiny brown roses on the wallpaper, bits of cotton crochet like shed exoskeletons prostrated over every surface. All of it was hers, her things, in her home.

No. That was wrong. I could not look for her in any of those things. I remembered that Mara would not have chosen the print on her wallpaper or the colour of her table and chairs. Some other person would have made those decisions. She wouldn't have known the things she lived among except by their sounds and surfaces.

I looked again at the small efforts that had been made to make the room cozy or comfortable. Over the sagging frame of a door at the far end of the living room, there was a narrow shelf of coloured bottles. Wine bottles, beer bottles, liquor bottles. All different sizes and colours. Maybe in the afternoon, there was a brief hour when the sun could be seen directly through the window, and it would hit those bottles and maybe someone once had thought it lovely, the way those different pieces of glass glowed. Someone who had picked out the wallpaper and the furniture. Who had tried to make a home for his blind wife.

"Jason," I said, "what about your father?"

He was pulling a couple of beers out of the fridge. "What?"

"Your father, were you close with him?"

He took two green plastic cups out of the cupboard and snapped the caps of the bottles off on the edge of the counter and then poured them into the cups. The beer made a longing, gulping sound that rose in pitch, almost gleeful, as it sucked and pulled air from the bottle.

"I think you know I wasn't," Jason said. He handed me a cup.

"I *don't* know. Not really," I said. "All I know is what you told me about how he died and . . . how he hurt her. But then why did she stay—did she love him that much?"

He drained about half the cup of beer. "She hated him," he said.

"Because he hit her?"

"You wouldn't have known it was possible for one person to hate another so much, but if you had, you wouldn't have thought it would be a wife for a husband that could feel that way. I don't know if I came to hating him on my own, or if it was just a habit I got into from watching her."

"But why," I asked. "Why did she stay with him?"

Jason stood up. "You see this chip off the edge of the table?"

I looked and there was a chunk missing from the end of one of the boards of the table, like someone had taken a bite out of it. A sheet of paint had torn off with it, and where it was left exposed, I could see the warm sheen of wood worn down by the oils on the hands of the people who had lived around it.

He said, "That's where one time he tried to bring the blunt end of a splitting maul down on her. He missed that time. But most of the time he didn't miss."

I felt the place—where was it supposed to be? my brain? beneath the left pocket of my blouse?—where I should have known something to say or wonder, and it was mute and dumb as muscle and bone. When I spoke again, I had to look somewhere else, like it was out of my liver or my lungs that I found the question. "Because she was afraid? That's why she didn't leave him?"

Jason ran his hand back and forth along the table, its edge in the gulf between his thumb and forefinger. "I don't know why people don't leave things," he said.

"Jason," I said. "Jason, did he hit you?"

He said, "What do you think." He said, "They had fights like they were fucking. It was the closest I got to seeing what it would look like if they'd loved each other, there was this heat in them, this way he'd look at her, as if he could hardly see anything else in the room. Sometimes if I got hurt it wasn't even on purpose—sometimes he'd hurt me because he was so haunted with her and wanting to do her harm that he just didn't notice I wasn't her. He'd go at her with a fist like he thought he could just flatten her into nothing. Into not being there. Not being anything at all."

I hated the wallpaper. I hated the bottles. I thought I shouldn't live here after all, and Jason shouldn't either. I thought we should just leave this town and take nothing with us. And now I understood why she had done it. It had been the only way she could leave. And she already knew that way of making an exit. "Jason, I know what happened to her," I said.

"What do you mean?"

"How she died." I looked at him meaningfully but he wouldn't return my gaze. "You don't have to tell me if you don't want to. But it's important you know"—I took a deep breath and told him what the psychologist Aunt Una had taken me to had said—"it wasn't your fault and there isn't anything, in the end, that can be done for other people except what they do for themselves. We can love them and support them, but that isn't enough for some people. Some people need something more that's meant to come from themselves, and for some reason they don't have it. Do you understand?"

Jason said, "You think she killed herself?"

I didn't know how to answer him. I was in the middle of realizing something. I'd been pulling Stephan out of drawers since I arrived, out of every thought and fear and desire and grief I had, and I'd thought what was left was all the missing-ness of Mara. All her absence, all my guilt. But now I saw that I'd been wrong. It was Jason that was left. He was so full, he was bursting out of containment in my thoughts or care, and he was what I was full of. Not his needs, but my own, what I needed to be for him. What Stephan and perhaps even Mara had not needed from me.

Jason said, "Say something." My mouth went looking for words and he looked at me then and said, "Say something."

"Do you," I asked, "do you have another story?"

He lowered his head. His hair was dirty and somehow much longer than when I'd met him, though it had not even been two months. It fell in pieces from a nucleus at the back of his head, where a coin-sized bit of bare skin showed, like a baby's hair. "Can it be just a little one?" he asked.

I nodded. I was looking at the table and all the places where paint was scratched or scraped away.

"Okay," he said. "You think you know what happened to her, but you don't. I haven't told you yet."

My father's people believe that if a pregnant woman dreams of a dead person, her child will inherit that person's soul. Old Woman had wanted a child for so long. She no longer thought it was possible for her to have children. She was too old, and her husband had never given her a baby.

Old Man had been angry with her for so long. He was tired of her face, the way it was always the same face in the morning that it had been in the evening. When she talked, she did not make him think of anything interesting. But it was not just her he was angry with. He had felt for a very long time that a trick had been played on him. He had thought he invented the world. He had thought he was an important person. The man from the beginning of things. He thought he would be busy forever with the pride of having made the world. But the longer he lived, the less the world pleased him. The animals had less and less to say. Eventually they would not talk to him at all. And he had made men and women to play on the earth, but because they were mortal, they were often bored and they never lost a certain kind of doomed expression that depressed Old Man. And because he was depressed, he decided that winter would not leave the world. He prepared more snow than he had ever made before and he let it fall until the men and women and animals did not know what there was to the world that was not snow. They waited for summer to come, so they could take fish from the rivers again, and so the caribou would run, but summer did not come.

At this time, Old Woman had a secret. She was with child. And so she did not mind anymore that her husband was melancholy and discourteous with her. And one night, as she slept with her head on the sea, as she often did, because it was such a soft place to rest her head, because even the frozen sea melted when Old Woman touched it, and her body between the sheets of snow, because the snow did not melt, not even when she touched it, she had a dream. She dreamt of long, green blades of grass that could cut your fingers. She dreamt of fireweed pushing up into a lit blue sky that did not darken for months. She dreamt of the quick water in the river full with salmon. She dreamt of the dumb, sad eyes of caribou.

She woke and smiled with the freight of her secret. In her belly, a little bigger each day, pushing and turning inside her, summer grew.

Mara

THIRTEEN

IN THOSE YEARS at the boarding school, I was more deeply happy than I have ever been since.

The girls respected me and did not ever seem to regard me as the strange burden I knew I had become to the rest of the world outside the heavy front doors of the school. They loved the stories I told them from the Bible and let me make up others too, or tell them about Da, or about how I had come to be blind. Some days I would tell them that my mother had been so mad before she hanged herself that she pulled our eyes from our heads while we slept. "If you could see me," I'd tell them gravely, "you would see only holes where other girls have eyes." Or, "Give me your hand and touch the glass eyes they make me wear. They feel real, don't they? They feel just like yours . . ." Or, if I was in another sort of mood, I would say it had been an ordinary childhood illness, such as any other child might have.

It was a kind of miracle, for which I was constantly grateful, that they never questioned the revisions I made to my account for myself. One day I might say, "A flight of birds descended on my eyes with their claws and beaks while my mother fought to shelter me from them but was too weak and could not run as fast as they could fly," and the next: "Cat-aracts." And the girls would make little bird-like sounds of their sorriness for me each time, and we would link our fingers together in the way that we had learned to do to comfort one another and remind ourselves that the darkness we lived in was not empty.

We were not entrusted with our own time at boarding school. Rather the nuns took our time into their care, and released it back to us in small parcels, with instructions as to how best to use it. I was so grateful to have them attend to time for me. There were no long hours with my cheek pressed to the glass of the window, straining to hear what might be on the other side. There was no occasion to question how I might better occupy myself or whether there was any true joy or relief in being so occupied, or where and how *she* might be occupied and why there was not a word from her, not any sign or evidence of her continued occupancy of the world itself, not even its faint consequence, the way a distant leaf might trem-ble on a distant tree because she had opened her hand. Instead, everything proceeded with a sense of hurry and urgency that was never panicked, only steadily, persistently brisk. All pro-cedures of our day's activity were as efficiently managed as was possible for such simple undertakings, stripped bare of any possible excesses of movement or hesitation. We learned to walk in straight lines, holding the hands of the children in front of and behind us. We knew precisely how to find our seats at the table with just a simple count of steps and a quick grasp of the back of the chair. It was as if a great engine lay beneath the school, turning us on a wheel that drew us from the dining hall to our classrooms, where we learned Braille and scripture and the few other subjects deemed applicable for children of our disability, and then from exercise in the yard to prayer to crafts to chapel and back to the dining hall. The fixed intent of that wheel, its unwavering progress, was a great comfort to us.

The girls were mostly soft-voiced and timorous, eager to please. I understood that many of them had come from homes where they had not been welcome. Those who were more confident or spirited were chastised so often by the nuns for being overly boisterous that their little clique lost its status among us and their exuberance became defiance. We were rewarded for three things at the school, and we knew the significance of those three things because they were constantly expounded: diligence, diffidence and deference. Excellence of other kinds—an especially high score on a test or victory in one of the exercise matches that the nuns reluctantly allowed once a year—was treated with mistrust and something akin to reproach, for, it was understood, such triumphs might rob us of our humility.

I did not come to know many of the girls individually, and most of them remained for me part of a single comforting entity composed of many gentle voices and soft, cold hands. Only Agnes, who was my roommate all the years I was at the school; Sister Margaret, who occasionally showed me affection; and Father McGivney, who took my confession and would tell me how to be forgiven with prayer and how many Hail Marys I was to say, emerged from the rest of the nuns and teachers and students. And they were enough. This little group of people who were mostly kind to me came to seem to be what was left of the world, and I did not feel that I needed more. Except at night, when all I could hear was the sound of Agnes's asthmatic breathing and perhaps, if Sister Margaret had consented to open the window, as I begged her to do in the summer months, the evening sounds of insects making their calls to one another, which might have been the same calls made by the same insects we had heard back home when we had fallen silent and lain with our heads together on the pillow, waiting for sleep. Then I thought of *her*.

Jason

~

mid-August 1996

FOURTEEN

IF ANYBODY EVER TOLD YOU to be careful about wanting things, you'd better believe the fuck out of them, I'd always known that. I knew for a fact that nobody with a closed hand ever got their fingers cut and so I went around like that all the time, with my hands in fists beside me.

Some folks didn't know any better than to take whatever they got. They had their hands out all the time, asking for whatever happened to them. It gave me a good feeling to see those people hurt themselves. I liked the looks on their faces, the little round Os of surprise they made out of their mouths when everything came to shit. Like the girl they loved turned out to like some other guy better, to have liked him better all over the back seat of his nicer car. Or they told you that you mattered to them, and then their mouths made little Os when you found some way to show them you weren't owned.

But there was a problem. A serious predicament, Peter would call it. The predicament had been living in my mother's bedroom for three weeks and was up before me every morning, with a pot of tea made, sitting at the breakfast table looking kind of happy and proud, like the teapot was a parade she'd thrown me. The predicament said stuff like, "I thought I

197

came here looking for your mother—isn't it weird that it was you I found and now that seems more important?" She told me she could see Ma in me and nobody had ever said that before. She said she didn't see it at first, but now she saw it all over the place, in the way my eyes moved or the way I talked so fast sometimes I'd gasp a little at the end, because I'd forgot to breathe. The predicament said she wanted to stay here with me, that she thought she could make a home of my town. She said I was her whole family.

So I made a little room for her, a little space in between things. I left a pause at the end of the night, when she'd stand there watching me before I closed my bedroom door, and it was enough time for her to get certain words out. And it wasn't that I hadn't heard those words before, it was that I let her get them out before I closed the door. It was that I drank her damn tea and got to thinking in the morning, going down the stairs, how it would be good to have a cup and might in fact be exactly what I wanted. It was that her face seemed kinder than when I first saw it, and I liked the lines it folded into when she smiled, and I liked, too, how nervous she was, how she had always looked ready for me to do something sudden or frightening. How I didn't even mind when she stopped looking ready.

One afternoon, I drove home thinking about the predicament, and when I got there, she was waiting at the kitchen table, smoking a cigarette and reading something, and she jumped up and switched the lights off, and while I stood there, staring at her, because even with the blinds drawn tight it was still bright enough inside to read a cereal box by, she leapt up and turned the lights back on and yelled, "Surprise!"

I started pulling my boots off but didn't take my eyes off her. It was hot as blazes outside, and sweat had sealed my shirt to my back. "What's this about," I asked.

She had that nervous, rabbit-y look about her. "I didn't know what you'd want. I mean, should I have asked Angel and Minnie, or Peter . . . ? I didn't know if you'd want a big to-do."

"Why would I want a big to-do?"

She had this paper cone hat on her head, and I had only the beginning of an idea what she was up to, but the hat was a big help. She gave a little tug on the chin elastic, looking embarrassed. "Well, that's just it. I thought you probably wouldn't. So I just made a cake, and—"

"You think it's my birthday?"

She stared at me, her big, wide rabbit eyes blinking, figuring. "It isn't?"

I dropped myself into one of the kitchen chairs. "We got any beer?"

She turned around, looking lost, and took half a step toward the fridge before turning back to me. "Yes, I got your fav—it isn't your birthday?"

I let myself grin a little then. She had the hat on and everything. "Nope."

"But the photo . . ."

I was just about ready to enjoy myself. "The beer, Aileen?"

She took it from the fridge and gave it to me in a glass, and then she ran upstairs. The really heartbreaking thing, it occurred to me, was the blanket she'd put up to cover the window over the sink that didn't have a curtain. It was poked through with tacks and looked about ready to come down. And it didn't make half a difference. You couldn't have hid a

199

shadow in the room. But it was the idea of dark. It was enough to make her think she could do something sort of stupid and heartbreaking like surprise someone in broad daylight in their own home, when it wasn't even their birthday. And then she hadn't heard the truck or had been so busy with whatever it was she'd been reading that she'd not even been ready when I got there. All round, it was the worst job of a surprise I could reckon, and I couldn't stop grinning about it.

I heard her feet on the stairs. That was like Ma, how light she was on the stairs. I spent about half a thought on it every time she went up or down them. Only the creaking of the stairs themselves let me know she was coming down. Chuckling to myself a little, I picked up the envelope she'd been looking at that had had her so distracted that she missed the sound of my truck in the yard. The address was typed in giant letters and in the corner there was only an address, no name.

"So you got a letter from Toronto," I said, as she walked toward me, holding something in her hands.

"Oh," she said, tipping her face down like she could hide it from me, "I just wrote to a lawyer. I wrote to a divorce lawyer, Jason. He had to write to Stephan's sister, because I didn't even know where he was." She dropped into her chair like an axe. "I didn't even know where to send the damn divorce forms."

"You okay about this?" I asked.

"Well, I'm not going to stay married to a man who doesn't care what end of the country I'm in, am I?"

"But he doesn't know you're here."

"Just leave it, Jason," she said. "Okay?"

"Sure thing," I said. "But did you ever think that maybe he's looking for you?"

She was white as a stone. "Yes," she said. "Yes, yes, I have."

"So the letter's from your lawyer?" I asked, and she looked at me without saying a word. I shrugged. "Well, it's your business."

"Look," she said, holding out the thing in her hands, which was a photograph. "See? On the back it says, 'August 11, 1984.' I had to use a magnifying glass to read it. Is that her writing or his?"

I'd forgot what day it was. "His," I said. I looked at the photograph. He had a cone-shaped paper party hat on hardly any different from Aileen's. Cavemen, probably, had worn hats like that. He was sitting beside me at the end of the table. There wasn't any cake, just a pile of cupcakes on a plate, with icing two inches high on top. The sign hung behind the table read, "Happy birthday, Jason." There were a few people around the table, but I could only guess who they were, with their backs to the camera, looking at me and him, who was the only one looking back at whoever was taking the picture. She wasn't in the photo. I wondered who had taken it, and why they hadn't waited for my mother to come back from the kitchen or wherever she had gone, outside the camera frame. "She couldn't write."

Aileen covered her eyes for a second. "Oh," she said. "Of course." After a moment, she asked, "So she didn't take the picture then."

"She was blind, Aileen. She wasn't a photographer." I would have been twelve years old, but I looked younger. I was looking at the cupcakes like they were happiness itself. It was my father's face I couldn't read. And I hated how much I recognized his face, not from remembering him but from the reflection of my own face and what it was turning out to look like.

"So why does it say it's your birthday then?"

"It doesn't. It was his." I gave the photograph back to her and took a slug from my beer.

"His . . ." She thought about that. "His name was Jason too?"

I gave a nod and slapped the table. "So where's that cake?"

"In the . . . I'll get it." She tucked the photograph into her apron pocket. "I'm sorry," she said quietly. "I didn't know."

"I know," I said, and then she went into the kitchen. "So what the hell are you doing with a cigarette," I asked, pulling what was left from the ashtray on the table and sucking the last puff or two out of it till I got the sweet, metallic tang of filter.

"Oh, I only do it from time to time. It's no big deal. I smoked in high school, you know."

"I can't picture that," I said.

"Did Mara smoke?"

I closed my eyes and imagined coming home to find her in the dark, a cloud of smoke rising around her, the dull, mechanical return of her hand from mouth to ashtray and back. "Nah," I said. "Hardly ever."

She set a plate down in front of me. It was about the sorriest piece of cake I'd ever seen. "I never made a cake before," she said, sounding angry.

"Looks good," I said. I took the fork she gave me and shovelled a piece of cake into my mouth. It was dry as dirt, but the icing was sweet and I figured I could finish it off no problem. Watching me eat seemed to be making her happy. "So how's the job hunt," I asked.

"Fine," she said. "I put an application in at *The Northern Light*."

"The newspaper? To do what?"

She looked down. "To write, I guess. I used to think I might like to be some kind of a writer. When he interviewed me, Melvin, the editor, made me come up with three ideas for stories. He said I had good instincts. I guess he liked my ideas."

"Melvin," I said like his name tasted bad in my mouth. Melvin weighed three hundred pounds on a good day and was from Alabama or some made-up place like that. He'd been in Dawson a decade and still acted like his feet didn't touch the same dirty ground the rest of ours did. "Here's an idea. Twenty-two years we've been negotiating our claims, and we're the only ones without a dollar to show for it. How's that for a story?" That morning I'd run into a buddy of mine who said it could be another year till we saw a cent. Or maybe we never would. His brother worked in the government and said that they were refusing to buy out the claim some mining company had on Tr'ochëk, where our people used to live. And we couldn't reach a settlement till somebody budged, and till then they were playing chicken with the feds. While the rest of us got old waiting to get what even the goddamn feds said we were owed.

She hesitated. "It's not really that kind of a paper. It's not really . . . hard news. More like cultural stuff, community pride, you know."

"Yeah," I said.

She looked worried. "Maybe, if I get the job, you could help me. You know, give your perspective on Dawson's history—"

"Just forget about it," I said. "It doesn't matter." When that money came I could leave. Go far enough away that I'd never find my way back even if I wanted it. Maybe take her with me.

She didn't seem convinced. "Jason, can I ask you . . . I mean, I understand that these . . . settlements . . . are important to you. It's a matter of justice for your people, okay, I get that."

"You think we're just looking for a handout?" I gave her the eyes I looked at tourists with.

"Of course not. I understand"—she fluttered her hands around her face—"they did something wrong here. White people just came and kicked you off your land—"

"They didn't kick us off it. They bought it for nothing. Our people back then didn't understand they were buying our land. They didn't know you could own land. They just thought the white folks were taking the little houses they'd built on the land."

She sighed. "So the government owes you the proper worth of your land. And reparations. I understand that. But what I don't understand is why this money is so important to you. You've got a house, a job. What do you need this money for?"

I took the pack beside the ashtray and pulled out another cigarette. "I don't know, Aileen," I said, with the cigarette clamped between my teeth as I lit it. "Guess that's a real mystery. Well, here's another one. How come this letter with a date of two weeks ago stamped on it is still all sealed up, tight as teeth? What are you waiting around for? You worried that lawyer's going to tell you Stephan signed the deal? Maybe all you wanted to do was give him a scare, getting a lawyer after him for a divorce, without even telling me a word about it. And maybe it didn't work. Maybe it didn't scare him at all to be done with you. That what you're worried about?"

She looked more tired than insulted. "You can drop it, Jason."

"Or maybe it isn't from the lawyer at all," I said, taking a long drag and feeling her want a cigarette of her own. Almost enjoying myself. "Nothing about this letter looks official to me. What's this address, Aileen? Who lives here?"

She rubbed her face, and I couldn't tell if that was what brought the red to it or not. "Yes, Jason, you don't miss a trick. The letter's not from the lawyer, it's from him. From Stephan. And that's our address on it, mine and his. And he used the magnatype. My special typewriter. He used the magnatype so I could read it." She picked the envelope up and stared at it, shaking her head like it was full of wonder. She seemed now hardly to be talking to me at all. "And that means he must have gone back to the house. Maybe he's there now, for all I know. And I'm not ready to read this letter. Maybe I should tear it up. Maybe it's him just sending back the papers, signed like you said. Or maybe it's something else and I should tear it up anyway. But I just keep thinking about picking up the phone. About just seeing if he'd answer if I called our home. About how good it would be to talk to someone, to really talk."

And somehow that made me feel a hot, dull anger in me, because what did she need to go to him for to talk of things. "I talk to you," I said.

"Yes," she answered slowly. "You do. But you don't listen much." And as she spoke, there was a crash at the window behind her. In the crack of light between the window and the closed blinds, I saw the body of a raven slide down the glass, dead, its eyes watching me as it fell to the ground below. Aileen seemed not to notice. I wanted it to fly again, as it was, the dead and broken thing it was now. I wanted it so hard I saw a flap of black feathers pass the window and head up toward the sky, past where I could see. I had wanted the bird into flight, and it made me glad to see that. "You know you don't, Jason."

It wasn't true. I'd heard all I wanted to hear of Stephan, but I always shut up when she got to talking of him again. "That's a lie."

"It isn't. You let me talk, I know that and I appreciate that. But it isn't the same as listening. And I know you're always so eager to start telling me your own things. I don't feel I can get help from you."

Faintly, I could hear someone moving upstairs. Aileen didn't seem to notice, but I listened to the steps, which circled toward us till they were standing just over our heads and then retreated. "You think maybe if we talked, like you said, you wouldn't want to call that guy anymore, you'd stop wanting to do that?"

She shrugged and snapped up the blind behind her and light flew into the room. "Maybe I would, maybe I wouldn't. But it's nice to talk."

"So talk to me then. You want to talk about Stephan? Tell me about him. Why don't you open the letter. What do you think it says?" I was listening harder for the steps upstairs than I was to her. But they didn't move. The footsteps themselves were listening.

From across the table, she reached her hand out and took mine. Then she tipped back her head and rested it against the window. Light was coming in all around her, blazing around her face. She was hardly there, in the middle of all that light. I tried to take my hand from her, but she held it tight. "See this," she said. "I don't know that I ever took another person's hand. It might be your mother's hand was the last one I held. What a thing to think."

She held it tight. "That's a lie. You talk like you think I'm stupid. You telling me Stephan never held your hand?" She held it so tight.

"We weren't like that," she said shortly. "Stephan wasn't . . . affectionate, not in an obvious way like that."

"What kind of way was he?"

Light nipping away at the edge of her face and her hair. Her at the centre of all that light. Till she looked like someone else. "Well, one time I remember, while we were still in college, he turned the palm of his hand out toward me while we were walking, and made mine face his, so they were touching, but we didn't reach for each other or move our fingers. So while we walked, our palms brushed against each other, just slightly, and with the rise and fall of every step I could feel that movement of him beside me, as if everything of him was there, in my hand, but only ever so lightly and just for a moment. He only did that once, but I never forgot it. Because it was how we always were. Separate—not dependent on each other like some couples, hanging on every word, calling every time we were apart, kissing every time we saw each other . . . but always that kind of closeness that was private and strange and our own, like a secret."

I nodded, slowly. "I get that."

"Well, I'm glad you do, because it boggles my mind, personally."

"How?"

"Because a thing can look a lot like love, smell like love, talk like love. But maybe, in the end, if it hurts you or leaves you, you're going to have to tell yourself, 'Well, that wasn't love.'"

"Why?"

"Because." The sun was sliding past the window, and I could see half her face again, the line of it with the sky behind it, everything as it was, sharp and true as something carved there. Till she looked like *her*. "Because, Jason, he's not going to come back. That was all I got."

"You know, I think you should open that letter—"

"I told you, I'm not ready yet."

"Well, when you are, you shouldn't worry about me. Doesn't have anything to do with me."

"Thanks," she said and stood up, pulling my empty plate away. "Was that any good?"

"Pretty awful," I said, grinning. "But not you. You're pretty great."

She had her back to me at the sink, but even from there, I could feel her smiling. And the thing upstairs was silent, or maybe gone. "You remind me of him a little, you know."

"I do? Of your husband?"

"Yeah, you do. I don't know why. You've both—and I don't mean any offence by this—you've both got something a little broken about you. A girl could go crazy trying to fix it."

I didn't mind that. "What do you mean."

"Well, take Angel. You want to tell me she hasn't lost half her mind already?"

I got up to grab another beer. "You sound like Minnie now."

"Well, it's cruel, Jason. To you, it maybe feels like something you can stop and start. But there's nothing about the way she looks at you that knows any kind of stopping."

"That's not true." I needed her to understand this, so I stood so close she had to turn the water off and look at me. I tried to tell her why she was wrong with my eyes. "You just don't understand how it is. Besides, she's going around with John now."

Aileen laughed, but her mouth wasn't smiling. "I wonder if you'd take it so well if you didn't know you could stop that any time you wanted. I've got this feeling she means more to you than you think."

"Shut up," I said, but tried to make it a joke. "You've got some mouth on you. Some big, dumb mouth."

"It's a funny thing," she said, turning the tap back on, and I got out of her way. "Broken folks—and I guess I'm probably one too—don't always look it. I'm an easy one, because you probably don't have to look at me too hard to figure it out, and maybe that's why people never take to me."

"I take to you."

She ignored me. "At first, I thought I loved Stephan because he was wholer than me, wholer than anyone else I knew. He looked clean as soap. Things *affected* him so much, but in a way that seemed good. Like he felt everything. But he didn't get bungled up in it like I did. Because he could feel something so much, and then a moment later, he could think of something else. I thought that must be the right way to live. And then, when I figured out I was wrong and he wasn't whole at all, I loved him because he was brokener than anyone else. Maybe I loved him even more then."

"I'll bet he was looking for you," I said. "Maybe that's what the letter is about. You don't have to go back to him, but I'll bet he misses you."

"Shit," she said as a glass slipped from her hands and cracked against the sink. She put her wet hands over her eyes, until I turned off the running water for her.

"It's okay," I said. "I'll clean it up."

"Jason," she said, uncovering her eyes. "I've got to know what happened to her."

I picked up the two halves of the glass and laid them gently in my other hand. It was a clean break.

"I feel her everywhere, Jason. I feel surrounded."

But it was a lie, because upstairs, her bedroom was the way she left it, but now it was full of Aileen's things, her clothes in her closet, and the bed never made. And I couldn't hear her there. Though I listened as hard as I could, I couldn't hear her there.

From behind, Angel looked like less than she was. But stronger too. You wouldn't be sure, looking at her walking away from you, if she was stronger than you were or not. From behind, you noticed how short she was, not much taller than when she was a kid. But with these hard muscles in her calves now. Everything about her soft, but then those hard, round muscles. And then, when you looked at her right on, the corners of her eyes. Her lips.

I watched her up ahead of me for a while before I caught her. I liked the slow way she walked, liked watching it. In everything she did, she was slower than everyone else. I was late to meet Aileen for lunch at the Midnight Sun, but I followed her anyway. And then when all of a sudden I found myself *missing* her, like there was something sad about her walking away from me, even going as slow as she was, I caught up with her. Without even hurrying, from a block away.

"Going someplace, Angie?" I asked her, and she turned around, and those eyes of hers looked happy to see me. They were like two dark, wet fish, her eyes. Shining and liquid and pointed up at the ends like two finned tails.

"It's the Moosehide Gathering, Jason," she said, like I should know that or did but was pretending not to. "I'm late. I guess you are too."

I shut my face as fast as I could so she couldn't tell I'd forgotten and wouldn't have caught her if I'd remembered.

Before he died, my father and some Elders decided everybody should be dragged up to Moosehide every summer to have a big party, like it was some kind of homecoming. But it was a lie. It was a lie that said we were fine. It was a lie that said everything was okey-dokey, because all we really needed was a goddamn beaded vest and some company. The lie said don't be angry anymore. The lie said we were proud, when I knew we were ashamed.

Moosehide was nobody's home now, if it ever was. My father himself had told me that our people had always travelled with the seasons and the animals. He said it used to be that only white people got stuck in the ground like trees, and we were like the wind. Moosehide was just the place we got shoved off to after white folks struck gold across the river from the closest thing to a home we'd ever had, the fish camp at Tr'ochëk. After that, I guess they started thinking those little houses across the water didn't look so shabby after all, and maybe they could buy them for a song from some Indians too dumb to know that when you sold your house you sold the land out from under it too. Tr'ochëk was the home we'd chosen for ourselves. Everywhere else was a place that we'd been sent to by a bunch of honkies who likely thought if they just shuffled us around enough, sooner or later we'd disappear.

I'd gone to the first gathering. It meant so goddamn much to my father. And then, after he died, I said to Minnie, "But it's pretty stupid, isn't it, everyone in those stupid costumes, banging around on those damn drums?" and she didn't answer, only looked at me and shrugged, like she wasn't on my side either. Her parents, like my father, were the last to live up there. When the school closed and the government said all the kids had to go to Dawson now, a few families waited a long time before they followed after, and hers and his were two of the last to leave. And he was only a boy then, but all his life, whenever he used the word *home,* it was Moosehide he meant, the way for Ma it always meant that sea-soaked nowhere she came from.

But I thought a home was a pretty poor thing if that was all it was, a place where something used to happen or an idea that had got caught like a kite in a tree. And after he died, I didn't go again.

So I had nothing to say to Angie, but she stood there looking at me like she knew everything I wasn't saying. "I'll walk you there," I said finally. "I'll walk you to the boat." We were already almost there.

"Jason," she said after a minute, "you know I'm with John now?"

"Sure," I said. "Old John, good old John."

"I just wanted to tell you. I guess I don't know why."

Minnie always told me to be careful with Angel. When my father was alive, he used to ask me if I'd noticed how pretty she was. "If I were you, I'd treat her like she was worth something," he'd say. "Some women have a gift for seeing good where there isn't much. It would be nice to wake up every day and be looked at by a woman like that."

"Maybe he'll take you to Vancouver," I said. "Fly you around in his plane. Take you to the city." There was a goat I kept behind the house a little while, when Ma was still alive.

It didn't last long. I kept it tied up the whole time. It would look at me like Angel did. I liked that goat being there. Sometimes I could hear it going on at night, and so I didn't have to look at it to know it was there. After I found it dead, I had to untie the rope. I could have cut it, but I laid that dead thing on my lap and pulled at the knot until there was nothing around its neck.

"Maybe," Angel said.

There was some true thing about her that I felt close to knowing, right then.

"Remember that time you went with Ma down to Whitehorse," I said.

"Sure," she answered.

"It was funny she asked you to go with her, not me."

She was staring down at the river like she was looking for something there. "Sometimes it was hard to figure out the things she did."

"Yeah." I looked at the river too and thought I wouldn't mind going for a swim in it like a tourist. It was hot enough I wouldn't mind that at all. "But it was funny though. Must have been weird, just the two of you in the car."

"It was."

"And whoever she got to drive. Three of you then."

She looked at me steady, with those eyes like dark and shining fish, and I understood nothing about her.

We were quiet till we got to the river, where all the boats were waiting. Then Angel stopped like she'd remembered something. "Jason," she said. "Does Aileen still talk to that husband of hers?"

"Nah," I said. "She got a letter from him a week ago, but she couldn't even open it."

213

I felt like I had to cover my ears not to hear what she was saying with her eyes.

"You're sure about that."

"What do you got to tell me, Angie?"

She looked away. "Saw her on the phone the other night. After The Pit, when she said she wasn't feeling good and left. I stayed another hour, and on the way home, I saw her on the pay phone."

"Must have been talking to her lawyer," I said. "Or somebody here in town even. Or she must have people back in Toronto or Halifax. She's allowed to call them, I'd say. None of our business if she wants to call them."

"Okay," Angel said. She looked down at the boats. "You sure you don't want to come."

It wasn't a question, not really. "I'll see you around, Angie."

"Okay," she said again. "Okay, Jason."

I watched everyone turn to welcome her and help her into a boat. Her aunts and a man I didn't recognize, all dressed up like they didn't know how stupid they looked in their feathers and beads. I watched how they looked glad to see her, and how she looked happy too, and I hadn't seen her look like that, not look at me like that, not for a while. They all had big, bright smiles on their faces. They looked like there was going to be something really special waiting for them when they got up to Moosehide. But none of them fooled me. There was no way they could fix up there all the things that were broken down here.

When I walked into the Midnight Sun, I saw Melvin before I saw her. He was sitting on one of the bar stools with his back to me, but I knew him from the spread of him over that tiny stool. He was the fattest man in town. You could forgive a guy for a lot for looking like a balloon stuck on the end of a pin. It was as if he'd sat there to be funny. What other guy would spear himself into a seat like that? But then I looked at the arms on the chairs around the tables, and it hit me that he couldn't squeeze himself between them. And then I remembered that what pissed me off about Melvin was that he didn't act like he knew he was fat. He always wore these big suit jackets that he must have got made specially, as if he thought he was somebody important.

I had to walk all the way around him to find her, slumped over the bar, a little unspooled, on the other side. At The Pit each night, I'd try to get her to drink with me but she almost never had more than one. She said she was afraid of embarrassing herself. One night Angie'd had to help her home, and she could hardly look at Angie the next day for the shame of it. But Melvin was a boozer and everyone in town knew it, and though it was still the afternoon, I could tell he'd managed to pour a couple drinks in her. I could count how many she'd had from just one look at her.

"Jason!" she said, pitching herself off the bar and out of her seat. I had to slow down to let her calm herself and sit back down. For a second, she looked like she thought we were going to hug, like I was her girlfriend or something.

"Well, let's get you a drink," said Melvin. "Did your aunt tell you we're celebrating?"

What I hated most about him was that accent. It sounded like he was making fun of himself, which he couldn't be doing, because no man in a suit jacket ever made fun of himself. So he was making fun of me or Aileen or whoever was listening. Talking slow like he was stupid, when he must have thought we were stupid, believing that phony redneck accent coming out of a big fat man that went to some fancy school in the States. Talking slow like we had all the time in the world to listen to him. Even when I let my eyes rest on his and didn't say anything, he didn't look bothered.

"I'll get you a pint," he said. "Two pints—or should I make it three?" he asked Aileen.

"Just two," she said, shaking her head a little too hard. "No more for me. Too many for me."

I was thinking about what Angel had said and how I could figure out if it was true. If she had called that man.

"Nothing for me," I said. "It's lunchtime," I said, eyeing the two of them. She should be embarrassed. Middle-aged lady, loose-faced this early in the day with some fat guy at some bar.

Her face showed she heard me, but I couldn't understand her expression as she stared up at me. I wished her face were an answer.

While Melvin called to the bartender, she patted the stool beside her, a little unsteadily. "Sit down, Jason," she said, her voice unsure. I wished her face were a sentence. I wished her face were a sentence that said if she'd called him or why she'd gone to that pay phone to do it and what she had said and what it would come to mean.

Melvin didn't show how many glasses he'd had, though his face was pink and beads of sweat kept appearing on his forehead, which he seized with a cloth from his pocket—it was the only gesture he made that didn't have a weird, ladylike feel about it. I wondered if he was a queer. I wondered what women or men ever saw the big, naked fact of him.

"So, Jason," he said. "I was just toasting your aunt. She's

got some darn interesting ideas, and a good head on her shoulders. She's going to make a great reporter."

On the stool beside Melvin, Aileen was still watching me with the same mystery of a look on her face. She seemed to be waiting for something, to want something from me.

"Jason," Melvin said, lifting his glass into the air, "your aunt"—and if he said it like that one more time, he was going to lose a tooth—"is my newest hire. I'm making her associate editor. That's a full-time, year-round job."

She was grinning at me. "Jason, I told you I was going to stay."

It didn't mean anything. I thought of all the things it didn't mean. So she'd stay in my house, it would be our house. Or I would help her find a place. An apartment, or maybe she'd buy a house of her own. So it was true what she'd said and she wouldn't leave. And it didn't matter who she'd called or hadn't called. September would come and all those other tourists would be gone, and she wouldn't leave.

The two of them looked at me with grins on their faces, but Aileen wasn't sure and hers slipped a little as I said nothing.

"So this is a celebration, Jason," Melvin said, and his smile had too many teeth in it. "Just a special little get-together in your aunt's honour. A remarkable lady." He swept his glass up into the air and tipped it at Aileen. "To this remarkable lady," he said. "My dear, welcome to the *Light*."

And then he turned to me. "Oh but you don't have a drink, Jason. Let me get you one, so we can toast your aunt." He waved at the bartender, but I shook my head and twisted my stool around to lean my back against the bar.

"I didn't tell you," Aileen said, whispering as if no one but me could hear, "that he would be here because I was afraid

217

you wouldn't come. I wanted you to come. I wanted you to hear him say it."

And she had a need in her that didn't need her mouth to tell it. She had a need in her and it wasn't Melvin or Stephan who could answer it. She needed me to say it was okay, okay that she had the job, okay that it was this joke of a man who would make it possible for her to stay, okay that she was going to leave behind everything she hadn't brought with her in the suitcase I'd carried to my house. And so I said it was okay, and she put her whole self in my arms.

Over her shoulder, Melvin raised his eyebrows at me and nodded at her empty glass. But it was not because of the booze that she had her arms that tight around me or anything else he understood.

Her voice was a whisper in my ear. "I'm glad I came, Jason," she said.

I'd held drunker girls before, girls who fell like this into me, their bones somehow gone soft and loose enough for them to be more blanket than girl, girls who whispered in that same wet way in my ear and wanted me to take their clothes off. But nobody wanted anything from me like she did. She wanted me to take her whole self and say that was okay too. She wanted all of me to be a family for her. She once told me that she came here to ask my mother to forgive her. And now that Ma was gone it was only me that could.

I poured what I could of her onto her stool again. Melvin put one of his big fat hands on her shoulder to hold her still and safe, and I knew the way he looked at her as he did that he would let her work at that paper as long as she wanted. He was her boss and wide as a door and maybe a queer to boot, but for a second I thought maybe I didn't mind him so much after all.

I told the bartender to get a beer for me, and when it came, I raised it up to her, and she gave me a big, loose smile. And as I swigged it back, I thought probably I'd forgiven her the first day she was here. Because she'd come that far to find me. And then because she stayed.

Mara

FIFTEEN

THE OCCASION OF OUR first meeting was Marla's wedding.
I liked that phrase. An actress in a film Agnes's mother had
once taken us to said it like that. In a voice that sounded like
she owned everything, she'd said, "How well I remember the
occasion of our first meeting." It was a glamorous, dignified
thing to say, so different from anything the nuns or anyone
who visited the school would ever say. Agnes and I took to
saying it to each other, and soon the other girls did too. We
were pretending to be something that didn't yet seem impossible. Only the older girls then had begun to suspect that no
such occasion might ever occur, and that there might never be
any meeting of anyone at all.

I never went to Marla's wedding, which was to a boy from
her hometown who worked at a pork farm and was said to be
not all there but very kind. But the nuns gave Marla permission to invite three girls on our floor to go to town to celebrate
with her the night before, escorted by Marla's older sister. At
dinner a week before the wedding, Father McGivney informed
me that I was one of the girls Marla had chosen.

We so rarely were allowed to leave the school that we
looked forward to the evening all week. We planned what

we would wear, and one or two of the nuns even, reluctantly, helped us find our nicest dresses from our scant wardrobes. Just before breakfast on the day of our outing, Sister Margaret knocked on my door and put something soft and silky in my hands. "I thought you might like to borrow my scarf to wear this evening," she whispered. "My mother left it to me, and it's a pity it never gets worn." She hesitated. "You don't know this, but you look very beautiful in green."

Marla's sister came to pick us up before we'd even eaten dinner, because she told us she would buy us dinner in town. I knew from the way the other girls discussed in whispers in the back seat what sort of restaurant we might be taken to that I was not the only one who had never been to one before. The car smelled of leather and smoke, and Marla told us proudly that it was pink and had a top that could go down in the summer. We all wished desperately that Marla had not chosen February for her wedding.

The place Marla's sister took us was not a restaurant but a café. Music played so loudly in the background that I could hardly hear the man who came to ask us what we would have. "Can't they turn the music down?" I hissed to Marla, but Marla's sister laughed and said it was not a record but a real band playing right there. I was embarrassed that she had heard me, and pretended to know the name of the band when she told me. Marla's sister went to art school in Toronto and was studying to be a sculptor. I felt overwhelmed by my luck at having taken the seat beside her. She spoke very gently to me, and often touched my shoulder warmly when she teased me, to let me know she wasn't being cruel. But she was quick to grow restless or bored, and sometimes I would find when I answered one of her questions that she had already turned to talk to someone else.

She ordered root beers for all of us and then read from the menu. "Well, what would you each like?" she asked when she had finished. None of us said a word, and she laughed, and when the man came to ask what we wanted, she told him we all were having hamburger platters.

By the time our food came, the band had stopped playing and so I could hear everything everyone said at the table, even the boy Marla's sister had invited to join us, who then took all her attention away from the rest of us.

"How are the eats?" Marla's sister asked triumphantly after we'd had a few bites.

"Better than anything," one of the girls said. "There's nothing like this at school."

"Like heaven," agreed another.

Mine was already cold and so greasy it soaked my hands and mouth. After each bite, I had to draw my napkin across my lips and fingers, and soon it was steeped in oil and useless. I tugged Marla's sleeve and asked if I could borrow hers, but she said no and sounded annoyed.

The boy told us a story about New York City and a musician he'd met there. He pretended he was telling the story to all of us, but I knew it was only Marla's sister the story was for. She pretended not to know that and started digging in her bag when he got to the funniest part. "You got a light?" she asked.

When we all had finished, she announced, "Well." I had to turn my face away from her, toward Marla, to keep from coughing at the smoke that circled me from her cigarette. "What do you say we get something a little stronger than root beer. This is a celebration after all. My little sister's hen party. Why don't we blow this Popsicle stand and find somewhere we can get a real drink?"

"I know a pub just around the block," the boy said, too eagerly, and then tried to recover. "My buddy's a bartender there. He won't have a problem serving a few minors if I tell him they're with me."

"Sounds like a plan, man." Beside me, she pushed herself out of her seat and I heard her cigarette hiss into extinction in her glass. "Come on, kiddos."

Marla's sister said it was too close to drive, though I was more excited about riding in her car again than I was about going anywhere else, so we held hands as if we were already back at school, and followed Marla and the boy to the pub.

The moment we were inside, I wished Marla had asked Agnes or any of the other girls instead of me. I'd never heard so many voices or so much noise all in one room. I suddenly thought the band at the café had not been so loud after all, and at least it had only been one noise, and a person could make sense of one noise, but not of all these different ones, all happening at once.

Marla's sister ordered a glass of something for each of us, and mine was sweet and strong and I was surprised by how much I liked it. I drank it down because I did not know what else to do with it, and then Marla's sister laughed at me and said, "Wait for the toast, greedy!" She rubbed her hand lightly in my hair and ordered me another one. "A little slower this time, please, little lush."

Then she said how proud and happy she was for her sister and made what was called a toast. And then people banged their glasses together, even mine, and after that I was allowed to drink again, and I drank this one even faster than the first.

After that the noise became something impenetrable, and I felt it push and pull me around the room as I tried to find my way to Marla or her sister or a chair. Suddenly I stumbled, the music and voices tugging me down, down toward the floor, and then I was in someone's arms, strong ones that plucked me out of the noise and dropped me into a chair.

"Well, well," said a man's voice. "For such a little thing, you sure are heavy on your feet."

I started crying then and didn't know why. The man got so close then I could smell cigarettes on him and something else, something salty and strong—maybe his drink or his skin itself. The smell was comforting, almost animal. It was the opposite of clean, but it wasn't dirty. He smelled like something teeming, full, rich, deep. "Where did they go?" I asked the man.

"Those friends of yours? I think they stepped outside. Gone to smoke a little hash with Joe, I think."

That made the tears fall faster and I was astonished with pity for myself. I rarely cried, and it seemed something very sad must have happened to me to cost so many tears.

"Don't you worry, I can go find them for you," said the man. He put his hand around mine and everything stilled. The room was, for a moment, perfectly silent as my hand disappeared inside his.

"Your hands are like Da's," I whispered.

"You want me to go find your friends?" he asked.

I shook my head.

"You want me to stay here?"

I nodded, tears stopped.

"You can't see, can you," he said, sounding sorry.

I shook my head again. It was so nice and easy just to say

227

nothing, though every time I moved my head I felt dizzy again. It was so kind of him to speak so I could be silent.

"What a pity. Pretty girl like you. What a tragedy. Were you always like this?"

Once more, I shook my head. Then, softly, shyly, I told him, "I still remember things. What my mother looked like. I had a sister. She looked just like me. It was a long time ago, but I still see those things, and that's not like being blind, is it. I can still see those things."

He squeezed my hand tighter in his. "No, that's something, I guess. That's something for sure."

"Will you—" I was so bold it amazed me. I wished Marla's sister could see how bold and adult I was. "Will you get me another one of those drinks?" I asked.

I heard him stand up, and he let go of my hand slowly. "I'll be right back," he said. He took a few steps away and then I heard him approach again. "Now, don't you scamper away," he told me before he headed back to the bar.

When he came back, he had a drink for both of us, and the one he gave me was stronger and more bitter than the last, but I liked it too. "How old are you anyway?" he asked me, and I told him I was eighteen. "Me too," he said, and we both knew that both of us were lying. But we didn't care, and he took me outside when we'd finished our drinks and couldn't see Marla's sister or the other girls there, and he thought maybe they went behind the alleyway, but when we got there, he said there was nobody there either. And then he told me how cold I looked, and he put his arm around me and said his truck was back there if I wanted to come in and warm up. And then when we were inside, he put the radio on, and I heard some woman singing about being alone, but I wasn't alone, I was with this man, who after a while turned down the radio and touched my cheek and put the heater on, rubbing his hands before it till they were warm and then he put them under my shirt, and I helped him take it off. The scarf that Sister Margaret said would make me look pretty got caught in my hair, but we took that off too, and then he had his lips on mine, and then, like I had made him crazy, made him an animal instead of a man, who would do anything, he put his tongue in my mouth, and it tasted like the drinks we'd had, and then he asked me, "Do you want me to take you back inside now?" and I couldn't say no, couldn't say anything, thought nothing except *How weak is thine heart,* but I shook my head and he understood and then he pulled me onto him like I weighed nothing at all.

"What is your name?" I asked when it was over, and he told me, "Jason."

Angel

~

late August 1996

SIXTEEN

THERE WAS SOMETHING I KNEW. And I kept it deep in my head, and I kept it quiet there, and I didn't tell anyone the thing I knew of myself, but went on knowing it, all the same. I knew it the way my heart beat and knew it beat. I knew it the way air found a way to my lungs and knew how it did. All of me was the fact of what I knew, a secret that was in me and part of me, and I told no one.

August now, and all the dying leaves and grass were shrinking into the dirt that they were made from. There was gold in the dying grass and the flowers that had become seeds. Gold even in the sky, which made a little space, at the end of days, for dark to come, blue and deep, for a few hours and then it was gone again.

And then one day, rain came. After all the dry weeks and days, rain came down, so hungry for the ground it fell all over it, fast and heavy, spreading slick, wet fingers over all, all. All the town was an appetite for the rain that fell, without stopping, from the long grey sky. I called to Momma that I was going out, and she yelled, "In this weather?" and I didn't answer.

I left my shoes on the porch so that I could feel the wet grass on my bare feet. And then I stepped into the road, where a thin river was hurrying along the tire tracks, heading downtown. I felt the cool mud slide between my toes and it made me smile.

And then I followed the road down to the end of town, and then I climbed down the bank to the river and by then the rain had turned slow and soft.

The river moved so fast. If I were to fall into it, it would carry me away and I would have no choice but to let the river change me, to make another plan for me and where I was going. I wondered if all the salmon we fished from the river were our people, and they had long ago fallen in the water and found it ran too fast to fight. I thought it wouldn't be such a bad thing to be one of those silver backs that flashed in the water. I imagined being snatched out of the pull of the waves and brought to land to feel for the first time what it was to not be carried by the water, to be urged toward something by every bone and scale. Some fishy thought in the salmon's brains must tell them the place where they are going. They must dream it will be somewhere beautiful and without pain.

And then I thought of the nets that would tear them from the river and all the beautiful, dark fish thoughts that they'd had there. They would feel air and all of a sudden, just like that, they would be full of knowing that air took them nowhere, led them to nothing at all. Open close, open close would go their gills. And their gills would not bring them oxygen, could not. Into the air, out of the net, back again. *Snap* go their spines, which cannot ever take them back to the river.

I loved salmon, which knew what they were and did not fight to be anything else. Their travel on the river was what they were made of. They could no more resist than have lungs or wings.

When I was a child, Papa used to take me out in his boat to fish for dinner for our family. But I would just lean over the side and watch those dark thoughts swim under the water. It would make him mad, most times, or sorry, shaking his head when he asked me to show him what I'd caught and I would have nothing to offer up to please him but a song I'd made up about the salmon. But the last time he took me in his boat, he said at the end, "Next time I'll take Charlie. Your heart is too good. You may well turn out to be happier for it. Hungrier, but happy." He went out one more time with Charlie after that, and then, another season later, he died.

I crept to the lowest rocks and sat. My feet were tucked under me and I bent to touch the water with my hands. It was so cold that it took all the feeling from my fingers.

I thought that I had not made so many decisions in my life. I would have liked to be like the salmon, but instead I had just always said, "River, take me where you will go."

And I had a thought that from time to time would come to me. The thought came to me as a knife can open something soft. I had thought that loving Jason was one single, fierce thing I had done. I thought I had swum toward him as if all the river ran downward and I ran up. I thought that was a good, brave thing, loving someone who didn't want it. I thought one day the river would say, "Angel, I am tired and you have never been tired. Let me take you to him."

But then I saw that it was possible also that all this time the river had been carrying me just behind him. And I had never, not once, been like the salmon.

It was that night I went to The Pit to find him. Not John.

A band that must have come from somewhere down south was playing. The singer's face was shiny with the sweat coming out of him, and as he sang, he would toss his head to take the hair out of his eyes, but it would stick to his face, and the sad way he sang made me sorry for him and his too-long hair and too-shiny face. This was true of white boys, and I had seen it before, how they would sweat for no reason at all, and make their pinky faces even pinkier. No native man I knew made singing a song look like hard work. But this kind of music sounded like work too, like the song was being scraped out of the singer and the band was trying everything they could think of to stop him.

And I sat there, listening and waiting, because I knew he would come. He came every day. He came to see me, I had thought once. It had gone through my head like a cloud passing over the sun, that thought, but when it was gone, there was the sun again and it would always be, as I would always know better.

And I watched the door open and she came in, without him. I had come to think it was for her he came to the bar now. If it had ever been for me, it was not now.

"Hello, Angel," she said.

"Hello, Aileen."

But I did not think it had ever been for me.

I watched her wonder if she should sit with me and then wish she had pretended not to see me at all. I watched her finally take a seat at the bar with her back to me. Because of how he'd looked at me the first time I told him, I hadn't let Jason know how many times now I'd caught her on that pay phone. I didn't think she'd ever seen me find her there, she was so swallowed up by whoever was at the other end of that line. So I couldn't ask him if he knew who she was calling or if he noticed she looked happy now, as she had not when she came.

And I sat there, turning the spoon in the grounds at the bottom of my cup, looking at her back and thinking of her sister.

I was only just thirteen when she came to me and whispered I was to ride to the city with her in her car. Since that day when she'd told me I was to watch after Jason and wait for him, she'd had a way of talking to me, like there was a secret between us. And then there was.

We were all bent over our bowls of oatmeal and listening to Charlie boast about the pretty mule deer doe he'd shot that morning that still lay staring from the bed of his truck. I had seen it there, and looked into its dull black eyes, and I had touched the sticky fur where all that was living in the deer had seeped out. And it was that I thought of when the phone rang, and Papa answered and then said that Jason's wife wanted me to go to the city with her, to pick out a present for my thirteenth birthday, though already it had come and gone. Papa said he wasn't sure, but Momma said, "Oh go ahead, she's a good girl and deserves a special treat, like a ride into the city with that white lady."

And I remembered what Minnie had told me she had seen, at the beginning of the summer, and wondered what Mara wanted from me and why she would ask to take me all the way to Whitehorse when she never went anywhere. But I had never gone away from home overnight without my brothers and sister, and felt a longing in me at the thought of a whole wide bed to myself and of coming back to tell June and Jude all I had seen in the city, so I said, "Please, Papa, I never went to the city before, and June went three times already," and he nodded very slowly and said, "*Tejù!* I have told you you must learn to ask for what you want, or others will take it from you." "I want to go to the city with Jason's mother," I told him then, and he said, "All right, little one. All right."

And I'd thought that Jason would be going with us, that he would drive, and I would ride in the seat behind him and his mother and feel his glance on me in the mirror maybe, while the wind blew in the window beside me and snatched up my hair, and maybe he would let me lean outside and feel the air beat back my hand when I reached it out. He'd only got his licence a few months before, but he'd been driving for years, since he was fifteen. Mara needed him to take her places, and she never seemed to want to ask the other Jason, her husband, not for that or for anything. There was a silence grown up between them like a bed of weeds. He never reached out his paddle of a hand to slide over her hips or bottom like Papa did when Momma passed him in the kitchen, and she never slapped his hand away, like Momma did Papa's, rolling her eyes with a look of happiness. Once, I sat beside Mara, showing her how to do beading the way they taught us at culture camp, and Jason's father came and stood in the doorway, watching her for a long time before he told her, "Mara? I'm going to make some dinner now." And she never showed she knew he was there, but I felt her hand tighten around the thread as soon as we could hear his steps on the floor, and all the time he stood there, she hardly breathed, and she dropped the beads for the first time that afternoon. And so I wondered what it was they both were listening to when they weren't speaking to each other, but I was too young and never knew the answer.

But when we went outside, it was not Jason's father's truck in the yard, but a car I didn't recognize with a licence plate from British Columbia. And inside a man sat at the wheel, and for a moment I didn't know who he was, and then I remembered he was the minister the Anglican Church had got to come stay for a year till they found someone to replace Reverend Wallace, who had been found frozen solid in the woods a year before, dead of a heart attack and left for days till Sunday came and he didn't, and someone finally thought to look for him.

"Reverend Eames is going to give us a ride in his car," she said, and so I got into the back seat, and she sat down in the other front seat, beside the white man from the church no one I knew went to.

None of us said anything all the drive there, and then when we arrived in the city, the man got out and took our suitcases from the trunk for us. We were stopped beside a hotel, and I climbed outside to look at it and almost missed the way the man looked at Mara as he helped her from her seat. His face had the kind of question in it that Jason's father's did when he looked at his wife, but now, for a moment, there was something in Mara's face that answered it. He had one hand around hers and the other behind her back as she stood up and turned her face to the sun, her eyes closed. They stood, like that, and I watched her face and his and tried to understand them, while they stood, his hand still around hers, his arm bent behind her back, and though everything else between them was separate, it was as if all his body and hers were pulled, each toward the other, as if though their hands were all that touched, only their hands kept them apart. Then the man got into his car and drove away, and Mara told me to help her to the desk, where she told the woman that she had booked a room for herself and her daughter.

"Where did the man go?" I asked her when we climbed the

stairs to her room. I did not know why it made me feel afraid to think of going into that room alone with her.

"It wouldn't be right," she said. "A man with a woman not his wife. And Whitehorse isn't that far from Dawson. And he has his career to think of. No, it wouldn't be right. There are gossips everywhere. Did you know Paul counted those who gossip as equal in sin to the haters of God?" She did not wait for an answer, but kept climbing the steps, her suitcase going *bump bump bump* all the way.

She made me unpack our pyjamas and clothes into the drawers in the room, and then she told me to order us bacon sandwiches from the phone. She said if I just picked up the phone, someone would answer, and that if I told them we wanted bacon sandwiches, they would bring them to us, and it was true, they did.

When we were finished, she sat on the bed and her eyes got fixed fast on the door, though I knew she couldn't see it or anything else.

"Is the man coming back?" I asked at last.

Her pale face went paler and I was afraid. Her hand hovered around her throat, shaking and fluttering around the necklace of beads she always wore there, and then she tore it off, and all those little beads that I'd thought were pretty went rolling here and there all over the floor. "Of course not. What do you think, what foul thoughts have . . ." She reached out the hand that had torn the necklace. I knew Jason would have walked toward it, as she wanted, but I would not. At last, she let her hand fall into her lap.

I could not look away from her pale, pale eyes. What could they see?

"I need you to take me to the doctor tomorrow. It is not

appropriate that Reverend Eames take a married woman, one not even part of his congregation. But you can help me, can't you?"

I nodded, but she waited, looking unsatisfied, and I remembered to say, "Yes." She made me say it again. "Yes. Yes."

"And you won't tell Jason of this?"

"No."

She smiled. And then she reached out her hand, and this time I took it, and she made me go and find her nightgown, and I watched, afraid, as she pulled the clothes off her bony body, with its white, stretched skin. Her breasts were loose as balloons with all the air let out, though her nipples were large and dark, and in the lamplight, they looked like marks of blood.

The next morning, she woke me and told me to dress as fast as I could because we were late. She told me we had no time for breakfast, and then we went down the stairs, to the desk, where she told the woman to make a taxi come for us. The taxi brought us to a hospital, and she made me wait on a chair among strangers reading magazines, while a nurse led her away. Sometime later she came back, and when I saw her face, I knew to put away the questions I had wanted to ask.

Another taxi took us back to the hotel room, and she called someone, and from the way she talked to him, I understood it was the man. She told him not to come pick us up after all. She told him we would find another way home.

She hung up the phone and left her hand on it for a moment, before she raised her face to me. "They did a test on me," she said.

I knew not to ask if she had passed. I knew it was another kind of test. Some other, grown-up kind.

"Angel," she said. "I am going to have a baby."

I stared at her. She was so old. And Jason almost a man.

"Maybe," she said, like someone in a dream, "the baby will help me leave him."

I did not know any words to say. I did not understand all she said after that, or even know who she meant when she said "him," but I knew enough to be afraid of her. And afraid for her. And Jason. After that, she told me to take everything from the drawers and put it into our suitcases again, and then another taxi took us to the tourist bus stop.

We spoke barely at all on the bus, which was full of tourists who pointed out the window every time a bird or creature passed. "You'll tell your father we couldn't find anything you liked," she said once. "That is why you are returning home with no present." Another time, she asked me to describe what the man in front of us was taking photographs of, because she could hear the click his camera made each time. I said I didn't know. All I could see were trees and water, sky.

After it was dark and the other riders were gone quiet, she reached out and took my hand, her eyes still staring straight ahead. I'd thought she was sleeping. "Angel," she whispered. "I did something. A few months ago, I couldn't stop myself and I did something, and I'm afraid. I'm afraid because I couldn't stop myself."

She held my hand till it hurt, but her voice was calm. "I can feel myself . . . coming undone," she said. "It has been happening for a long time. Jason knows. He helps me. But I don't know if he helps put me together or take me apart. I have to stop whatever is happening to me. It happened to my mother, you know. We watched it happen. That is the last thing I remember seeing. How my mother turned out to be made of a long knot of string wrapped around and around itself, but I didn't know until the last little piece had come unravelled and all that was left of her was a bit of string there on the floor."

I didn't know if she really meant it, or if it was the kind of story she always told Jason. I didn't see how a woman could be a mother and a piece of string too. So I just sat very still and let her hold my hand all the rest of the way, as though it didn't hurt at all. And I thought of what Minnie had told me and knew it was true, and of what Mara had said and thought it might be a lie, that the thing she had done, she had done not once but again and again. And if it was a lie, only Jason could tell me and he wouldn't. I knew he wouldn't ever tell me that.

When we were home again, I walked her back to her house, and Jason came running down the steps, looking worried. Only later I found out she hadn't told him or her husband she was going to Whitehorse. She bent down—I always forgot how tall she was till she needed me to lean on—and whispered in my ear, "You'll remember what I told you. Wait for him. He'll need you."

I thought of her voice then, those words, and the soured-flower smell of her breath, and I sat at my little table, turning my spoon in my cup. And it didn't surprise me to see Jason push open the door of The Pit and stand there, seeing me, suddenly filling the room with whatever the thing about him was that made me stop breathing. I could tell from there he was in a good mood, because of how he stopped to look at me and didn't wait to come and pull out the chair across from me and fall into it.

"Hello, Jason."

"Hello, Angel." He picked up my empty coffee cup, and then he pushed it back to me. "Slim pickings."

"I'll get you a drink," I said.

"No need." He turned and made a nod so slight I hardly knew he'd made it, and Eloise, across the room, nodded in answer and began filling a glass. "There's some chill out there today," he said.

"It's almost September," I answered. "No southerners here tonight except the band."

"And Eloise."

"She's from Whitehorse, that doesn't count."

"But she'll leave just like the rest of them." Eloise put a pint down in front of Jason, and he grabbed her hand. "Tell me, when you leaving, Eloise?"

"When the season's done. Start of September. I've got to get back to school."

Jason nodded. "Thanks for the beer, sweetheart."

He was looking at Aileen's back. "Go on," I said. "Tell her to come over."

He pulled a used-up sugar packet from the pile I'd made on the table because I liked sweet coffee, and rolled it between his hands. Then he flicked it from his open palm and hit her arm where it lay resting on the bar. She got up right away like that was the call she'd been waiting for.

The two of them talked while I tipped my chair back and thought about the thing I knew. And then Gary, an old drunk whose sister had drowned right in front of him years ago, while he watched from shore because he couldn't swim, hobbled over to me on the crutch he'd been going around on all summer and said, "You ever had a pain that just came out of nowhere and wouldn't go away? That the doctors didn't even know what to do with?"

"No," I said, "I guess not."

"That's my foot," he said. "I'll have to go to Whitehorse and see if they can do anything there. It hurts so bad I could almost cut it off. It'd hurt less to cut it off."

"Oh," I said.

"But if it weren't for that, I'd ask you to dance for sure."

"I know, Gary," I said.

"Jason there'll probably want to dance with you. I've seen the way he looks at you. You stole that boy's heart clean out of him, I'd say."

Jason didn't even look up. I smiled at Gary. "Not sure Jason's much of a dancer. But I'll be coming looking for you for a dance, just as soon as that foot is better."

He beamed at me and waved the crutch in the air, before he limped back over to the bar.

Aileen was laughing so hard, I didn't want to stop her. She had her head back with laughter, and in the light that came down spilling over the bar, it wasn't possible to see any grey in her gold hair. Jason wasn't laughing, but he had a smile that slid up the side of his face every time he looked over at Aileen.

In this dim room, smoke made a cloud over our heads the shape of a ghost or a dream. For a moment, I looked, really looked, at everything around me. At the bright-coloured Christmas lights strung in loops along the walls. At the things on the shelf that ran around the room—a broken clock; a plastic doll with a papoose on her back; empty liquor bottles, one shaped like the body of a woman; money from the States and Japan and Germany; photos of customers and people who worked here, their arms around each other and grins on their faces. I looked at the singer on the stage and his band, at Eloise, at the people at the bar and at tables, and just coming in the door. I knew them all, except the band. I knew every face in the room. Then I looked back at the coffee cup in my hand.

"So I've got another story for you, Aileen," Jason said. He glanced at me. "You mind if I tell it, Angel?"

"No," I said, letting my eyes slide over him again. "No, I'd like to hear it."

He leaned over the table, peering again and again at Aileen, his eyes wide and eager. Only lately he'd begun to look that way. All summer I'd watched him hold himself back from her so he was always out of reach and unknowable. Now I saw him giving himself to her in armfuls, as if she'd just reached out a hand and he would fill it with everything he had.

Old Man knew Old Woman's secret. He found out one night when he lay listening to her sleeping beside him. Because he knew there was something she wasn't telling him. He noticed how her smile looked like a jewel in her mouth, and he knew there was something she was keeping that was hers and not his. And he knew that he could only learn what she wouldn't tell him when she was sleeping and her lips were loose with dreams and their honest ways, so he let the lamp go out while she lay beside him, and when her breath was long and deep, he lit it again. He looked at her and found her beautiful but in a way that made him draw back from her. He saw her eyelids flickering and knew she dreamt. Then he leaned close and listened to what she would say, but even in her dreams, she kept her secret. She whispered dream thoughts and dream stories, but they were hollow, gutted of meaning or information. She dreamt only of light, water, insects moving very slowly. He was frustrated and almost left her, when he heard something she could not silence or hide. He pressed his ear closer to her to be sure. Only by the man who made the world could it be heard, but beneath her own heavy woman's heartbeat, there was its reflection, a soft, steady sound of life just starting, being just beginning.

And so while she slept, he put his seed in her. He put another child there, inside her. A twin. And as he made the child, he thought only of dark and hard, cold earth, of silence. He put winter's twin there in her. She did not know the child was there until she woke and remembered her dreams and how they'd changed in the night. She felt the third heartbeat in her, and knew a different season grew there to haunt the first. At breakfast her husband wouldn't look at her, and she put her hand on her belly and carried his child and hers.

When he finished telling his story, I pulled at my hair, wrapping and unwrapping it around my fingers.

"I don't know if I understand these stories," Aileen said.

Jason shrugged but looked pleased with himself.

"You know, I had a dream about your mother," I said. They both turned to me as if I'd surprised them. "She was just walking by the river, holding something in her hands, trying to find a place to hide it. I kept calling her name, and she wouldn't answer. Finally I got close to her, and she held up both her hands and all that was in them was a little bit of string. She said, 'He already took the beads.'"

Aileen stood up. "I think I'm going to head home. You coming?"

Jason glanced at me. "You want me to stick around?"

I didn't answer. I was remembering what Minnie had told me, six years ago. I remembered what she had figured out about Mara and Jason, which was why I never said anything to Minnie or to him or anyone else about what Mara told me in Whitehorse. And then later, as we watched Jason lay flowers against Mara's stone in Brookside Cemetery, Minnie whispered what had happened to Mara and ordered me never to speak about it to Jason or anyone else. And I thought it was best I had never told anyone why Mara had taken me to Whitehorse. And I knew not saying anything was how I could do what she had told me to. It was how I would watch after him. And it was how I would love him.

After a moment, he shrugged at Aileen and said, "I'm going to stay here with Angie for another round."

He reached his hand out and set it on mine, still in a good mood, still looking to make me smile. "Can I buy you a drink, Angie?"

I looked at his dark, dark eyes that were still, even then, beautiful. "No," I said.

I knew already then, had known for days, before even checking the calendar or counting the month on my hands. I hadn't known till I felt it what it would be like to be so certain, to feel a fact in your body, to have knowledge about yourself that came out of the pounding of your blood, the weight of your breasts, the roundness and hardness of your body. I knew before I went to the nurse's station and asked for the test, and I knew even then, waiting for the test, that I wasn't really waiting, that there was no question to be answered. There was only this thing I knew.

I sat beside Jason, knowing this and saying nothing. And

it was strange, what I didn't think of as we sat side by side in quiet, and later on the walk home. I didn't think of the girls in my high school who'd got pregnant at fifteen. I didn't remember how I felt a kind of envy in me, a hunger for the way those girls got larger and larger, while I felt that a wind could have taken me away. Their shapes in the hallways grew and left no room for the rest of us. Until they quit school and became part of our mothers' world and not ours any longer, part of the mystery of sex itself. I didn't think of how I was my mother's last child, and how the day I started school, she wept over being left alone at home and wished she'd had eight or ten children more, and she said to me then, "Don't wait too long." Or how another time, when I was older and spent too long staring in the bathroom mirror, dreaming about what I might become one day, "Don't hurry."

Just before I told him the thing I knew, as we walked home together, I remembered how the first time it had happened, he had stopped suddenly, when we had just begun, and he went fumbling in his pants for one, and I said, "Don't," and he said, "You don't want me to?" and then he looked like he understood and said, "Oh, you're on the . . ."

But I wasn't, and it was Mara I thought of then. And on the way home, as I stopped him, and put my hand against his shoulder, I remembered how that night he'd wanted to use one and it was Mara who had made me think maybe something like a miracle might happen. And the funny thing was, it wasn't that night I was really thinking of even then. It was Mara herself, and how she had not been able to see anything at all.

Mara

SEVENTEEN

MARLA'S SISTER WAS FURIOUS with me for having left the bar, but Marla told me she wouldn't even have noticed except that the other girls had got worried. On the way back, Marla's sister said we weren't to breathe a word to anyone at school about me leaving the bar with that old Indian. The other girls and I were all astonished to learn that it had been an old Indian I had gone off with, and one of them asked me in a whisper what it was like, and I said I didn't know what to compare it to.

I didn't think much after that about the man called Jason. After our short time in the city, it was especially thrilling to return to the old routines at school, and I found myself enjoying everything more, the tasteless food seemed saltier, the nuns kinder, and the words we read each day with our fingertips from the Bible seemed to speak to me directly.

It was Agnes who noticed. One day, I was struggling to fasten the zipper that ran up the back of the heavy wool tunic we all wore, and she heard and came and tried to help me. "It won't go, Mara," she said at last. "You'll have to tell them."

"Tell them what?" I asked. My breasts had grown larger

lately, and I was ashamed of having eaten so much that my belly pushed open the pleats in my tunic.

Agnes linked her finger around mine. "I've heard you in the bathroom. I've heard you be ill, I mean."

I felt my face heat. "That's private," I told her. I had only gone when I thought no one was there. Lately the hymns in chapel had made me feel dizzy and faint, and I'd sometimes had to hurry away to the toilet, though we weren't supposed to leave chapel till after the last prayer. Sometimes the nuns reading to us made me queasy too, as if their voices and the priest's too had all entered into my head, pushing their words inside me, more and more, deeper into my belly, which was already too full with their words.

"You don't know?" Agnes asked. "Do you not know?"

I squeezed her finger, knowing I hurt her a little. "Of course I know," I said.

She didn't believe me. "Mara, when is the last time it came?"

It took me a moment to understand her. "I don't know," I said.

"Do they hurt? Your tits, I mean?"

"Yes," I whispered.

She leaned closer and said in my ear, as if she were sharing a secret, "My sister said her bosoms always hurt and it didn't come anymore. And I would always hear her sick in the bathroom, like you."

"What do you mean?" I asked her, becoming frightened. "Is something wrong with me? Am I sick?"

"Mara," Agnes whispered, her voice delighted with the secret and the thrill of it all, her voice happy for me. "You're going to have a baby."

I didn't understand at first what she was saying to me. "What do you mean?" I asked. "What do you mean?"

"Mara." She squeezed my finger tighter, and then her hot, moist hand took all of mine in it. "I've tried to figure it out. Was it when you went to town? Or was it . . . one of the priests?"

I put both hands on my belly and wondered if it could be true, what she said. I wondered if I might be able to do something like that, make a person out of nothing, inside me. I didn't see how I could. I had never done anything but try to be nothing, nothing bad, nothing wrong, nothing loud, nothing in the way of other people. Sometimes in my own prayers I thanked God for making me blind so that I couldn't see how every day I got a little smaller. I was so tiny now, it was no wonder that the people I once loved had lost me. No one came looking for me because no one looks for nobody. I was a mistake in space, and that was all. A body where the hole of *her* should have been. And that was why God and my mother took my eyes. To make me disappear.

But if it were true. If I could make out of nothing another person, it might not be so very different than having a hand reach out across the dark and take yours, as if you were one soul housed in two bodies. My body might be a house for another, and then, if that were true, it might be like what the whole world looked like if you had two eyes to see it.

"Mara?" Agnes asked. "Mara, why are you crying?"

Jason

∼

late August 1996

EIGHTEEN

SHE WAS DOWN ON THE BED, on her stomach, with her arms bent at the elbow and her hands up in her hair, over her head. Her face was turned sideways, away from me.

The night before, she'd told me, and I broke everything in the house. Not when she'd told me she was pregnant with my baby, but afterwards, when she told me she was going with that old man of hers to Vancouver to raise it like it was his. My baby. Inside her, I thought in wonder, and looked at her, the black of her hair in piles on the dirty sheets of the bed. My child and hers.

The house was carpeted with the glittering bits of glass, smashed plates and broken frames. There was nothing left but walls and floors and furniture that was too large to be crushed or thrown. Angel had watched me calmly as I began to break the things that hung on the walls or sat on the shelves. When I began opening cupboards and drawers, she went outside and stood on the grass with her hands on her waist, her back to me. It took hours to finish breaking everything, and then I had to check to make sure I hadn't missed anything, left something buried, whole and intact. Aileen came downstairs and I heard her and Angel talking, in soft voices, and then Aileen got a bag from her room and left the house.

When I was quite sure I'd got it all, I sat down on the kitchen table (the chairs were legless, backless, on the floor) and Angel came and leaned beside me. "I can stay here tonight," she said, "if you want." I couldn't speak, but I nodded my head and she led me by the hand up the stairs. She gathered the four corners of my blanket, littered with the waste of things I'd once owned, and lifted it off the bed and then fell asleep. I sat on the side of the bed and looked at her for a long time, and then I went back downstairs, crushing broken things into smaller pieces with my heels on each step as I passed. I didn't sleep.

As I cooked breakfast, in the morning, I could hear the bed creak upstairs, but when I brought it to her, in the pan, she was still buried in the blankets, her face turned away from me. I shook her shoulder, and she turned her wide-open eyes to me. She took the pan and asked if I wanted some, and I didn't answer. The eggs were hard in the middle like she liked them, and she cut them into pieces and then cut the sausages and tomato slices up too and mixed it all together. I watched her eat.

I thought of calm things. I pictured a piece of wood, long and perfectly smooth. I pictured a hand sanding it even smoother.

"Does he know?" I asked.

"Not yet," said the girl on the bed.

I took the empty, greasy pan away and laid it in the kitchen sink. When I came back upstairs, she was lying like this with her back to me.

"Let me touch it," I asked. I reached my hand toward her stomach, I knelt by the bed. Outside, the grass was August-bleached, straw-coloured like it would be when the snow melted back the next spring.

"No," she said. "Not now."

"Are you angry with me?" I asked.

There was silence, and then, "No."

"Did I scare you last night?" I asked.

"No," she said, and she turned to me then. "I wasn't scared."

I'd never seen a better-looking girl. She was like a model. She looked like a magazine page. Her features as perfect as an animal's, her little fox teeth. Those deer eyes. I knew it was wrong, with all this, but I wanted to fuck her, right then. I didn't even know if you could fuck pregnant girls, but I wanted to have her by those skinny hips, to be in the bed with her there on the dirty sheets, with everything broken around us.

"I keep thinking about your parents," she said. She sat up and stared out the window. I knew without looking everything that was out there.

"They were so happy," I said, fast.

She looked at me. I couldn't read her face. "Jason," she said.

I talked fast so she couldn't interrupt me. "No, they were so in love. I didn't know it till I was old enough to understand, but that was what love looked like. They fought, you know that, but they loved each other. You could always tell the kind of love they had. It was like it made them mad, loving each other like that, it drove them to strange things, crazy things, hurting each other sometimes. And it's so hard to tell the difference. When I was a kid, sometimes I'd think they

261

were fighting, but they were, you know, kissing or doing other stuff, all close, and it was a different kind of love, sort of fierce in a way, so I'd get mixed up because I was a kid and didn't know about sex or anything, and it would almost look like a fight they were having, when they were in love, just kissing maybe, or him wanting her, or something like that."

She said, "What do you think it was like for her? Coming so far, coming here. She said she couldn't ever seem to get warm. You think it feels colder if you can't see?"

"She loved it here," I said. "Remember how she was always going for long walks all the time? In the snow, or by the river in the summer . . ."

Angel shook her head. "I don't think I remember that. I wonder if she missed her home."

"It was such a long time ago," I said. "She probably hardly remembered it. She was glad to come away."

"People always want to do that," Angel said. "Leave places."

"They do," I said, "they do."

She made her hair in a braid, without even looking at it, and lowered her feet to the ground. I worried about her bare feet on the floor, where everything was broken. She was humming something.

"What are you singing?" I asked.

She shrugged. "I never wanted to go anywhere but here," she said. "I always loved it here."

"Then stay," I said. The pain felt as if my ribs were pulling apart, a hinge opening. "You can stay with me, Angie. You can stay right here."

"I'm going with him." Her voice was soft and I was in love with her.

~

A few hours later, she left. She said she had to go home or her mother would worry, and she didn't want her mother looking any too close at her. She said June already suspected.

I stood where she had left me in the hall and listened to the front door close behind her downstairs. For a long time I stared down the hall at the door to the room where Aileen hadn't stayed. I had the feeling someone was inside and listened but heard nothing. A bug bounced around inside the glass lamp that was mounted on the wall, even though it was bright as day out, even though the lamp hadn't been switched on in months. I didn't know if it was a fly or a moth, but I could hear it light and flap against the glass. I took off my shoe and smashed the lamp. Even then, the door at the end of the hall stayed closed, and whoever was inside was silent.

Then I heard the front door open again, and I knew she had changed her mind. I ran downstairs, where Aileen stood pulling off her shoes.

"Where have you been?" I said. "Where did you sleep last night?"

"Jason," she said. "Jason, Angel told me."

"You answer me. Where did you sleep?"

"I got a room at the Downtown Hotel. I thought I should give you—"

"Are you calling him?" Surprise on her face and then defiance. She would have said, "Who?" I saw her mouth forming the word, a lie on her lips. I wouldn't let her. I said again and louder, "Are you calling him?"

She stared at me, the lie taken from her. "Why does it matter if I am?"

"Both of you. Both of you."

She grabbed me, her hand on my neck so I couldn't turn

my face away. She never would have touched me like that before. I let her get brave like that. My fault. "What, Jason?"

I could look straight at her if it was what she wanted. I could let my eyes tell her what my mouth said. It was her choice to stuff my face in it, like a dog in his shit, to leave me with no chance. "Whores. Both of you."

She dropped her hand and her eyes stopped looking at me and got real focused on something far away. "I'm going upstairs."

"I don't give a shit where you go."

"You know, Jason, you ought to figure out what it is you want and how to ask for it. You want to be with Angel now? What has this changed? And you don't want me to call my husband—why, so I have no one else and nowhere to go but here, so I can just hang around you all the time, like a hungry dog, or like I'm your m—" She went pale. "I'm going upstairs."

She climbed the stairs, and I heard her moving around in my mother's room. I heard how she was a ghost in this house. I heard how not even the walls could get rid of her.

She hadn't even noticed that everything was broken.

"Did you break the mirrors?" Minnie asked.

"Yes," I said.

"And the light bulbs?"

"Yes," I said. It would be weeks before I'd miss them.

"And the windows?"

"No," I said. "I didn't break the windows."

Minnie thought about that.

"Well, not all the windows," I said. When I got home, I'd break them. I hadn't thought of it.

Minnie reached for the pitcher and refilled my glass. The waitress had brought her a glass, but it was untouched.

"How come you never drink, Minnie?" I asked. I felt glad to be here with her, where there was no way to know if Angel had come back.

She shrugged. "It wouldn't help things," she said.

She said it serious, but it made me laugh a little. "You don't think so?"

"I know so," she said, still serious, and then she grinned. "And then who would look after you?"

The way Minnie listened to me and the things she said made me know she understood so well that sometimes it felt like I didn't even need to talk. Sometimes I wasn't even sure what I'd said out loud and what I hadn't, she was just there nodding, getting everything I said and didn't.

"So what," Minnie asked, "you want a kid? You think so?"

I thought there was something hungry then about the way she asked that. I thought about how I'd never seen her with any guys since she left her husband, not ever. "I don't know," I said. I thought about asking her about her kid, and if she'd wanted him. And if she still did. Some mothers brought their kids with them everywhere, even out to the bars, up till all hours. But I hardly ever saw Minnie with Amaruk.

"She would have gone with him anyway," Minnie said, like she was agreeing with something I'd said. "It doesn't make any difference."

I swallowed. "But if I wanted her to stay. If I told her that."

"I wanted somebody like that once. Didn't change a thing. If she goes," Minnie said, "she'll be happy there. It will be good for her to see that you won't follow after."

"I will. I'll go and find her. When the money comes. I'll be a rich man and I'll buy her and our baby a house, a huge house somewhere a million miles away. In Texas or Australia or China."

She shook her head. "Jason, none of us is ever getting rich."

"The money's coming. You know it is. Everybody got it but us."

"Doesn't mean anything."

"Of course it does. Why wouldn't we get it? What would the reason be for it to be like this for us, only us?"

"Fuck reasons," said Minnie.

I put my head in my hands. "She'll change her mind. She'll come back." Minnie shook her head again.

"No," she said.

I didn't think Angie would come back that night, but she did. She came home hours after me. She was a little unsteady, I thought. I was standing there, because there wasn't anywhere to sit, not really.

"Where'd you go," I said. She stood at the sink, drinking water out of her hands.

She looked at me and then looked away, wiping her hands on her pants. "This is the first cold night," she said.

"Did you tell him," I said, so loud, and she didn't even look startled.

"He wants me to come," she said. "He's buying me a ticket. An airplane ticket."

I grabbed her then, my hands feeling so clumsy, like there were three of them or they were too big. "You don't want to do this, do you?"

She turned back to the sink and put some water on her face before turning the taps off, like I didn't know she just wanted to shake me off, didn't want me touching her. "I do," she said. "And so does he."

"Sure he does," I said, fast, "sure. He's so damn old, it's the only shot he's got. He'll be so proud to be with a girl young enough to get knocked up, he won't care who put it in her. This is the only chance he's got, an old man like him."

"He has a daughter already. Down in Vancouver. With his ex-wife. He loves her. He'll love this one too."

I thought of the way a bird drops sometimes, its wings spread, over the river, and if the wind is going the right way, it can just hang like that in the air, not even moving a thing, and not go forward or backwards. Just be there, in the air.

"You're so slow," I said, as I watched her untie her braid, and every smooth, shining hair that it had snared fell on her shoulders. "The way you do things, everything. You look like you've got more time than everybody else."

"I was always like this, Jason."

"Ma said, 'The devil says there's no hurry.'"

"I don't know how to be any other way."

"Ma would say, '*Redeem the time, because the days are evil.*'"

"I don't know what that means."

I loved the way she moved. Like gravity. Heavy as gold. I never saw her stumble or do anything that didn't look like part of a plan only she knew, a plan she revealed only step by step, with each flicker of her eyelids or gesture of her hand. "I don't know what it meant either," I said.

"He says I can go to nursing school there, that I could start after the baby's born. When the others went away to college,

267

Momma told me just to stay at home a little longer and then I could go away too and get my training to be a nurse. But I didn't want to leave her to go to Whitehorse or anywhere. And if it weren't for this, I wouldn't have. Jason," she said, "I'm in love with him."

"My mother," I said. "You dreamt of my mother."

"What?"

"You dreamt of my mother."

I saw her look like she was looking in her own brain, finding something. "Oh," she said.

I felt very, very hot. "You know," I said. "You know what it means. When a pregnant woman dreams of a dead person, she is carrying that person's soul in her. That's how the dead tell us they're coming."

"It's just a story," she said softly. She didn't even hesitate.

"My mother," I said.

I was sitting on the floor now and she squatted down in front of me, put her hands on my feet, but I wouldn't look at her. "You really believe that?" she asked. "I don't know where the dead go or what they think about there. But I think the dead must be very, very tired. I think they must stop worrying about us. Maybe they just sleep. Wherever they go, they just sleep there."

"You believe that?"

"I don't believe anything. But I don't think the dead are thinking about us."

I woke up in the night, on the floor, cold. Something broken was sticking in my back. I stood up and realized why I'd woken. Through the window, snow was falling, blowing in on a wind, dropping lightly on the floor. The wind was icy, and the night was ink black. I would tell Angel in the morning about the snow and she would say it was a dream. She would lie to me.

As long as I could remember, I'd wanted to leave this town. The way my mother hated it made me hate it. The way my father loved it made me hate it. I didn't know how the town wouldn't want me to leave. How it pulled at me. Pulled me back every time I left.

The first time I left, I was halfway to Whitehorse before I noticed what was happening. Every mile I drove, my truck got a little heavier. I stopped a couple times, thinking maybe I blew a tire. But there was nothing wrong with the truck. By the time I crossed the border, it was too heavy to turn or keep straight and it kept swinging for the shoulder of the road. It wasn't till I parked the truck outside a motel in Fort Nelson and pulled my duffle bag out of the back that I realized what the problem was. It was me. I didn't look any bigger, but I weighed more than the moon.

Three times I left, and I lasted as long as I could. But it got so bad I could hardly stand. I would wake in the morning and not be able to pry my body from the bed. I went back home, and the higher I climbed on the map, the lighter I got, till my truck was almost flying off the road, and I was so angry I could cry.

I woke so early there was hardly any light between the curtains I'd forgot to close. Angel was still asleep in my bed. I left her there and went to Aileen's door.

"Get up," I told her.

She was already awake, sitting at the edge of the mattress with her back to me. "What? Why? What's going on?"

"You said you wanted to see the claim."

She stood up and went to the window. "Not today, Jason."

And I didn't blame her and didn't know why I wanted to go either, except not to be there when Angie woke up. But I said, "Get your clothes on if you're coming." And then I waited in the truck with the engine running until she came.

Driving down the dirt road to the site, I took the turns hard and liked the way I'd get thrown against the door or her each time, and how every bump I hit set us loose from our seats till we banged down into them again. I liked how she knew not to complain.

I parked in front of the excavator, beside the pit. I didn't want to get too close to Peter's cabin. This early on a Sunday, he and Pat would still be sleeping. "This is it," I told Aileen.

She got out slowly, and I pointed up to the cab of the excavator. "So. That's where I sit all day." I nodded at the sluice. "I dig up dirt from that pit, dump it in the sluice, and the water washes away everything in the basin that's lighter than gold. Which is everything."

Aileen went to the edge of the pit and peered up at the machine. "Gold is heavy?" she asked, like she didn't believe me.

"Heavier than lead. I'll show you."

She was still staring down into the pit. "I don't know what I was expecting," she said finally. "Something else, I guess."

"Like what?"

"I don't know. A river full of gold. Or a cave with twinkling walls. Stupid of me."

270

I shrugged. "Well, now you know." The field all around us was full of mountain avens gone to seed, waving in the wind. For no good reason they made me think of Angel. "Come on over here."

In the spring someone had broken into the cabin, and after that Peter moved the safe into the camper. He'd made a point of telling me where he'd moved it, so I'd know he didn't think it was me who'd broken through that window and banged a dent the size of a fist into the safe. I hadn't told him that I'd known the code for years and would have taken it all if I'd wanted to.

I led Aileen up into the camper and found the safe in the corner. I entered the code and the door swung open, and I pulled out the Ziploc bag inside.

"That's it?" Aileen said. "That's all you'd get in, what, a week?"

"That's the whole summer," I said. There were a few good handfuls of flake and pebbles almost as big as the eraser on a pencil. "So, you don't believe gold's heavy?"

She frowned. "I didn't say that."

I grinned at her. "Hold out your hand."

She did, her face confused, and I set the bag in her open hand. It dropped right through and she gasped and doubled over, trying to catch it before it thudded to the ground. "My god," she said.

"Gold's heavy," I told her again.

She shook her head. "It looks like nothing," she said. "Hardly anything at all. How could it weigh that much?" She picked the gold up from the ground with both hands and held it up to her face, turning it back and forth in the light from the window.

271

When she was finished, I returned the gold to the safe and we walked back to the truck. We stood for a while, leaning against the tailgate, looking out across the big dirt pile and the hole I'd spent the summer making, across the field to the woods in the distance.

"Aileen," I said.

"Yes."

"If I had money, enough to take us wherever we wanted to go, would you go with me?"

She turned to look at me. "What are you asking, Jason? I told you I'd stay here with you. Nobody needs to go anywhere."

"Tell me if you would."

"Are you thinking of going after Angel? Is that what this is about?"

"I just need to know. Would you go with me if I had enough money to take us anywhere?"

She thought for a minute. And then she said, "Sure I would, Jason. Sure."

Then we got back into the truck. And I thought about Angie. I thought about why I never asked her before to stay the night or have a baby or anything at all. Come home, Angie, I thought as I turned the key. Come home and take your jeans off. Let me put my fingers in your cunt and say you are the sweetest girl I know.

Angel was waiting when I got home. She told me June was going to take her to the airport the next morning. She had her suitcase by the door. Aileen looked at her and at me and said, "I'll leave you two alone," but I told her, "Stay."

That night, I watched Angel in the bathroom, unbraiding her hair. Washing her face with something from a little blue tub. I knew she wouldn't like it if she saw me watching there. The light was low and long through the window. Everything was gold in the room. Angie herself had light all over her, the shine of it even in the mirror, where she was looking back at herself, licked in yellow light. And how, I wondered, was a mirror I had broken two days before now on the wall again, fixed and whole?

She surprised me, turning suddenly to leave, and caught me there. "I'm going to bed," she said.

I knew I'd pretend to be sleeping when she woke and dressed, and only when I heard the door close would I run downstairs to watch her from the window as she crossed the grass to the waiting car, leaving. I would watch her steadily, standing in the door, so she couldn't leave without me letting her.

At the end of the hall, the door slid open, and Aileen stood there. She looked at me and began to close the door again, but I called her name. "Come out," I said. "I've got another story for you."

"Not tonight, Jason," she said, through the crack in the door. "I'm tired tonight."

My fist made a hole in the wall. "Tonight," I said. "It's a story for tonight. You too," I told Angel.

Angel put her hands over her face and sat down, just there, on the floor in the hall. She put her head against the wall, and her feet reached across to touch the other side without even her legs straightening out. After a moment, Aileen stepped into the hall and pulled the door closed behind her.

My fist didn't hurt. Not one bit. I liked the hole in the wall and I would have liked to make another one. I thought and thought about a story. Then I started.

Old Woman bore her two children. The girl had the eyes of a fish, slick and dark and deep. The boy was as pale as a white man. Even though her husband had given her this second child that she did not want, while she slept, Old Woman loved the boy as much as the girl.

When the girl was twelve years old, she was walking in the snow and saw that it had blood in it. She looked for the source of the blood and then knew that it was her. She lay down in the snow as she was meant to do until her people found her. Girls of that age wore warm clothes all the time, because when the blood came, it might be days until someone found them, and they were not permitted to move until they were found. The first woman blood is dangerous for the woman and for her people. What she does in the first months of bleeding will write the story of her life to come. She must go and live in a brush house outside the camp that her father's clan builds for her. She must learn to control the power of her bleeding. It might take weeks or years to learn this power. During this time, she must wear a long hood that covers her face and body, reaching out an arm's length in front of her, so that no one can see her face. She must wear copper and hooves strung around her so that hunters can hear her coming and take another path. If she cuts wood during this time, she will cut her lifeline too short. If she eats fresh meat, it will anger the spirit in the meat. However hungry she is, when food is brought to her, she must throw it on the ground and let other women eat first. When her time of seclusion is over, she returns to her father's family, but she can never speak to her blood brothers again.

A husband had been chosen already for Old Woman's daughter, and a wife for her son. The husband and wife were nearly as old as Old Woman and Old Man, and they had taken the boy and girl to their houses to raise them so that they would grow up right and be a good wife and a good husband. It was almost three days before the girl's husband-to-be found her. He called her mother to her, and she and other women came to take the girl to her brush house. As they walked there, the girl looked back to see the bloody path of her footprints behind her in the snow.

The girl was known to be a strange one. Her hands and cheeks were never cold and when she sang it sounded like water running on stone and when she spoke it sounded like grass talking in the wind. Out of the drops of blood she left behind her, small red flowers grew up out of the snow, though it was deep in winter.

The girl was left at the brush house, hungry, for days. During that time, animals came to visit her; even those that slept in winter woke to make their way to her house. Around the brush house, the snow melted. She ran out of wood and grew cold in her house. Then the trees outside her house said, Cut us down. So she cut the trees and burned them in the fire. When she was outside, the sun shone down and warmed her till she could not bear to wear clothes. Take off your hood, said the sun, and dance as you were made. So she took off her hood and was naked, and danced like that in the forest. She grew hungrier and hungrier. Then the caribou said to her, Eat of me. So she slaughtered him and ate the meat, cooked on the fire. Then she was hungry again. At the river, the ice turned to water, and a fish leapt from the surface and said, I forgive you. Eat my meat. So him, too, she cooked on the fire and ate.

When her mother's people arrived, she had just finished the fish and its fat was still on her mouth and hands. She lowered her hood so that her face could not be seen.

What are you eating? asked her mother.

Nothing, said the girl.

What are these bones on the floor? asked her mother.

I don't know, answered her daughter.

Then the girl's brother appeared beside the brush house. I saw her, he said. She chopped down wood for the fire and unfastened her hood and went without clothes. She ate of the caribou and of the fish. I watched her from the forest, and she did not know I was there. I am ashamed to call her sister. I will spit at her when I see her. We must leave her here to die.

Old Woman cried bitterly because she knew she must leave her daughter. Your husband will not want you now, she said. You will have to stay here alone and raise yourself. It would be better that you had starved, for the shame you have brought to our family.

Then the women left the girl, and they wept as they walked back, deep into the forest. The brother, who had been scolded for coming to this women's place, hid in the trees. He saw his sister sit down on the ground, and the snow melted around her. He saw a caribou lick away her tears. He loved her like no other. She was his sister, but they were the children of gods and all other girls were only human girls and he could not love them. Now, he thought, now she is mine alone.

The brother made a little house in the trees, far enough away that the girl could not see him there, and he watched her every day. When she was old enough, he would make her his bride. But after many weeks, the brother noticed that at night his sister had a visitor. A tall figure would emerge from the other side of the forest, and knock on her door and she would let him inside. She no longer wore the hood. The fourth time the man visited her, the brother could not stop himself from looking at the man's face as he left the house. The man was horribly tall and dark, and his face was that of an animal. It was the Bushman, the terrible monster that lived in the woods and ate men and women.

Sister, cried the boy, beating his hands against the door after he had waited for the Bushman to disappear into the forest. Sister, let me in. It is I, your brother, here to protect you.

Opening the door at last, his sister led him inside, where she sat down near the fire. She had grown fat and smiled a deep, true smile at her brother. I have missed you, she said.

Why does the Bushman visit you? he asked, breathless.

She smiled still. I cannot tell you that, Brother.

You must not invite him in or he will hurt you, he cried.

She licked her wrists a little and held them to the fire. He is not the Bushman but Fire-man. Our people have long seen him in our dreams. We dream of his house of white clay and stone. He has taken me there. In the house there is a small table with a hole like a mouth behind it.

What is in the hole? the boy asked his sister.

Even if I were not so in love, I could not tell you, answered his sister. If you dream of it, you must not ever look there. Oh Brother, she said, do you know what it is to love so that it is like a knife drawn inside of you, like the violence of an animal eating another?

Her brother looked into the forest. Yes, he said. Yes.

$\sim$

Angel stood up without a word and slipped past us to my bedroom, closing the door behind her.

"What's in the hole," Aileen said.

I shook my head. "I can't tell you," I said. "I can't tell you."

The next morning, I woke to the sound of her leaving me. The door shut behind her, and through the window, I watched her throw a match against the wall of my mother's house. She burned it to the ground.

Mara

NINETEEN

ALL MEN WHEN I imagined them looked like my father, slightly. He had been the last man I saw. So when I liked a man enough to think of what he looked like, I would give him a little piece of my father. I gave the man called Jason his hands. I gave Father McGivney Da's rough, curled dark hair and long smile and his ears that stuck out like mine. He already had his way of talking, of making *r*'s stay on in his mouth when other people would be done with them. It made everything he said sound gentle, even when the words themselves were not. Even when he said, "*I will show unto thee the judgment of the great whore, who sitteth upon many waters,*" the word *whore* in his mouth was so pretty that I saw her in my mind as a beautiful woman, with Mother's long yellow hair, streaming down to the shining ocean she floated on, as if she weighed no more than a leaf on the tide.

And when I sat in the confession box, and I knew he knew it was I, I thought of the whore floating there, a golden feather borne by the waves, as I told him I had lain with a man. He asked me who the man was, and I said he was a man not from here. Then I said I thought he might be an Indian man. He was from somewhere away up north. I said how I couldn't think of it getting any colder than here in Edmonton, and said how I could never feel the tips of my fingers when we went on our exercise walk, not for months now, but Father McGivney interrupted me. He didn't tell me how many times to say the Hail Mary, he only said, "Where is this man now?"

I said he was gone away now. I said he'd only been there for the night, on his way back from a job down in Calgary. I told him that after, when we went inside from his truck, he'd even asked me to dance, and we'd had two whole songs before Marla's sister found us. I never thought anyone would ask me to dance, and when Jason did, I cried because I didn't know how. And then he showed me how.

Father McGivney didn't want to hear about the dance and only asked me why I hadn't told him sooner, and I said I didn't know I was with child sooner, but now I knew I was because I wasn't bleeding anymore, and I could feel that my stomach was fatter than it was, and Agnes had said, "Do your tits hurt?" and I said they did, and she said that's how her sister said she always knew for sure.

I was waiting for Father McGivney to tell me how many Hail Marys, but he never did, he only kept asking me questions. Then he told me, "Get along now," and one of the sisters would come get me from my room later. I picked up my cane, which I had only just been allowed to have, because Father McGivney said we must learn to be self-sufficient and the canes would make us weak, and pushed open the door, and then I went around the side where he was and knocked.

He was angry and surprised, I could hear it, but I said, "Please, Father, how many Hail Marys?" I was frightened because he had never sounded angry and surprised before, he always sounded like Da before. He always touched me a little, just like I was a little cat, he'd touch my hair or down my side, and I heard him say to Sister Rose that I was a pretty girl, and I was glad of that.

But he told me to get back to my room, and said, "Don't you have the sense to know you've ruined yourself," and I didn't have the sense to know that, I didn't know what he meant at all. He said, "What chance we try to give you all, and look how you came to us, to our charity, to give you some sort of a life, something small but your own, and you're as stupid as you are blind, you humiliate the body God gave you and make a slattern of yourself with the first boy who'll—" And then he stopped and he said, "Get to your room now."

And I went there and sat on my bed for a long time, until Sister Margaret came, and she said we'd have to find the boy who did this and make him come back and marry me. And they told me later that they'd found him, that Marla's sister asked the boy she'd been kissing at the bar, and he knew who the man called Jason was. And she said he'd come to the chapel and marry me, and she helped me pack my suitcase that was a present for my wedding from her, and her face was wet when she kissed me, and I hoped she was happy for me, because I was the youngest girl at our school to get married, and we knew that many never married at all, and I knew it would mean I would wear a long, scratchy dress like Marla's. I'd thought we'd stay and maybe I could finish the year, but they said I had to go now and start my married life, so the man called Jason came to get me and he had bought a new truck, because the old one was broken, and he took me away in it.

The place he was from was called Dawson and after he put my suitcase in the back of the truck, he shook out a big piece of paper, and then made me put my finger on it. "That's where we are," he said. Then he pulled my hand so my finger dragged up along the map, and he said, "That's where we're going."

"What's it like there?" I asked him.

He said the people were nicer than in Edmonton. Then he said his sisters would be nice to me and take care of me, so I wouldn't miss Agnes and Sister Margaret at all.

He helped me into the truck, and pulled out something and put it in my hand.

"What is it?" I asked, rolling it between my fingers. And then I knew. "It's a necklace," I said. "It's for me. It's a present for me."

He took it from my hands and put it around my neck. "I saw it and I thought of you. I didn't know then that I'd ever see you again. But they made me think of you. The beads are beautiful, like you. All different colours." He touched my hair. "I wish you could see them."

I liked how strong they felt in my hands. Like something that would last. I'd had a crucifix on a chain once, but the chain had got caught in my hair and I'd broken it. I never could find where the crucifix had fallen, not even when the nuns looked for me. But I felt that this one was stronger, and I wrapped the beads around my fingers, and held them, tight in my hand, as Jason started the truck.

Aileen

❧

late August 1996

TWENTY

I WAS AT MY DESK, bent over the galleys for next week's issue with a magnifying glass, when the door was pushed open so forcefully it banged against the wall, and he stood in the doorway, staring at me.

"Jason," I said.

His face was somehow altered, as if something had come loose in it. His mouth gone soft, the sharp line of his brow no longer guarding whatever expression might cross over his widened eyes. "She burned the house down," he whispered.

Beside me, Melvin paused in the tapping of his typewriter keys. "Shall I place a phone call?" he asked me.

"Jason . . ." I said. "Jason, tell me what happened."

"I woke up and she was gone. I heard her shutting the door downstairs, and then she threw a match behind her. And maybe she had already set fire to the house before she went outside. She must have lit a match and dropped it on the stairs before she left. That's what she must have done."

"You mean Angel," I said slowly. "Angel burned the house." Beside me, Melvin picked up the phone and began to dial. I almost stopped him. I didn't want the authorities called until I knew. But I felt ashamed to doubt him.

Jason nodded, his eyes unstill, glancing from me to Melvin, unsure now of himself.

"Jason, is this a lie?" I asked him, and he didn't answer. Beside me, I heard Melvin speaking low into the phone, unalarmed as always by disaster. In that moment it seemed like less trouble if Angel had burned the house to the ground.

"False alarm," Melvin said, hanging up the phone. "Neighbour says the house is fine." He studied Jason for a moment. "Must have been mistaken. These things happen."

"Will you come to lunch with me?" Jason asked.

I tried to understand what had come undone in him. I'd thought, in the end, losing Angel would be like everything with him, something that was happening in his imagination as much as in the world, the idea of suffering more than pain itself. I had not been prepared for him to stand before me and come undone. "Okay," I said, and looked to Melvin, who nodded without raising his gaze from his typewriter. "Sure, let's get something to eat."

We walked out together onto a street that was black with crows, a sea of hooked beaks and dark, shining feathers. There must have been a dozen or more, and not one of them flying. Just creeping around one another, scratching at the dirt. Some had their wings unfolded above them, waiting.

"A murder of crows," I said, remembering the word. It had been our mother who taught us that there were names for the gathering of all animals. *A gulp of cormorants,* she'd called the big, bent-necked birds that roosted near our beach, and the inky marks against a sky they darkened with their wings were *a clutter of starlings.*

"What did you say?"

"Our mother taught us that," I said. "That's what you call a whole bunch of crows. Not a flock, but a murder of crows."

"No," Jason said. "These are ravens."

"Okay. A murder of ravens then."

"No," he said, looking at them with something like sorrow. "There's another word."

"Jason . . ." I tried to understand his face. "Did you read the article? Is that what this is about?" Though I'd been afraid of how he would take the story I had written about my sister, I was, too, proud of it. I wanted him to read it. And did not have the first idea what he would say or feel when he did.

He shook his head. "I didn't read anything."

"About your mother? It came out today . . ." His face was blank and I believed him. Then it wasn't that but Angel who had him looking like this. I'd blamed him before for not giving her any reason to do anything else, never till the moment she said she was leaving showing any sign he wanted her to stay. But now, and suddenly, I felt blindingly angry with her.

"I'll buy you a sandwich at Klondike Kate's," he said. "I've got money."

"Okay," I answered and tried to keep pace with him. It was all I could do to stay beside him as he led me up the street. Only once did he look back at me.

"An unkindness of ravens," he said.

At first we ate in silence. The hunted look on his face seemed to preclude conversation.

"There are no bugs here," I said at last, as I watched him cut his meatloaf into tiny, even pieces. He was a surprisingly delicate eater. "You ever notice that? I guess it's because there's no nighttime, and that's when they come out. I've never seen a summer go by before without a single mosquito."

"They spray in the spring. A helicopter goes over and shakes out dust and we have to keep our windows closed."

"Oh." I took the wrapper from my straw off the table and threaded it between my fingers. "I see."

I thought those might be all the words that would pass between us, but then he laid his silverware on the table and looked at me earnestly. "I need you to tell me something, Aileen."

I nodded slowly.

"When it happened to your husband—Stephan. After he fell, how did you know."

I felt suddenly cold and pulled my jacket more tightly around me. I cleared my throat. "Know what, Jason?"

He looked at me with clear, calm eyes. "That he'd gone crazy."

I looked at my half-finished chicken, like something naked on my plate, and my stomach turned. I drew a leaf of lettuce over it with my fork. "Well," I said. "There were doctors."

"So the doctors told you."

"Sort of." I remembered how his doctor had busied himself whenever I'd tried to talk to him, fussing with papers at the nurse's station or flipping the pages of Stephan's chart. I'd known he didn't want to look me in the eye. "I went to see the doctor when something seemed wrong. I asked if something could have happened to his brain to . . . change him."

"That's it," Jason said triumphantly. "How did you know that something seemed wrong?"

I turned my head from side to side. "When you're married to someone . . . When you're that close . . ."

"You just know, right?"

"Yes," I said softly. "I guess you just know."

"One day he was himself, and the next, he wasn't."

"He was distant," I whispered. "He just wasn't entirely there anymore."

Jason was radiant with satisfaction. He returned to eating his lunch, spearing several mouthfuls at a time on his fork. "That's what I thought of this morning. It was after she burned the house. That was how I knew. We weren't married so it's not like you and Stephan. It took me longer to figure it out."

"Figure out what." I felt deeply, deeply tired.

"That she'd gone crazy." He poked his fork into his mouth and gave me a closed-lip grin as he chewed.

"Jason, it's not the same. That's not how it was with Stephan."

"How was it with Stephan?" he asked cheerfully, still chewing.

I closed my eyes. Thought of the strange, awkward girl I'd been at twenty-one. How I'd had to order in special large-print textbooks and sit in the front row of every class to see the board. How it had taken meeting him to know I was pretty or must be, because there was no other reason he would have looked at me that first night like I was the only person in the room. How long it took me to understand he looked at everyone that way. How he walked into a crowded room like a starved man sitting down to a meal and it was only then I understood that what was truly terrifying wasn't other people, it was being alone. "He had a brain injury," I snapped. "Angel didn't fall off a roof."

"No. That's true." Jason thought about that. "But sometimes people just go crazy for no reason at all. Don't they?"

Yes. "Yes," I said.

The thousand taxi rides home. The endless series of silences that ended all the nights. All the giddy, beer-eyed chatter and the showing off. The way he'd forget about me and disappear into a crowd or a corner and then appear just when I thought he'd gone home without me, like a star in a dark sky. How he worked that wonder, that joy I felt when I thought I'd lost him and all of a sudden he was there again, like hope itself, his waiting face the world's tiniest miracle.

"I should have known right away," Jason said, shaking his head. "First there was that old man—she'd never be interested in him. And then wanting to leave here, when nobody loves this town like she does. And burning down the house—"

"Sometimes," I said. "Sometimes, Jason, it looks like someone's crazy and it's something else. It's that you weren't really looking at things right. Maybe it's you who changed. Or maybe nothing has changed at all." One day, a year after the accident, I'd looked at him lying on the couch reading a magazine and realized that what I was looking at, not just then, but had been looking at for years, was a very tired man who didn't love me. Not in any way that mattered. "Jason, you know I call Stephan every night now?"

He nodded without looking at me.

"I thought you should know that. It wasn't just once or twice."

"So?"

"There's something I didn't tell you about him." I watched my sister's son, finishing his lunch, pretending nothing I could say could matter very much to him. "He wasn't always . . . He wasn't always very nice."

Jason turned his head to the side and narrowed his eyes. "What about now?"

"Now?"

"You talk to him every day now, you said. How come. Did he change?"

"Did he . . . ?"

Once, after a fight we'd had, I'd found Stephan in the kitchen standing in front of the freezer, in the dark. He had his head bowed, like he was looking in the freezer, and I waited for him. But then I realized he was crying, and I'd never seen him cry before. His shoulders shook, as I watched him, standing there in his underwear, lit only by the street light through the window. I didn't know what to do or say, but suddenly there was nothing left of my anger. I touched his back with my hand and he pulled away as if he thought I'd hurt him, as if the touch of my hand was a threat to him. "Close the freezer," I said. And he did. I wondered why he'd even opened it. I couldn't think of anything else to say. I'd like to have been some other kind of person.

"I don't know, Jason," I said at last. "I don't know if people change."

He leaned forward. "Angel doesn't." As if he was trying to convince me. "She's been the same all my life. Till she went crazy."

I sighed. "Then maybe you're right. Maybe she'll come back. Maybe she just needs to be talked out of it."

"That's it," he said happily. He reached out and touched my hand, just for a moment. "I knew," he said. "I knew you'd understand."

Then he stood up and went to the bar to pay the waitress, refusing to accept my share. And then I followed him outside and we walked home together without speaking.

～

That night, while Jason sat at the kitchen table, dialling Angel's hotel again and again, refusing to leave a message each time, I laid a newspaper beside him and went upstairs to shower.

When I returned to my room, dressed for bed, my hair wrapped up in a towel, I found him blocking the door. I saw the paper in his hand and raised my chin. I was not ashamed of what I had written, however it might trouble him. She was my loss too, and if he chose to grieve for her in sulks and stories, I could damn well grieve for her in print.

"I wanted to surprise you. It's a new section," I told him. "Melvin thought of it. I came up with the name, 'Journeys North.' Everybody here has a crazy story of how they got to be in Dawson. I mean, not you or people who were born here, but everyone else. So we thought we'd pick a different person every month and tell their story. I thought it would be something special to start with Mara. It's a tribute to her, don't you see?"

"Aileen," he said. I pushed past him and he followed me through the door. "I've got a story for you."

"Jason, I need to go to bed," I told him.

"I read your article."

"Yes," I said. "I know."

He stepped closer. "It was all lies."

I sat down on the bed feeling suddenly deeply tired. "But it isn't, Jason."

"You didn't tell anything about what happened to her. And you didn't say how she came here, or what she was like, or how she died."

"I don't know those things, Jason," I reminded him. "You wouldn't tell me. I just wrote what I knew."

"And you didn't tell about her mother's shadow or the blindfolds or . . ."

I stared at him. "What are you talking about?"

"You didn't tell about how her father put blindfolds over her eyes and yours, so you wouldn't fall in love with a landscape that could teach you despair, the way it taught your mother. Or the way your mother's shadow disappeared before she died. Or how you betrayed her, taking off the blindfold, so you kept your eyes and my mother didn't."

I felt overwhelmed by the endlessness of his fantasies, his damage, his lies. I was exhausted of it all. "Jason, I don't know what you're talking about. It happened like I told you it did, like I wrote in the article. And I betrayed her because I never looked for her. Because I just let her go, like she had never—"

"He killed her," he said.

"What?"

"It's just a short story tonight."

The sister left her house the next day, and was gone till the sun had already made its brief trip beneath the world. Her brother was tireless watching the house. Finally, he saw smoke go up in the dark, and he went there and found her already in bed sleeping, and he made his knife go across her throat and then she died.

"Jason," I said. I realized then that he was more confused than I had understood. I'd thought we were two misfits of a kind, like a cockeyed vaudeville duo, this sullen, defensive boy and his aging aunt. I opened my arms to him but couldn't bring myself to step closer or draw him into them.

295

"Get out," he said. "Get out of her room. I'm sick of you and your lies."

I hesitated. I made so little money and had already spent too much of it at the hotel the other night, trying to give him and Angel space to figure things out. "I've got nowhere to go, Jason. Do you really want me to—"

"I don't give a damn," he said. "Stay or go. I don't give a damn what you do."

He slammed the door behind him, and I immediately felt as if I were trapped inside the room, as if I couldn't open the door again now that he had closed it. And so I climbed into bed, and lay awake for hours, listening to him slam down the phone downstairs over and over. And I thought about how I hadn't called Stephan, and how last night when we'd spoken he said there was something important he needed to talk to me about.

Mara

TWENTY-ONE

It was early May already when he drove me up to Dawson. For the first day and night, I listened to him talk, and then the second day, I tired of him talking. He was so worried for me. He kept asking if I was hungry, if I needed to stop and relieve myself, whether the music was too loud or not loud enough. He wanted to know too many things about me. He asked where my family was and why nobody had come to our wedding, but there was no one that showed up for him either.

The second afternoon, I picked a fight with him, over the radio. He tried to please me, but it only made me more angry and I didn't know why.

I had been proud to leave school, and then, very suddenly, I wasn't anymore. I thought of my bed in my room and how I liked to sleep to the sound of Agnes snoring. I felt as if we were driving too far and might go off the map altogether. I didn't want to fall off the side of the world with this man I hardly knew.

I stopped answering his questions, and then I stopped saying anything at all. He was even patient with that, and said silence was a blessing and it was his shortcoming to forget that blessing too often. But I could hear in his voice how worried he was, to have married a blind girl with no family, whom no one had ever come to look for. Hours later, when he stopped for gas, I slipped out the passenger door with my cane and went walking down the road. I forgot my shoes.

I didn't know if he would drive on or look for me or wait before he gave up. I thought maybe he'd be relieved or even glad. I thought I'd just go walking down that road and see what happened. It wouldn't have mattered very much if he didn't ever come to put me back into the truck.

The night wind was a crack in the warm evening. It was cool and dry and tasted of burnt things. Already dark was settling. I stumbled often. Sometimes cars passed me and I heard them slow, noticing me, and I hoped it wasn't Jason, not yet.

After a while the sidewalk ended, and I swept the curb with my cane and found my way down to the road. It was easier to walk there, I found, than on the rough sidewalk. I could still hear the worrying, hissing noise of a transformer, and knew there were homes near me. I smelled green—things, soft, wet curled things, dreaming of the sky from deep underground. I smelled the sweat of them, the way they were fighting. I smelled earth, still warm from the day, damp and both perished and living, taking more dead things into it and then pushing living things out of it. I smelled the earth letting the green things win. If I opened my mouth, I could taste all that I smelled. The air tasted like things *still,* not things not moving, but things *still* moving, things unstopped.

And the Lord shall scatter thee among all people . . . There was the sound of people near me, not so far from me. Maybe across the road, or somewhere behind me was a house. I heard a screen door open, close, open and then slam, far in the distance. I heard it slap against a wooden frame, falling closed one last time behind someone leaving.

A dog barked, rang his chain. A woman was laughing, high and loose, and I had heard very few women laugh in my life. The nuns only smiled. I'd got so I could hear them smiling.

My mother never laughed. But *she* did. When *she* laughed, after he made the bandages go over our eyes, sometimes I'd have to touch my mouth to know it was her and not me laughing.

Far away, a man yelled, "That's what everybody says!" I couldn't tell if he was talking to the laughing woman or someone altogether different.

Jason had said his sisters would be kind to me, but he didn't know that. They might not like me. They might think me a bad wife for him, or make fun of me because I couldn't see. They might find me strange. Agnes had said lots of people did, but she liked me anyway. What if they didn't like me anyway?

I had never thought of where I would go when I was done at school. I had thought they would tell me, when it was time, what I would do next, and there would be a place I could go to, not a school but another place with a little room for me, a little bed, a place to be when I was awake, to lay me when I was sleeping. It didn't surprise me that this had been what came next. Only Jason surprised me. I hadn't thought there would be someone else with me when I went to the next place.

The baby was moving. At first when this happened it had frightened me. But now I was glad and I put my hand there so it knew that I loved it, even though it was not even a baby yet, only something inside me, just started, new. I put my hand there because even what it was already was mine.

A strange thing was happening. It was growing brighter. I looked up and all the dim colourlessness of the world was brighter. Night had never come, just day, like this, like something throbbing. Day beat again, harder, deeper. It was holy.

Bird sound. Like the thrush. I remembered that from nights we had left the window open and in the pale hours before we were allowed to rise from our beds, when Mother would be waiting in the kitchen rolling oatcakes with a wooden pin and calling our names when it was time to leave our room and see her again, at the start of a day. The thrush sound was the first we heard in summers. Then the crows. *She* liked the crows best, but I loved the thrush song. That slippery flute sound, the water of it, the stream and rush from one note to the next, like water moving fast over rocks. But the crow sound, that sad, distant winter sound, the spread of its long arced call, its hysterical grief, hanging over frozen fields, that was *hers.*

From the one end of the earth even unto the other . . . Now I could hear trees bending near me. Old trees, the wind whistling in a dry way between them. I must have been past the town now. For a long time, the soles of my feet had hurt like the pain of something reminding me, each step the bloody feel of the road and its stones, the weight of my body pressing against each soft foot, down against that pain. Now I could not feel them at all. Now it was as if I were walking not on the ground, but inches above it, the air between my feet and the earth skimming past, bearing me up this road, to the north place where I'd be home now.

"Your father lost his name," I said to the child moving in my belly. The man called Jason had told me he was not always called Jason. It was a name given him at the school he'd had to go to in the white village down the river that his family finally followed him to. The white teachers had given him the name Jason, and for months, he'd gotten in trouble for not answering to his new name. He didn't understand how a name could be a thing that changed.

"I'll give his name to you," I told the child in me. I knew he would be my son. I knew he would suit that unwanted name. Because I hadn't known I wanted him until he was already a thing that had happened, and then I knew I wanted him most.

A vehicle passed me, and only as it did did I realize none had for some time. But it stopped ahead of me; I heard the stones hop and skate along the pavement as it slid over onto the shoulder of the highway, just ahead of where I was walking. And then I knew it was my husband.

He threw open the door and came to get me. I heard his steps in the loose stones beside the road, heavy, running. He shook me and told me, "Where did you go? Mara," he shouted, "Mara, why did you leave me?"

He asked me what the fuck I was thinking. He said he had looked for me for hours, everywhere searching for me. He asked where I had been. He said, "I don't ever want you to do that again. You understand me, do you understand? Not ever again."

The sky was getting hotter. I asked him why did night not come. He said, "Up here in summer the sun doesn't go down."

"Not at all?" I asked.

"Gets close," he said, "but doesn't ever get there."

I didn't know why I was crying. I pushed the cane into his hand to take for me and then I wrapped both arms around one of his. With his other arm, he opened the door and helped me inside, into my seat. There was a bird somewhere above us, again, I heard it passing over us, calling out. This time it reminded me of the bird sound *she* loved, but the cry was deeper in its throat, more rasping and more desperate.

And then I wanted to punish him. As he got into his seat, he reached out a hand and set it down on my knee. Without a thought, I bent at the waist and snatched up his hand between my teeth. I bit as hard as I could, feeling my teeth burying themselves in his soft, yielding skin. He gasped but didn't draw his hand away. There was a moment when he said nothing, and I let the weight of my head fall in my lap, easing the grip of my jaw on his hand but not removing my mouth. I stopped the tears that were dropping from my cheek to his hand. Nothing he or I could do could change anything that had happened to us. "Why," I asked him, in a whisper, "does God not forgive us?"

His other hand came down and stroked my hair. "What is it, honey?" he asked. "I can't hear you with your face buried like that."

I raised my face and pushed his hands away from me. "Tell me about it again," I said. "What it will be like."

"Well, first thing, we'll go to Aida's house and she'll make us something to eat. She'll fuss about you. She'll call Joannie to come over and meet you."

"No," I said. "Tell me what it will be like." He was confused and while he hesitated, I thought of what it would smell like. If the stove would already be on when we opened the door. The smell of something warm and ready, a pot of something smelling darkly of meat, hot, thick food smells, waiting for us. His sisters opening their arms, the laundry smell of their blouses, the soap and flowers of their hair, the coolness of their cheeks, the warmth of their hands. *Let us take our journey*, I thought as I waited for his answer, *and let us go, and I will go before thee.*

Minnie

～

late August 1996

TWENTY-TWO

IF I DIDN'T HAVE CIGARETTES, I would need people. I said
that to my sister all the time. "Oh, you don't need me?" Violet
always said. "What," I would say. "You don't think I could
pull some drunk off a bar stool and have him watch Amaruk
for me? That boy's so good, you don't have to be able to see
straight to watch after him." Violet would then make this *tsk
tsk* sound our mother used to make when she was pretending
to be annoyed with us.

Right now, I was sitting in Violet's kitchen, watching her
iron, and I was thinking about my cigarette but I decided not
to say it out loud. A joke could run itself out if you weren't
careful. It wasn't really a joke anyway, because I knew it was
true. Since I was a girl, I had been independent. Our mother
always said the day she gave me shoes was the day I was out
the door. Violet was different. Though she was a year older
than me, she always did things after me. She hesitated. You
could just ask her a simple question, and she'd stop and you
could see her weighing it out, how to answer. She was cautious. But cautious wasn't a bad thing. She got married later
than me and look who still had her husband. And the kids and
the ironing to go with it.

It was a cool, clear day, but sitting up on the counter with my back against the window, I was heating up. "Can you get a sunburn through the glass?" I asked Violet.

Violet paused and tucked her long bangs back behind her ears. She had cute ears. Little and round, like a monkey or something. I always envied her ears. "I don't know," she said slowly. "It would definitely take longer than if you were outside."

"That iron's heating it up here too," I said. I liked my sister's house well enough, but it was cramped for just her and her husband and their four kids. With me and Amaruk in there too, it felt like it was getting a little smaller every day. And the kitchen was teeny to start with. I admired how Violet never seemed to get tired or feel sorry for herself, but it exhausted me to see how full the basket of unironed clothes was and how empty the basket of ironed clothes was. And we'd been there near an hour already. Some chores weren't rewarding. I liked vacuuming, in a really dirty house. Somewhere where you could see the difference you were making. Ironing seemed unreasonable. So much work over just a few wrinkles that would be back next wash anyway.

But she didn't take the hint and just kept going back and forth, up and down, with the damn iron. Last year, for her thirty-second birthday, her husband, Hughie, had invited everyone over for ice cream and cake, and he called us all into the kitchen so he could give Violet her big birthday surprise. And he showed her how he'd built an ironing board into the wall so it was hidden away in a little cupboard, and then you could just open the door and pull it down from the wall on a hinge. Jesus, I thought and I looked to Violet to see if she'd show she was mad in front of guests or fake a smile and wait till they were all gone to tell him why an ironing board was not an acceptable birthday gift for your wife. To my surprise, Violet walked up to the cupboard and ran her hands along it, opening and closing it like she just couldn't believe it (a door! open! closed!), and then she looked at him and had tears in her eyes as she thanked him, like she was the luckiest girl on earth.

"Just a few more weeks, anyway," I said, as Violet sprayed one of Hughie's shirts and the iron hissed.

"A few more weeks, is it," she said. I saw that she was sweating a little too. And this room really was too small for a big family. Just the two of us and a stack of wrinkly clothes and it felt filled to burst. I didn't like the fussy wallpaper she had got put up the year before, with its little blue flowers all over. It made the place seem even smaller, even more *indoors* somehow.

"Till I'm back at the Baders' place," I explained. I wondered if she would say, "You could stay with us all year if you wanted," like she sometimes did. I house-sat for a German couple through the winter—they had a whole big house but only came to it in the summer. A year ago, I'd got fired from my bartending job when Amaruk got sick with pneumonia and I had to miss ten days straight of work right in the middle of tourist season. I hadn't been able to find a decent job since, so I'd been living on what I could string together and the money Ed, Amaruk's father, sent, scrimping pennies while I waited for something to come along. In the meantime, Violet and Hughie put me up in the summer, and they always seemed like they wished I'd stay longer. I wondered if Violet was lonely.

"I know," said Violet.

"You know that's when I'm back there, or you knew that was what I meant."

"Both," said Violet.

311

"So June said Angel called home finally," I said.

Violet stopped and set the iron on its end. "Oh," she said. "How is she?"

"Dunno," I said. "I didn't talk to her. But June said she didn't think she was going to come back till after the baby's born."

"Has she called Jason?" Violet said.

I shook my head. "Maybe. I wouldn't know."

"You sound like you're mad at her."

"Well," I said.

"Now why would this make you mad?" Violet asked.

I shrugged and lit another cigarette and listened to the thump and hiss of the iron while I looked out the window into the scruffy, stunted fir trees around the house. "Your window's dirty," I said. I touched a handprint on the glass. Small. Maybe the size of Amaruk's hand.

"I'm going to go out tonight," I said. "Maybe I'll swing by and look for Jason."

"Maybe you should leave him alone."

"Huh," I said. "Well, anyway, can you watch Amaruk tonight?"

"Of course," said Violet. She never came out to the bars. She had made Hughie promise the day he married her that he wouldn't drink anymore, and she didn't either to make it easier for him. I told her she could come out and just drink coffee, like I did, but she said that was tempting fate.

There really was something about cigarettes, I thought as I put mine out in one of the ugly china ashtrays Violet always set in front of me, as a protest against me putting them out in the sink or on dirty plates. Every single time I finished one, I wished I were just starting it.

~

I went straight to Jason's house. Along the way, I passed Rita's little cabin, where I knew Amaruk would be somewhere inside, playing with Rita's son Sean. I decided not to stop. Amaruk would want me to stay home. When he was young enough for me to still pick him up and carry him home, he would look at me with deep, sad eyes when I was getting ready to go out. But he wouldn't say anything. Even once he learned the words that he could have said if he wanted to, he never did. I'd thought, at the time, that those eyes were worse than whatever he could have said. Sometimes I'd hardly known why I even went out at all; half the time I was bored sideways by everyone, and just depressed with thinking of those eyes, watching me from the doorway as I dressed, watching from the screen door as I left. Then for a while, he grew so attached to Violet, he couldn't stand to be away from her. He'd cry when I came to bring him home. Sometimes I'd have to give him a little slap to stop him crying for her. And I thought that was worse than those sad eyes. But for more than a year now, he'd got so he'd come and beg me not to go out, he'd ask when I'd be back, and he'd tell me he would not sleep until then, and when I came back, if I went up to his bedroom, I'd find him there, watching the door, with his thumb in his mouth, which he still wouldn't stop doing, though at least he knew now not to do it in front of other kids. And that was worse.

Aileen was out sitting on the steps of the porch when I got there, and I wasn't expecting that.

"Hello," she said.

"Hello," I said, and I stopped there, looking at her.

Aileen had her hair pulled up with pins on top of her head

313

and she was wearing a pale pink cardigan, buttoned up wrong, so it buckled on one side. She had a long, flowered skirt on that went down to the ground, and she'd tucked her feet under it. I couldn't figure out if she was dressed like a little girl or an old lady. Something was changed in her.

"Anyway," I said. "I came by."

"Are you looking for Jason?"

I said I was and followed Aileen in. It had been a few years since I'd been in Jason's house, I realized, as I discovered how weird it was to see things just as they'd been. I wondered if Jason had kept it that way on purpose, to honour her, or if he just hadn't bothered changing anything.

Jason was on his knees in the kitchen, putting wood in the stove.

"Is this the first fire?" I asked.

He looked up at me and shrugged. "I guess so," he said.

"We haven't lit the stove yet. There's been a couple nights we could have used it though. It's getting cold early this year. Going to be a long winter," I said.

Neither Jason nor Aileen answered me and so I got tired of trying to make conversation. I sat down at Mara's old pine table that still had Mara's old flowered tablecloth on it. "I brought some beers," I said, pushing them down the table toward Aileen.

She pulled one out and offered it to Jason. He shook his head and she opened it. I watched her take a long swallow. I remembered one time when I was a child, I was walking home from my cousin's house at dinnertime one evening, and suddenly, between the road and the house I was passing, I saw a body in the snow. I went closer, not quite scared yet, still just interested, and saw it was a woman, her reddish hair stretched out in the snow and over her face, her arms and legs bent up into a ball. I touched the lady's shoulder with my boot, and she moaned a little but didn't move. I had to get my mother, who helped the lady stand up and then drove her to her house, me in the back seat, trying to see the reflection of the lady's face in the window she was leaned against. After my mother came out of the lady's bedroom, she told me the lady would be fine and we could go home now. "Too much alcohol," she said. It was the first but not the last drunk I saw passed out in the snow, but I always remembered her. Sometimes when I was talking to white people, women especially, I'd remember the lady. Aileen made me think of her, how her hands weren't even in mittens, just little fists in the snow.

"So, you doing okay?" I asked Jason.

"He's fine," Aileen said, and you could tell she didn't want us to talk about it anymore.

"Maybe it makes sense that she'd be the one to go. She was the last one to leave of the three of us. Maybe for her, it will take. While me and you grow old here."

"Shut up, Minnie," said Jason. I looked at him more closely then, and honest to god he looked like when Mara died. Not a lick older either. He was almost as white as Aileen.

"It's okay," Aileen said. I looked at her, her face all open, like she was exposed there, even if that was just another way of lying. "This is going to be all right. Jason is going to be all right."

"She doesn't have any right though," I said.

They both stared at me.

"Angie's like my own sister. But she doesn't have any right to take that kid from you, Jason."

Jason had left the stove door open and it was hot, hot, hot.

315

It was just dim enough outside that you could see the patterns of the flames shifting the light around the room.

Jason said, "I was going to tell Aileen a story."

"You and your stories," I said.

"He's got two left to tell me," she said. "Only one after tonight."

"Well, you're going to live here now, aren't you. All winter long. I'm sure you'll get to hear lots more stories."

For a moment, Jason and Aileen had the same pinched face. Then Jason pulled a chair out and turned it around and sat on it backwards, so his arms hung over the back. "Pass me a beer, Minnie," he said. I gave him one, and he said, "She had a child."

"No, she didn't," said Aileen quickly.

"She did."

The brother cut his sister up into small pieces, so he could hide her in the ground, beneath the snow, where she'd be eaten by spring. It took him hours to clean up all the blood, and as he was cleaning, he heard the sound of someone crying.

Be quiet, he said, thinking it was an animal looking for food. Go away!

But the crying continued, and he thought perhaps it was the wind, and he closed the door.

But the crying continued, and the brother became very afraid that it was Fire-man, come to cry for his dead woman. She's gone to walk in the woods, he called, in case Fire-man was listening. She'll be back in the morning. I am just making some breakfast for us now.

But the crying continued, and finally, the brother went to

316

find the crying sound. In a little cradle in the corner, he found a baby. It could only be a few days old. He knew it was the child of his sister and Fire-man.

Then he became afraid, for he knew Fire-man would return, looking for his woman and his child. So he wrapped the baby in some caribou skins and took him in his arms and left the cottage. He went deep, deep into the woods, and waited for the sun to rise, so he could find his way home to his people.

But the sun did not rise. He waited many days, but the cold got deeper and darker. He had to sleep on boughs of fir, blanketed with snow, the baby close to his chest so they would not freeze to death. He heard the trees around him whispering, Get the caribou. He did not want to see what the caribou would do when they came, so he ran and ran, the baby in his arms, and the sound of hoofbeats behind him. He stopped by a brook and made a fire to melt the ice so he and the baby could drink, but he heard the water say then, Get the fish. He saw, then, salmon frozen in the ice, and their tails began to move, slowly back and forth. They are only fish, he said. They cannot hurt me. One rose to the surface and watched him and the baby with its wet eyes, then it disappeared into the frozen brook, and he saw the flash of it moving in the ice, travelling far, far upstream. He left the brook then and began to climb toward the mountains, when his father and mother appeared before him.

The fish say that you have killed your sister, said his father.

The caribou say that you have taken her child, said his mother.

He wept and said it was because he loved her. He told them how she had disdained his love.

Fire-man is looking for you, said his father.

He will find you, said his mother.

He lay down on the ground then and held fast to the child. I will not let him take the child, he said.

The fish have eaten the child, said his mother. And he looked and saw the child in his arms was eaten.

The caribou beat out its brains with their hooves, said his father. And the brother saw that it was true, and he opened the bloodied caribou skins on the snow and wept upon them.

I will kill you, said his mother. He raised his hands up to her to plead for his life, but she rose taller above him, till all the sky was her face, and the trees dwindled to bony sticks beside him, and the snow grew deeper, and the wind more bitter.

Hide me, he said to the wind, but the wind blew harder. Bury me, he said to the snow, but the snow made a valley around him. Shelter me, he said to the trees, but they were only sticks and could shelter no one.

His father then appeared by his side and said, You are my son. I will not let her harm you.

I have loved you, Father, he said, his tears ice in his eyes. Do not leave me now.

I will not leave you, said his father, because you will be always with us. No one will be able to leave you. You will be cold. You will be ice. You will be the snap of frozen branches that betray the feet of hunters. You will be the moonlit glare of the river. You will be dark. You will be the sleeping of all living things. You will be waiting that does not end. You will be time that ages without passing. You will be the endlessness of all things, of all endurances, of all suffering. You will be weather and winter, and there will be no summer again.

The brother thought to change his mind and ask to be only a mortal, not a god or a season but something that could, at last, die, but it was too late because already he had no mind to change, only snow and the thin light of the moon.

I was quiet after Jason finished. Aileen stood and turned her back to us, but we could see that she put her hands up to her face.

"Well," said Jason. "I feel like getting out of here."

"You want to go down and see who's at the bar?" I asked.

"No," said Jason. "I mean out of here."

"Let's go up north," Aileen said suddenly.

I laughed at how seriously she said that, and how she said it like it was a place to go, but Jason answered her seriously. "Where would we go?" he asked.

"I don't care where we go," Aileen said. "We could take the Dempster Highway. We could cross the Arctic Circle. Get away from all of this."

Our mother used to say, "Be careful not to take yourself too seriously." I thought about saying that to Aileen sometimes.

"I could call Peter tonight," Jason said. "He won't care if I don't show up tomorrow. We could be gone by tomorrow."

Aileen leaned against the window, her forehead pressed against it. "Good," she said.

Then neither of them said anything. If we'd been out, I could have gone and talked to someone else, but I was in Jason's house at Jason's table, so I had to just wait and watch while the two of them sat there so quietly that the ticking of the clock seemed to shake the walls.

The first time Lopita spoke to me, she had said, "You gonna come sit down here or did nobody ever teach you you can't fuck with your eyes?" I had just got the job, my first real job, and was still focused on busing the tables fast enough that the waitresses would slip me five bucks from their tips. I was hardly twenty and as shy in Vancouver as I'd been ballsy in Dawson. I hadn't been looking at anybody. Not even Lopita, who was more beautiful and weird-looking than anyone I had ever seen before. But when I looked at her then, I realized I didn't want to stop looking, and maybe that was why Lopita had said that. To make me look. And keep looking.

"I gotta go to the bathroom," I said. Jason nodded and Aileen seemed startled to see me standing there. Jesus, I thought, as I found my way to the same old white-painted plywood door that you had to pull open and closed by a tiny round hole in the wood you could hook a couple fingers through. I'd always been surprised by how rundown this place was. Growing up, I thought, well, Mara had enough to do with Jason and being blind and all. But there was really no excuse for Jason not fixing the place up.

I had to give a good tug to get my pants down. I was getting my mother's ass. Violet had four children and was still as thin as a stick. The window in the shower was open, and cold air was coming through. The toilet seat was ice-cold. I pissed and listened to a dog barking somewhere outside.

Lopita was from Mexico, and had a broad brown face and narrow black eyes. All her features were narrow and doll-like, lost in her wide face, except her mouth, which was much too big. It was full at the centre and then got thinner as it snaked up into her cheeks. It was a bent mouth. It was never closed or open in a normal way. It was always twisted or laughing and showing too many teeth. She wore coral lipstick. She made me sit down at one of her tables that first night while she counted all the money she owed the restaurant and separated out her tips. She didn't give any of her tips to me. When she was finished, she put the biggest pile of money in an envelope, and the smaller pile she stuck in the back pocket of her jeans, which were too tight. Then she leaned across the table and put her hand under my face and kissed me.

I let the water keep running over my hands after I finished washing them. The hot water felt so good. In the cold, my fingers always stiffened.

Lopita had said, "Why did you get a job here? You'd make better money downtown." I had explained, "Back home, a few times I heard American tourists ask why there were so many Mexicans in the north. One asked me once if it had been hard for me to get used to the cold. No one in the city wanted to hire me, and I thought maybe they would here if they thought I was Mexican. I never had Mexican food before, but Raul gave me a quesadilla after I filled out my application. I thought it was delicious. I never had anything like that before."

"Well," I said now, as I walked back into the room, "I should get going, I guess."

"You just got here," said Aileen, who was washing dishes at the sink. "Let me put some coffee on for you."

"If you're going on a trip tomorrow, you'll have to get ready," I said. "I'll stay out of the way of that."

Jason was still in his chair at the table. "I'm glad you came by, Minnie," he said. "Thanks," he said.

"You can keep the beer," I said. "Take it with you on your trip."

"Wait," said Aileen. "I'll walk you out." She slipped her

feet into a pair of worn leather sandals and pushed open the door, without looking back at Jason.

I let her go out first and then closed the screen door behind me. "Yes?" I said.

"I just wanted to walk you out," she said. I found lies so boring. "Well," she said, "I guess I wanted to ask you something, but I'm not quite sure even what, or how to ask."

"I've got to get home," I said.

"I know," said Aileen. "I know. Just wait a moment. I'm trying to figure something out and I don't have anybody to talk to about it."

"Except Jason," I said.

"But it's especially him I can't talk to."

I nodded slowly because I knew now where she was going.

"I used to think that right was always something you could think up in your head. That if you did the wrong thing, it was because you hadn't thought about it enough. Shit. Let me start again. You've known Jason a long time, haven't you?"

I nodded again. "When we were kids, I'd babysit him. Mara needed lots of help watching him. I mean, the watching part. Later we got to be friends."

"I know how much you matter to him. You must really know each other well."

"I don't know that he wants to be known that well. But I know him better than anybody else, I guess. I guess that's true."

The words came out of her mouth like she was chasing them out. "Stephan—my husband—he wants to try again. He asked me to come home. He said he gave it a lot of thought and he wants me to come home."

"And you figure that's back in Toronto."

"That's back in . . ." She scowled. "Say it to me straight."

"The way I heard it from Jason, you thought your home was here now."

"I did. And maybe I still do. I haven't figured it out. I just haven't figured it out. Maybe I could take him with me. Or maybe we should both stay here. But I wanted to ask you, do you think, if I were to go . . . Or even just with Angel gone . . . Do you think he's going to be okay?"

"Well," I said. "I don't think that really has to do with either one of us. And I don't think it's anybody's business to say that about anyone else. Are you going to be okay? Am I?"

"I know," she said. She sat down on the porch steps, where she'd been when I arrived. "But everybody let him down, didn't they. He told me about what his father did to him. I'm sure you must know that. And then when Mara died, it must have been like she was leaving him."

"I don't know what you mean about 'his father did.' What did his father do? He didn't do anything wrong to Jason."

Aileen's eyes widened and then got sad. "So maybe no one knew then," she said softly. "His father used to hurt Jason and Mara."

"No, he didn't," I said.

"Minnie, he did. He wouldn't lie about a thing like that. He told me about the fights they'd have. He showed me where the table was broken from him once trying to hit her with the back of an axe."

"God, Jason," I said. I thought of how he never spoke about his mother and of what he must have got going on in his head about her. I remembered the day, a couple months before Mara died, that the three of us were in the kitchen, and she wanted Jason to go split some wood for the fire. But Jason and I had planned to drive to Alaska that morning, to see my cousin Deke about a job. Deke said he could get Jason good pay for a job on his boat, and Jason had just finished school and thought he might like that, being out there on the water all the time. "Well, you've got it wrong," I said.

"He has a scar, Minnie," she said. "I've seen it. He left a scar on his son."

"He didn't," I said simply. "It was her. It was always her."

"What do you mean?" She stopped. "You mean my sister?"

"You can't even blame her, not really. She was troubled, that's what my father would say. She knew the Bible inside and out but she didn't know anything about being a mother. There wasn't anything Jason could do right. I saw her come down on him like a pack of wolves over nothing. She was half crazy when she shouted at him, every time she told him how worthless he was. Maybe all-the-way crazy. Because she loved him. Jason couldn't tell that, but I could. She was obsessed with that boy. Even more than his father, and he loved Jason and was just heartbroken to watch her grind him down. But he was a coward and he worshipped Mara, and he could never get her to leave Jason alone. I remember once she came to get Jason from my house, and my mother and I watched from the window, her dragging him up the road and hissing something mixed up about hell or sin, and he didn't even try to defend himself. He let her treat him like dirt and convince him that he was. My mother said, 'That woman is as sad as the stones. Look at her try to beat her love out of that boy. Who do you think she's punishing.' You know, if she hadn't been blind, somebody might have thought to take him from her. But the whole town pitied her, and Jason's father too, and they were miserable enough to be their own punishment for whatever wrong they did. And no one thought of Jason."

"But he loves her," Aileen whispered.

"I know," I said. "He did then too. He'd get angry at his father if he tried to get between them. I think he hated him for letting it happen, but he wouldn't let him try to stop it either. And Jason was always so protective of Mara. She never had a cane or a dog or anything like that, so the only way she'd get around anywhere was if Jason took her. And everywhere he took her, she'd be telling him that he was less than nothing. And as twisted as it was, I thought I understood. I thought I got it and why he put up with it. I thought there was something more between them that only they understood, and it wasn't anyone else's business. And then one day, I saw her hurt him."

Aileen flinched, like I had hit her myself.

"I didn't see it coming. She was angry, but she was always angry with him so I didn't make much of it." It was one of the few times I had seen him stand up to her. He'd been so excited about that damn trip to Alaska, and he told her he'd be back in a couple days and would do the wood then. There was no earthly need to be cutting wood that time of spring anyway, and it was like she'd made the job up, like she needed a reason to stand there, in the way of the door, so neither of us could leave without moving her from it. And finally, Jason tried to push past her, and she had the splitting maul in her hands, and brought it down over his head, and I closed my eyes and when I opened them and saw the axe on the floor where she'd dropped it and the table cut from the blow, I didn't know if she'd missed or he'd ducked. I wasn't even sure he would have. That was the way they were. If she had wanted to bring that axe down on him, he would have stood there and taken it. "I've seen mothers slap their kids when they mouth off, or give them a smack on the ass to shut them up, that's not something

325

anyone I know would get in a twist about. But this wasn't that. She brought an axe down on her son." But it wasn't even that, the axe or that moment. As I'd opened my eyes and seen the axe on the floor, he went and stood before her. He put his hand around her wrist and waited, like he knew what was coming. And she hit him hard enough that he stumbled. He knocked his face on the door as he fell. It took weeks for the cut on his cheek to heal, and after that, I'd look at the scar and think, It must have happened before. He'd walked toward her like it was something he had learned to do. "I told Angel what I'd seen and she agreed with me that it must not have been the first time. That he might have been keeping this secret as long as we'd known him. And we decided to get him out of town as soon as we could. But then, before the summer ended, she was dead. And not long after that, his father too. And after that, you'd move a mountain easier than you'd get him to leave this town, and we thought, well, maybe it didn't matter, now that he was on his own and free. And then you showed up."

I shut up then, and Aileen got to her feet. She looked so shaken I almost felt sorry for her, her eyes like burnt holes in a white rag. "I didn't know about that," she said finally. "Thank you for telling me."

I shrugged and watched her walk back up the steps, leaning against the railing and pausing on the last step with her back to me. "She worried about him as much as you do," I said quietly. "It wouldn't be any different if she hit him and asked, 'Is he going to be okay?'"

Aileen was closing the door as I walked back toward the steps and called, "Aileen, I had a baby when I was young." She hesitated and looked back at me, but with the light behind her, I couldn't see her face. "I wasn't much older than Angie.

He's seven years old," I said. "His name is Amaruk. He's a good boy. You know, it's not Angel that Jason cares about. It's not even that child. It's that he thinks somehow it's her."

"Who?"

"Mara. He thinks somehow that baby's her."

"You mean that story, about pregnant women dreaming of dead people?"

"It isn't just a story to Jason. Some people around here wouldn't disagree with him either."

"Why are you telling me that?"

"So you understand what matters to him. You think you care about him, but the only thing he ever cared about was her."

She nodded and then closed the door behind her. I watched the lights go out downstairs.

"I never heard a name like yours," I had said after the first time we slept together. I was half dressed, but couldn't make myself leave the bed, even though I was already almost an hour late for work. Lopita smiled and slipped her hand under the waistband of my cotton underwear. "It means 'the valley of the wolves,'" she said. "It's a saint name. What does yours mean?"

"I don't think it means anything," I answered. "It was just the name of a friend of my mother's at school."

Lopita lit a cigarette and pushed herself up onto a pillow. I put my hand on her long, plump thigh, but she ignored it. "I want you to go to school," she said. "It's stupid of you to just be like this. Cleaning tables forever."

She was taking night classes at the university and wanted me to do the same. I started saving that night. I put ten dollars in a jar after every shift. But the money added up so slowly. Weeks went by, and I still didn't have enough for even one class. That night I had also, for the first time, told Lopita I loved her. But not till after she was gone. I wasn't stupid. It would be months till I could tell her to her face, and by that time, she would be sleeping with her professor. "I never thought I'd fuck a Marxist," she'd say, "but my cunt is apolitical." By the time Lopita moved in with him, the jar would still have less than a semester's tuition in it, and only a few weeks later, I would lose it to a truck driver after falling asleep hitchhiking home.

The next day, I was by myself at the bar, just drinking pineapple juice and staring at my reflection in the mirror behind the liquor bottles, when Aileen came in.

"Pull up a chair, stranger," I said.

She shrugged her shoulders lightly, looked at my glass and then away. "I just came by to look for Jason. We're supposed to leave this afternoon to go up north, but he didn't come home."

"Any word from Angel?" I said.

She shook her head. "I don't think so."

She had a funny energy about her. She was glowing, like she had a fever or a sunburn. "You're going back to him," I realized.

She pulled her purse off the bar stool and slung it over her shoulder. Her grey-blond hair was shining under the yellow bar lights. "I haven't decided. I already told you I haven't decided."

"What you mean is you haven't told Jason."

"Minnie . . ." She squeezed her hands over her eyes, like

she could change what was right in front of her with her fists. "That thing. That thing you told me. About her. I can't stop thinking about it. It makes me wish I'd never come here. It makes me want to leave."

"Well, there you go. So you want to leave and hubby wants you home. Sounds like everything's on track." I stood up and walked around the bar to grab a beer. I waved it in the air at the bartender, who was over at a table and nodded back at me.

"Minnie," Aileen said quietly. "I know what you think of me. I think it myself. But I can't figure it out. He left me and I thought it was a tragedy. Then I got here, and I started thinking we were just two unhappy people clinging to each other and thinking that was a marriage. So which is true? How can I tell?"

I looked at her tired, worn-out face, so much like Mara's. Skin as white and thin as paper. People that stupid could make you feel sorry for them. If it weren't for what they did to other people. And I remembered when I first realized what Jason had done. It had taken me days to figure out, me who had thought I understood him better than he understood himself. He'd told me he was taking his mother out in his boat. Even at the time, I thought it was strange because she'd never gone out in his boat before that I knew of. And then Jason came back and his mother didn't. When I went to see him the next day, it was only Jason and his father there. Jason's father said that Mara had gone missing. His eyes were wild and frightened. He said he'd started spreading the word. He pleaded with me to search for her. He didn't want to leave the house in case she came home or called. He kept telling me she was blind, that she couldn't be out by herself because she was blind, as if it were something I didn't know. And Jason watched his father shake me and plead, and he didn't say a word.

The whole town looked for her. For days and weeks. And then, even months after, every hunter had an eye out for her yellow hair when he went into the woods, though no one thought they'd find her alive. And I noticed that Jason didn't leave his house all the time we searched for his mother. And he never said to anyone that he'd taken her out in his boat that day. And then I understood the look he'd had on his face since his father said Mara hadn't come home.

I went by his house and found him lying on her bed, just staring like he was looking at something, but there wasn't anything there. "I know what you did," I told him. He didn't answer. And I said that if anybody asked, he'd have to say he brought her home from the boat, no matter how much he thought he could trust the person asking. He lifted his head then and told me he hadn't touched her. And the lie, the way he looked me in the eyes to tell it, made me sure of what I'd only guessed before. I could have been insulted he didn't trust me with the truth, but I'd known him all his life and knew he'd never learned how not to lie. I waited till he was quiet again, and then I told him I would keep his secret. I told him I'd tell Angel not to ever say anything about it to anyone. It was too late to hide it from her, when I'd already told her what I'd seen Mara do, and she knew Jason as well as I did and might come to suspect on her own whatever I might try to keep from her. But I knew I could trust her. I told Jason only we two could understand what had went on between him and his mother and why he'd had to do what he'd done out there on the river in his boat. And when, later, I told Angie, she didn't hesitate. I remembered how she'd nodded like I'd confirmed something she already knew. I knew from how she loved him and from how she looked at me then that she wouldn't betray him any sooner than I would, and that she understood what Jason did had not been a matter of murder but of survival. As I knew, the second I lay eyes on Aileen, that sooner or later she was going to ask a question that he would want to answer with the truth.

"You know," I told her then, "I think you should go back to him."

"Do you mean that? Or are you just being spiteful?"

"No," I said honestly. "I think it would be best for everyone." And then I told her the lie I'd known I'd have to tell since the moment she'd first told me who she was. "You know, Aileen," I said, "Jason won't ever get around to telling you what happened to that sister of yours. And I can tell you why he won't."

She stared at me, speechless and unsure of herself.

"Because it isn't a good story. He likes what he makes up better, so he'll keep making it up for you. I wouldn't believe anything he tells you. The truth is always less interesting. But worth knowing. Don't you think?"

She shook her head a little. "I don't—I don't know. What are you saying?"

"I'm saying all that happened is your sister went out for a walk in the woods one day. Looks like she tried to climb down the hill toward the river, but she slipped. Hit her head. Landed at the river's edge and drowned in three inches of water."

"She . . . drowned?"

"What do you think. You like Jason's stories better? Well, go on and listen to them then. You suit yourself."

She had her hand over her mouth, and behind her hand she was mumbling something.

"What?" I demanded.

She dropped her hand to her lap and sighed. "She was so afraid of water."

I shrugged. I could have liked Aileen. If she had all the way committed to being decent or to being a stubborn, selfish piece of work, I could have liked her. But what she did instead was worse, maybe, even than what Mara had done to Jason. She got halfway to caring and then she lost her nerve. I leaned forward again. "I want to wish you luck with that man of yours," I said. "And you know, Aileen, maybe you're right." I made my eyes as wide and empty as I could. "Maybe things'll work out better this time."

Her face seemed to hesitate, looking for something in mine, and then she smiled, so brightly that for just a second I felt sorry for her. "Thanks, Minnie," she said. "I'll see you when we get back."

I nodded slowly, and she left the bar, leaving the door swinging open behind her.

Everyone thought I'd married Ed because I was pregnant, but I didn't. I did it because he asked. I'd never expected anyone to ask me to marry them. And I believed him when he said he would have asked even if I hadn't been knocked up.

Everyone also thought I was cruel, the way I left him, but I wasn't. I did it because I needed to do something kind for him. Because I owed him so much and had given him so little. I owed him Amaruk, but I knew I would take him from him. So I let him go, not even a year after we married. And not even two years after that, he was married again, to a nice girl down in Teslin, where they bought a house and had three children of their own.

I finished my beer and walked out of the bar into the dirty street. I thought maybe I'd go home and see if Amaruk was still awake. If he had waited up for me, I'd let him come sleep in my bed and would let him talk until he fell asleep, mid-sentence, his soft baby hair and the light weight of his head on my shoulder.

It was almost dark out and maybe in another hour or two, it really would be dark. In another week or a few days, I'd be able to walk outside this time of night and see the stars. People went a little crazy in winter sometimes. There were nights I looked up at the stars and thought I saw a face there. I lit up a cigarette, and the flare of the match made it seem darker outside. Thank god for cigarettes, I thought. It filled my mouth and I didn't need anything, didn't need anyone's lips or hands.

Ed was so happy when I told him I had named our son Amaruk. He was an Inuk from Chesterfield Inlet and had been sent to a residential school, where a Québécois priest gave him the name Édouard. Later, he had to change it to the English spelling. "A good Inuktitut name," he said. "Amaruk." To the blond-haired nurse, who stood smiling a thin smile and holding her hands out to take my baby back to the nursery, I said, "It means wolf."

Mara

TWENTY-THREE

THE SUMMER THAT I carried my son came and passed like a
turned page. Around my son and me, things changed. The sun
burned for many days. Its heat sickened us. And then it slid
away, and then it did not come again for a long time. And then
it was colder than I had ever known possible.

Around us, Jason worried and tried to think what to do to
please us, but we were not pleased. The last few months, we
were ill and spent most days in bed. His sisters were always
at the door, always wanting to cook things or lend things. We
wanted them to go away, but he would not send them away.
He whispered to them that they must understand it was a difficult pregnancy and I was not myself.

And I was not myself. I was us both.

But all these things, the words and worries of others, the
fickle seasons and their moods, happened very far away and
did not interest us. So much else was at work. My son grew
nails and ears and lungs. My belly stretched to give space to
my son, to contain him. He grew eyes.

I began to have terrible dreams. I stopped sleeping. I was
afraid he would escape if I were not awake to keep him inside
me. In the dreams, I found him in other rooms of the house, or

other houses altogether, half formed, thinking nails might keep him safe, thinking ears and lungs and eyes would be enough to face the world with.

He grew hair. He moved.

I felt something altering in me, something deeper and more important than my body. I felt how I would not ever be safe again once he had left me. I felt how hard it became to hold on to another thought once I'd had that one.

His eyes opened and closed. He saw light.

I saw how I had known very, very little of the world. I realized my piece of it had been very small. I saw that what choices I had made had not been the right ones.

When he left me, he hurt me terribly. He left me slowly and cruelly. And I thought that what was happening was more awful than anything else I had lived. And then I was myself again.

But I was not.

Because they put him in my arms. And I saw that the way he filled what had been empty between them was the way that he would mend all that had been broken. And I understood that nothing else had happened before him. I understood the past was something very light, like a kite or a balloon. It could all be blown away. Or drawn back and unspooled again so that it happened just as I told him. And so I met his father in a jail. I read the Bible to him. I was blind and immaculate and he fell in love with me like a person might fall in love with the sun.

And maybe already then I saw that something in me had come undone. Maybe then was the beginning of knowing what I spent my son's life learning. That I would hurt him. That I would hurt him as badly as he hurt me when he left. That everything I did to keep him safe would ruin him.

Angel

~

late August 1996

TWENTY-FOUR

EVERY NIGHT WE ATE dinner together at a plastic outdoor table that was not outdoors but inside John's apartment, and every night he apologized for not having a proper dining table, and every night I said I didn't mind and thought I'd rather eat on that white plastic than on marble. We sat beside each other in a row, John, his daughter and me, so we could look out the big window together as we ate. John's apartment was on the fifteenth floor and we could see the ocean far away.

Felicia, John's daughter from his first marriage that he never talked about, was only four years younger than me and she had a way of looking at me sideways with her eyes to let me know she wasn't sure about me yet. She was quieter than I was but had purple hair, and I kept thinking that maybe her hair was like something to say; her hair was her trying to start a conversation.

One night as John was sliding the fish sticks straight off of the pan onto our plates with a wooden spoon, he said, "Angie, we're big fans of having you here, aren't we, kiddo."

Felicia gave me her sideways eyes and then turned back to the window.

"We've talked about this already, but I wanted to make it official. Felicia and I would really like it if you'd stay on. Here with us."

"I'll be back with Mom as soon as school starts," Felicia pointed out.

"Yes, honey. But you'll be here on weekends."

"You want me to stay here?" I said.

"Yes, here. With me." He put the pan on the table then and took my hand in his, which was sticky with something from cooking, but the pan wasn't set right on the table and it crashed down on the floor between us. "That's okay," he said, "that's okay," and he scooped the fish sticks off the floor in his bare hands and blew on them. Then he put them on his plate and grinned at me, but his ears had gone red and I saw that. "We washed that floor last week. It's good and clean," he said.

"Dad, are you asking her to marry you?" Felicia asked. She stuck her fish stick on the end of her fork and looked at it with one eye closed, like it was the fish she was asking.

"No," he said.

I smiled, and he said, "I don't think anybody's looking to get married. Not right now." Then he made a worried face and asked me, "Is that right?"

"Yes," I said, and it was true. I didn't care if I ever got married. "That's right."

"Well, is she saying yes?"

"Honey, don't call her *she*. Angie needs time to think about it."

But I didn't. "But I don't," I said. I took his sticky hand in mine and the smile that was on his face then was like a sunrise.

Of course, hours later, after dinner and dishes and TV on the couch with my feet in his lap and Felicia on the floor in front of the screen like she was looking for something inside it, after sex, fast and sweet with his hand clamped on my mouth to help me be quiet so she wouldn't hear, after he'd fallen asleep beside me with both his hands around mine, I lay awake and wondered. I could hear the TV still on in the other room. The window was open at the foot of the bed and the air coming through was cold, but I liked the air on my face and then the rest of my body hot with the weight and warmth of him against me.

I'd not known before that moment, lying there, that there was a way to be so happy that it hurt you and made you afraid. I knew there was no other answer I could have given him. I loved him truly. I loved him with all the heart I had to love. I loved even Felicia, whose face softened sometimes when I touched her hair to ask her to turn the lights off when she went to bed or when I stood beside her at the sink, washing dishes while she dried. We hadn't yet even told her of the sister I was growing for her, but I knew when we did, she'd be glad, as we were glad. And then there was the smell of the sea and I thought even the city might be something you could get to love. I liked how it was never quiet, not really, outside. With the windows open, even from way up there in that apartment building, we could always hear the sounds of the city, steady as a heart far below us beating.

But even though John promised I would make new friends when I began my classes at the college after the baby was born, and would be so busy with being a mother and then, later, a nurse, that I would hardly have time to think of Dawson, I knew my thoughts would always be full of the only place I'd known till I came here. I would miss my mother and my sister and even my brothers, though they hardly ever came home anymore. I would miss Minnie and the other girls I'd grown up with. Jason. I'd never thought to leave them. I'd gotten used to people leaving town and I had always been the one that stayed behind.

I would always be wanting to know the ways their lives would change in the years I was away. What happened to them there. I would visit whenever I could, but I knew how that would change, too, because I'd seen it happen first to Charlie and then Jude, and then so many others that I'd gone to school with. The visits were like so many beads spread out on a string, and the longer you were away, the longer the string got but there were never any more beads.

Every night, I'd know they were there. I'd be able to see them in my mind as if they were on the other side of my bedroom door. Drinking and laughing at The Pit as the days got shorter and people got tucked up inside themselves with their secrets for the winter. I'd miss them like it was my own teeth or hands I was missing.

Some people couldn't ever leave Dawson. Some came back twenty years later, thinking they were old and changed, but we'd recognize them right off, and they'd feel like they'd come home. It might be like that for Jason. He'd been trying to leave for years and maybe Aileen was that last thing he needed to get out the door.

But I knew, with all my heart, that no matter how long he was gone, one day he'd come back. He was the type that wouldn't ever leave Dawson really. It might be ten years or forty till he came back, but I knew he would. I don't know what that thing was that would pull him to it so he wouldn't ever be gone, truly gone, but when he did, I'd bring his daughter to meet him there.

Mara

TWENTY-FIVE

YEARS AGO, WHEN EVERYONE was younger, my son had a kind of reputation around the high school. People would want to move away from him when he was nearby. When he'd be walking down the hall, everyone made themselves a little narrower, so there'd be room for him. I could tell he liked that, but I could tell, too, he didn't know that it wasn't just that he frightened them. There were ways that people talked about him, like he was not all there. Like he was this idea of himself, just walking around. Like they didn't believe in that idea.

And I never told him that, because he thought he was better than they were and he liked to think that. He thought how much better than being a person to be an event. To be a storm or a fight or a mood. He made himself as angry as he could be, so people wouldn't know anything about him except that. He thought they didn't know anything else, but they did. And I did.

He thought no one knew how vain he was. He loved mirrors. He wished there were a mirror where you could see yourself like you looked when you weren't looking at yourself. He wanted to see the side of his face. His eyes, fixed in the distance. When he walked by windows, he'd turn sharply, suddenly, to look in the glass and try and catch a glimpse of himself before he'd turned. Once, he left gym class to go to the bathroom, and on his way out, he stopped to watch himself in the mirror. He leaned right over the sink, till he could have pressed his two faces against each other, and his eyes looked at each other for a while. He was still looking at himself like that when a kid from his gym class came in the door. He stopped and stared at Jason, and Jason was ashamed of himself and of how he liked to look at himself in mirrors. So he got the kid by the hair and hit his head against the wall a few times, then he went back to class.

He did that so the kid wouldn't tell anyone he saw him staring at himself in the mirror, but when people asked what happened to him, he said, "I saw Jason staring at himself in the mirror, and then he hit my head against the wall."

Once, he and Minnie's sister had to go and pick Minnie up down south, when she'd had her money stolen by someone on her way home. On the way back, Violet let Jason drive, even though he was only thirteen. After only a few minutes behind the wheel, he suddenly swerved the car and they landed in a ditch. They had to get towed to Whitehorse and wait a day while a mechanic fixed the left axle. When they got back, Minnie said an animal had run out onto the road, but I knew Jason had been driving with the window down, his arm out resting on the side of the car, and leaning his head to the side to look at himself in the mirror there. *"The Lord knows the thoughts of man,"* I whispered to him, *"that they are vanity."*

Though I was blind, I saw what he was. I saw his weakness and his desires and his longings and his fury. I saw what he was and I did all I did to stop it. I was for want of words to tell him certain things. To show him what fastened us together, that he was mine and bound to me. That I feared for him. That I feared to be the thing that bound him and for him to be unbound.

And then, as he grew older, I felt him drawn from me. I felt that what pulled at him was stronger than I would ever be, though I fought to keep him. And one day he told me he was leaving, heading across the border for some job he'd heard about. And I knew that this was what I'd feared, that the steps he took out the door that day would be the ones that took him away from me forever. And I knew I had to stop him. It was the only thought I could hold in my head.

I stood before the door and had almost forgotten I held the axe still in my hands. And then I remembered and thought perhaps I could frighten him, make him afraid as I was afraid. I raised it only to stop him for a moment, to make him listen to me. But it was too heavy. It fell from my hands, and I knew from his silence he'd thought it was only an accident that I had not hurt him. And he took my wrist in his hand so that I knew he was offering himself to me, and it was a challenge, it was his way of showing me that not even my hands could stop him from leaving me. I was for want of words, and my fists made themselves into the shape of mouths. And with my fist, I tried to tell him what my mouth had failed to speak.

It happened once. And it was all I needed to know the truth of all I'd feared.

Aileen

~

late August 1996

TWENTY-SIX

I WOULD NEVER HAVE GOT in the boat with him except for the way he asked. The way he asked made me wonder if Minnie had said something to him.

We never went north after all. On my way to meet him at the house, I ran into Annie. She hugged me like we were old friends and asked what had happened to me since she saw me last, and I couldn't answer. She told me she had just got back from hauling a load to Florida. "I thought it would be a nice holiday to stay over there. Play the slots. Go see some dolphins. But it was hot as hell. Good to be home." She said, "We should get together sometime. Get a beer. You know, Jim still asks about you." I shook my head and didn't know what to tell her. "You been all right?" she asked, concern in her eyes. Like I belonged here. Like there would be time for her to get to know what things worried me. I said, "I have to go."

When he came home, I had my suitcase packed to leave, but he said instead, "Let's take the boat out." And his face made me say yes.

Or maybe it wasn't either of those things but what I knew I was going to tell him that made me think that getting into that boat with him was one small thing I could do. It didn't really make any sense. Like he would forgive me or not because of a boat. But I wasn't thinking right. I was thinking of Stephan.

The last time I called, he had asked me one more time.

"Have you bought your ticket yet?" he said.

"Not yet," I answered. I was afraid he'd get impatient, or cold as he sometimes did, that he would end the phone call with me wondering if he had changed his mind.

But after a moment, he laughed, and it was like everything else faded away into that sound, his voice, forgiving, ready. "I guess," he said, "I wouldn't be in any hurry to book a four-day bus ride either."

I hesitated. "You know," I said. "I think I might fly."

"Really?" And I heard the pleasure in his voice. It had always frustrated him that I was afraid of flying.

"Yeah," I said. "I think so." I could imagine it already, looking out at the tarmac below as it started rushing past faster and faster and the plane built up the speed to take off into the sky, as everything heaved and shook.

"Leen, I want you to buy that ticket today. I want you to come home."

"I'm going to. I will. I just need, I just need a little more time. Just a day or two more."

The quality of his silence before he spoke let me know I'd annoyed him. "I don't see what you're doing up there," he said at last. "What's so goddamned interesting about that town?"

When Stephan had asked me to come home, it occurred to me for the first time that probably love was always imaginary. That it was something two people agreed to put together out of thin air and stare at for the rest of their lives, so as not to ever really see each other. So love wasn't something you found or fell into, like all the clichés described, like "oh look, there's some love, over there," but something you kept inventing out of nothing for each other every day.

But I knew I could explain none of that to Jason. It would seem as if I were deceiving myself. It would seem as if I were going back because I was afraid. And so I found myself wishing I could leave Jason without a word, without a trace. He was beyond my help or understanding, and I hadn't known that until Minnie revealed the depth of his lies. I did not know whom to blame for the sickness of what had happened to his mother, who had once been my sister. But though I knew it was wrong, I hated him for it. For what had become of her while I wasn't looking for her.

I would write to him, if he let me. Maybe I could send him money, even let him visit someday. Or maybe it would be better for me to come to see him here, alone. I didn't know how I could explain him to Stephan. I'd never told Stephan about my sister. I'd never told him anything of where I'd come from. And there was no reason to confuse things now. The way he knew me was pure, free of my family or my past. It was a better way to be known. The rest was . . . misleading. A tenuous thread that led somewhere uncertain and dark. A place I no longer wanted to go. And I could cut that thread now, if I could just choose the right words to tell Jason that in a few days, I'd be gone.

As I climbed into the passenger seat of Jason's truck, I thought of what I'd tell Stephan about my time away. I didn't know how I'd ever explain what had led me to that strange town, far up past where anyone would go if they weren't looking for something or lost.

Mara

TWENTY-SEVEN

AFTER IT HAD HAPPENED, the thing I was afraid of, I stayed away as far as I could from my son. His father thought things were better between us, because I did not scold Jason or make him sit for Bible study anymore. But Jason knew I hid from him and why.

And it was that summer I had met Lewis Eames. He was new in town and not staying long enough to trouble himself with fitting in. And he had no gift for attracting the notice or interest of strangers, so he was left alone, mostly, even by his congregation, who were mourning the minister they'd lost in a snowstorm that winter. He came to my Bible study class and I felt him watch me as I read. He was so interested in my Bible and made me show him how the ends of my fingers read the dots and made them into words. He reached out to the page and his hand touched mine.

None of it would have happened, but I needed help and feared to ask for it from Jason. And Lewis was lonely, so he came to call for me most days, to see if there was anything I needed, or anywhere I wanted to go. And the sin that we committed, after only a few weeks of knowing each other, was not so great as it might appear to one who did not understand. Even what I did with Lewis, there in the little room he'd rented across from the church, was to keep Jason safe. Because I knew what I had done to Jason once, I would do again. And so I hid from him, I hid what I had done and might do to my son in the sin I committed in Lewis's bed.

And then one morning, I went to Jason and I said, "Take me out in your boat," and he agreed, as he always agreed to whatever I asked of him. I wanted to walk, and so we went together, his hand at my back, all the way to where he'd docked the boat his father gave him. I climbed into his boat, and though the rocking of it in the water made me clutch at the sides with both my hands, it was not that that I was afraid of. And what I did then, I did to save him. And what I thought of was how for three seasons, I'd carried him inside me. Like a secret. Like something deeply precious, and safe.

And I remembered how, when he was a baby, he'd suck on my finger. The nurse said he had jaundice and that I had to stop breastfeeding him. So I'd heat up formula and give it to him in a bottle, but he'd refuse it so often, I thought he might starve, my little skeleton boy. He was so thin and so small. But he'd always want to suck on my finger, and sometimes I'd cry because he wanted my finger and not the bottle and I was not a good mother.

Then, and even later, when he was a teenager, some nights when I knew he was fast asleep, I would creep up the stairs and lie with my back to his door.

All these years later, I still could feel his mouth, open and wanting. I knew how he was like an appetite. How he went into the world unfed.

When I had once sat outside his door, when he was a sleeping child, I whispered to him, "I will never leave you." I said to him, "If I fail you it is because I love you." I told him, "Pay no attention to what I do or say. What I tell you now is what I truly feel. You are loved."

Jason

~

late August 1996

TWENTY-EIGHT

WHEN WE GOT THERE, she looked down at my boat and said, "I'd thought it would be bigger, like those awful ones we see out on the river sometimes." It was an aluminum shell with a twenty-horsepower outboard motor screwed on the back. I shrugged and said it did the job. Together we untied the boat and waded out into the water.

"Jump in," I said, and she obeyed. I pushed the boat out till I was knee-deep, and then threw my leg over the side and climbed into the back. I yanked the pull cord, and the engine began to growl. As I turned to face out to the bow, where Aileen sat, clutching the sides, the boat leaned far over onto its side and then, suddenly, we were skimming along the surface of the river and the town was far behind us.

We were a couple of miles out before Aileen leaned over and, grabbing the bench seat in front of her, began to climb toward my seat at the stern. "Get back," I shouted.

"I just want to talk to you," she said, sitting down on the middle seat. "I told you boats frighten me. I'm afraid of falling out."

"It's dangerous," I said. "Too much weight in the back. Let me cut the engine."

The sound of the engine died away, and immediately, the current caught hold of the boat and began pulling it forward, taking it back to sea.

"Come sit beside me," I said. "It's okay," I added, as she hesitated. "It's safe now that we're just drifting."

She sat down beside me and looked over the side, down into the river.

"I don't see any fish," she said.

"They're there."

"You didn't bring your fishing rod?" she asked.

"I'm not fishing today," I replied. Then I said, "Aileen? I don't want to stay here anymore. Now that Angie's gone."

She looked startled. "Did Minnie talk to you?" she asked sharply.

I didn't understand what she meant. "I should have left years ago. I never could, but I was thinking maybe if, like you said one time, your husband got me a construction job. Maybe if we went together"

Aileen let her hand reach down into the water, so it disappeared from sight and the waves at the surface splashed around her wrist. "This will be hard, Jason," she said. Then she took her hand out of the water and rested it, wet, on her lap. She looked at me and said, "I'm going back to Stephan."

My eyes left her face and, without moving my head, my gaze slowly slid back to the boat, and then far, far down the river.

She touched my knee and then pulled her hand away. "You know, I'm not even gone yet, but already this summer feels like a dream to me. This is home for you, Jason, but for me, it was only ever a dream. It's time to wake up." She smiled like she was already gone, and I wanted to take that smile off her face with my hand.

I turned my head from side to side as I put together what I had missed before. What Minnie had been warning me about her all along. She was so caught up in herself, she couldn't see straight, so wrapped up in whatever it was she wanted, she'd got herself tied up in knots. She was a fucking fool. If she'd had sense in her head, if she'd ever had sense in her head. But then maybe she'd have left town as soon as she arrived. Maybe it was only because she was this stupid that she'd stayed as long as she had. "That's all right," I said. "I'll go with you. We'll go together. And you can go back to that guy. And I'll find my own place. We'll go together."

"Jason . . ." Her eyes were wet. "I can't take you with me."

"Did you and Angel talk about this?"

She shook her head. "Jason, you're mixing things up. This has nothing to do with Angel. I know myself. I can wish I were someone different, but that won't help either of us. Maybe this sounds cruel, but I'm trying to be as straight as I can with you: I just don't have room for you. These are two different worlds, the one that Stephan's in and yours. I can't live in both."

"I have money," I said. "Is that what this is about? I can pay my own way. I have money." I began breathing deeply, quickly, and then I grabbed the side of the boat. "It's all right," I said, slowing my breath. "It's all right. I won't go with you. I won't go with you, like you said. I should let you go first. You need to make things right with your husband. I should finish the season with Peter. Maybe I should wait here till the money from the government comes, in case—just in case."

She just shook her head again. "Maybe I should never have come here. Maybe she was better off without me, and you will be too."

A cold feeling was creeping over me, like little icy spiders

crawling up my arms and legs. I couldn't feel anything anymore. I could have pinched my own skin and felt nothing.
But I wasn't worried, because I saw clearly now how things
would go. "I'll come visit you in the city. In a little while.
When everything's ready. By then, Angel will have come back,
and we'll have our little baby."

"Jason." She was as white as the sun. "Angel is gone."

"It's okay," I said and I smiled at her. "You'll see, we'll be
like a family. I just need a little time. Then I'll come visit you.
I'll drive down. I'll come every weekend."

"You can't come every weekend," she said. "It will take
you days to drive there. You're not thinking. You're confused,
Jason."

I was staring over my shoulder to the trees along the riverbank as we floated past them. "I heard a story once about a
man that came here looking for gold," I said. "He was crazy
to find gold. But it was after the rush was over, and everyone
laughed at him, showing up years later, when there was nothing left in the town but the gold teeth of the whores. He was
furious at being made a fool of, and he picked up a handful of
dirt on the useless claim that he'd been sold. And he squeezed
it and put all his anger in his fist. And he squeezed that dirt so
hard that he released the water in it, he released a river. The
river flowed out of his hand through the dry, worthless dirt of
this town, and he got in a boat and he sailed that river to its
end, and there, where the river washed onto the shore of a distant land, he found more gold than he'd ever dreamt of. That's
how angry he was. And that's just what I will do. I'll squeeze
that hard, I'll make a way to you and my baby . . ."

"Stop," said Aileen, pressing her fists against her head
and looking wound up like a toy, "stop. I'm so tired of your

stories." She twisted her mouth to one side. Her eyes were wet but she wasn't crying anymore. "Every word, Jason. Every word is a lie." She said, "You can't make water from dirt. And that story of yours about our father and the blindfolds . . . You take what's true and you make it into something else. It's more than a lie, it's an insult to the truth. My mother drowned herself and my father never was right again. He was a lousy father. And my sister and I inherited the cataracts that ran in my mother's family, and they never got treated because he was so wrapped up in his grief, he hardly knew we were there. Your mother's were so bad that they cost her her sight. That's all that happened."

My mouth opened but said nothing, like the mouth of a fish. I had just begun to understand. I had been so stupid for so long, and only now, at last, I understood.

"Tell me one true thing, Jason. I've been here all this time, trying to make things up to you, to her. But you can't tell me one thing that isn't a lie. You can't even tell me what happened to her."

"Ma," I whispered and it was all I could say.

She stared at me, pretending she didn't understand.

"Did you plan this? Were you planning this my whole life?" I gasped as I realized how big the lie was, how it had surrounded me all my life. It was a net I'd always been caught in. "You made up that story about your sister and told it to me since the day I was born, so I'd have no choice but to believe you. So you could fool me for so long without me guessing. So you could come back and pretend to be her and leave me all over again . . . you must have already known, from the day that I was born."

She grabbed the side of the boat and leaned away from me. "Jason, what are you saying?"

"I didn't think you would come back. I told you if you left not to ever come back. And I knew you never would. I thought you never would."

"Jason. You think I'm . . ."

"In the boat, when you said you were going to Calgary with that minister, I was so angry. I was ashamed. I couldn't tell anyone what you'd done. How could I tell them why you had left? That you wanted him and that baby more than us. But you came back. You came back for me."

Her eyes were wide, like they were trying to see right through me to the other side. "Jason, do you mean that she left Dawson? Jason, you have to tell me right now. Are you saying my sister is still alive?"

"Maybe I knew. Maybe I didn't know it but I knew. Maybe that's why I told you those stories, like the ones you used to tell me. Maybe it was so I could know if it were you. Because you would know what they meant."

Her hand was covering her mouth so that it was hard to hear what she was saying. "Jesuschrist, jesuschrist," she said over and over. She squeezed her eyes shut and I could hear her breathe, it was that loud and deep. I could hear my mother breathing.

"And you do know, don't you. You know what the stories mean, don't you, Ma?"

"The stories . . ." Her eyes had stopped flicking toward the river like maybe she could escape there. Now she was staring right through the boat that held us, shaking her head slowly. She sighed and all the air went out of her. "Yes. Yes, I think I do understand them, Jason."

I looked at her and saw her for the first time. I had missed her so much. I had searched for her everywhere. I had heard her in my house long after she was gone. "Ma?" I said again, even more gently.

She pressed her lips together but wouldn't look at me. I wondered how it was that she could see again. It was a miracle. She said, "All those stories are about hurting the people you love. It's not an accident or cruelty. It's something else. Do you understand that?" She took another breath deep into her. "The point is nobody knows why. Nobody means to. But nobody knows how to stop. It's a warning, Jason. You were warning me."

I was still confused. I covered my eyes. "But why did you go?"

She smiled sadly. "If she left you, I don't think it was you she was leaving. My father used to say that a fish could love a bird but then where would they live? Our mother was like a bird. She never really made a home with us. But there is no real place for a fish and a bird to live together. Only in a story."

And then I knew she wasn't going to leave me again. "But there is one place," I said, softly.

"Jason, you have to take us back to shore now." She looked worried again. I reached out my hand to calm her, but she pulled hers away. She'd said she hadn't held another hand but mine since her sister's.

Here on the river, which was as bright as a mirror, I could remember everything from that day. I felt as if all the world was spinning, and the only thing that didn't move was my boat and her in it. It was then and it was now at the same time, and both times she was going away, twice, and all at once, she was leaving. The first time she told me, I'd wanted to hurt her, to leave my prints on her, to stop her with my hands. I wished then that I'd hurt her, and all the years in between I'd known that I should have. It was so hard to be free of her but so hard, too, to keep her. All you could do to make someone yours or still was to murder what was in them that wanted to go away from you or ever could. I said to her then, "I should have hurt you."

She was twisted around in her seat, staring at the shore, and she hardly looked at me over her shoulder. "You should have . . . What did you say, Jason?"

"You didn't believe me about the man who squeezed a river out of dirt. But it's because you don't understand how hard he squeezed," I told her. "He wanted it enough, he was that afraid of losing it, that he squeezed a river from a fist of dirt. He squeezed that hard."

"It's not true," she said. Her voice was clear as a bell as she said to me, "You can't make water from dirt." She said, "Say it, Jason. Say no man could make a river out of dirt. Say your mother hurt you and then she left—"

"Ma," I whispered. "Let me show you how hard he squeezed." And I showed her. I showed her. I showed her.

Her throat in my hands was soft and my hands were hard and the thrust of her pulse in her throat in my hands was hard but my hands are harder, my hands are *this hard*, and even when she cried my name, Jason, I don't answer and I don't let go until the pulse has stopped and her breath, its eloquence, is stopped and everything stops.

And then you are there before me, let loose, let go, like your long yellow hair, you are all over streaming in front of me, you are in my arms and you are gone. You are leaving me, I grasp you by your long faded yellow hair, but that, too, is leaving me. I say your name to you, and you don't answer because you are leaving me. I cry for you. And you are so cold that you don't shed any tears, Ma.

I can't believe you are here in my boat. That you are like this in front of me, all your secrets open to me. You will finally tell me your secrets, where you went and why you left, here, today, in this boat, on this river. What a special day it is. I laugh at how you are opened like a page in front of me.

And then you do the strangest thing. It's night now, and we're still floating, I guess we are going slowly away, to the ocean maybe. I guess we're going to leave, like you wanted. But we'll go slowly. We'll take the long way. I tell you this joke, and you don't laugh, because you are doing the strangest thing. You are changing. Your yellow hair is gone, and your legs and your eyes and all the shape of you and all the look of you, it's all gone. Instead, what is left is your shining scales, the fan of your tail, your fins, your eyes that see nothing but water.

You become a fish, Ma.

You leave my boat for the river, I watch as you snap your tail and release yourself into the air and then fall down, deep into the water. I watch you, the colours of you, moving against the waves. You don't tell me where you're going. You don't say goodbye. But I smile as I watch you, because I can see how happy you are.

"Ma," I whisper to you. "I haven't told you your last story." I know you can hear me, under the water you have perfect ears. So I tell you your story.

Winter came that year like a disease that had no cure. Old Man would watch the mortal men and women peering out of the windows of their snow houses, looking for a spring that did not come. He took to walking by himself in the woods, thinking deeply. His wife never came home. The loss of both

373

her children had left her silent and hard-faced. She had lain down along the frozen river and let the snow bury her deeper and deeper. Sometimes Old Man would call to her, from far above the drifts of snow. He would order her to come home to him and cook his food. But she didn't answer. Then he would call softly down to her, My love, I am lost without you. Then he would think perhaps he heard something, and he'd press his ear to the snow to listen harder. But she was so far beneath him, and there was so much snow between them, that all he could hear was the sighing wind that blew over the snow and buried her deeper.

He went home, but he was no longer accustomed to his loneliness. He looked to the world of men and women for amusement, but they only made him sad. Without the hope of spring, they had returned to their old despair and boredom. They were cruel to each other and rarely rose from bed during the day. At night they would lie around in each other's arms, without love, and grow hungry thinking of the past.

At last Old Man could take it no longer. He knew he had made terrible mistakes. He wished he knew what his wife's deep, under-the-snow thoughts were. Why did she leave him and what place had she gone to down there where he couldn't follow? In the pale city winter, would she one day, suddenly, brush one hand against the other and feel how, palm to palm, lightly, softly, rising and falling, they felt like a late-summer river and a regret. If she were in a boat and she ran out of words, say she was only sorry, sorry and wordless, till the boat ran ashore, and she climbed out weeping, and she left the boat and got a bag, and she took that bag away with her, and after that she was gone, and where she went after that was unknown, a hole at the centre of a zero that made a ring around everything, what was left in the boat—a lie? A man?

And so Old Man made a flood and it covered the world, it rose even higher than the snow and covered that too. When everything was gone, he said down into the water, This will not be the end of you. You'll go on in some way or another. But I have failed and been failed by you. So I will try again.

I will make a new world. It will be better than the last. It will keep no secrets from me. There will be no seasons to begin and end and teach us to leave each other. The new world will not be split by snow and sun or by sky and sea. I will make a land where winged fish and finned birds live in watery skies, in an in-between place, where there is neither ice nor grass nor stars nor sun. Without light or dark, I will find her there. She will say, I'll never leave this place.

Mara

TWENTY-NINE

I DON'T KNOW HOW she found me. There is no phone call to tell me she is coming, no warning at all. But I know, the moment I open the door, that it is her. I don't know what tells me, if it's the sound of her breath inhaled all at once, or something about her, a smell I couldn't put words to that something in me recognizes. Or maybe it is true what they say about twins and something else connects us that can't be broken, not even after thirty years.

My hand goes out to hers, without thinking. Upstairs I can hear him calling, "Mara, who's at the door?" And before I can even have the thought that I should be ashamed of reaching for her, as if we were still children, as if there weren't all that time and half a country between us, hers is in mine.

It takes us ages to begin to explain to each other, and longer still to really understand. She asks me if I forgive her and I don't know how to answer. Then she tells me she went to my son first to be forgiven and it was he who sent her to me. I hold her hand still tighter. After a moment, she says she'd like to go back there someday, to see him again. I tell her we will go together, and then we are quiet, and I know we both are thinking of how far away it is and what a long trip it would be.

There is something I want to ask her but I am frightened of the answer. If the thing I did was the right thing to do, she is the only one who can tell me that. I'd give anything to be told it was. "Tell me," I beg her at last. "Tell me if he's all right." She starts to answer and then I interrupt. "Tell me a story about him."

Minnie

~

December 1996

THIRTY

STILL, EVERY FEW WEEKS, someone comes and tells me what
he's got to saying, and I have to find him, tell him again.

Sometimes I'll find him sitting in the kitchen with a suitcase at his feet. "Angel called last night," he'll tell me.

"So I hear," I'll say.

"The baby's born. She's pissed I wasn't there. I told her
I had to get things settled around here first, but she didn't
understand. She'll forgive me when I see her. I know she will."

"No, Jason," I tell him, and then I tell him again what
happened.

Once his neighbour called me because he was sitting in
his truck for hours with the engine not started, wearing just
a flannel shirt and jeans. It took me and the neighbour half
an hour to get him back in the house, though he could hardly
move from the cold and I was scared he'd lose a toe for it. He
said he was going to pick his mother up from the airport, that
she was finally bringing her baby home.

Folks are saying his mind's come unhitched, but I know he
knows. The only time he was sure enough of himself to fool
me was the night two months ago he told me, as I drove him
home from the bar where he bought everybody a round and

said he was the father of two new baby girls, that he'd buried her on the bank of the Klondike River far out past town. I saw him look scared then, and he said, "Minnie, she's haunting me."

And I tell him again that he must never speak to anyone of Mara, and he shakes his head and says it's Aileen he means.

And I did wonder. I did wonder because nobody saw her go, she left so fast, and it wasn't till I saw he'd got a letter from her—he left it on the table in the kitchen and I read it in front of him and he said nothing—that I could be sure. She asked his permission to visit and I wondered if he'd give it. He shook his head and I knew that much at least was true.

And Nora at the post office said the letters from Toronto came for him often. She said most times he just dropped them in the trash by the door. And I thanked god to know she'd got away and was gone where she couldn't hurt him, and I thought maybe once she understood that no reply was coming, the letters would stop and he'd be free of her.

A month ago, something else came in the mail for Jason. It came in a little square envelope with only one line from Angie to explain it. Just a shadowy smudge of ink on a bit of shiny paper that she said was her. Their child, not yet born. I gave it to him and said, "This is your daughter," and asked if he understood me.

And he took it in his hand and I looked away from his face because nobody should ever let everything show like he did then. He said, "Tell me again."

So I do and then I make him tell it back to me, as many times as it takes. And I can see him fight that wish that comes into his eyes. It isn't that he doesn't know what happened. I know that, if no one else around here does. It's that he isn't content with things as they took place. But who wouldn't slap somebody who said that to them, when not one of us knows a way around the things that happened except straight through, and if we did, wouldn't we all be there together trying to get around that other way. And that's what I tell him. And I see him understand, but he's got such a hankering in him for something that would make a story worth listening to that he can't stop finding a different way to tell it, and he makes me think of an animal chewing off a leg to get out of a trap it set itself.

But now I see him with that photo, gone tattered from him holding it. He'll sit there looking at it in his hand, and sometimes he'll say, "She isn't born yet, is she?" Or, "Her mother took her to the city." And once, "Do you think she'll ever come up here?" And that's why I told Angie she'd better make sure she brings that baby home as soon as it gets born. I think he could be a real father to that kid and that's more than anybody else let him be. And maybe if he weren't wishing things were some other way, he would start to see what way they are.

So I tell him I can see our two lives and it's not something you would tell somebody, but this is how it happens, what you don't write or say, we just continue, loved and let down in all the ways we were. And it's quiet around here now, everyone who's leaving gone and just us left. I don't mind the quiet or the cold. And I wouldn't trust somebody who couldn't go three quarters of a day without a sunrise. These long nights, I go outside sometimes and the moon just lays on the snow, and dark is the last word for it. Whatever might be there, underneath where you can see, beneath the snow, is no less a part of things for being hidden. And in the end it doesn't matter much, what is and isn't there. We know something, those of us that stay after the snow comes. Some nights, I can see everything.

ACKNOWLEDGEMENTS

A number of people and books were critical to my research for this book. I regret that I cannot name all of them here, but I am grateful to every one. I was assisted by the following books especially: Helene Dobrowolsky's *Hammerstones: A History of the Tr'ondëk Hwëch'in*; Minnie Aodla Freeman's *Life among the Qallunaat*; Sherrill E. Grace's *Canada and the Idea of North*; Renée Hulan's *Northern Experience and the Myths of Canadian Culture*; Catharine McClellan et al.'s *Part of the Land, Part of the Water*; Ken S. Coates and William R. Morrison's *Land of the Midnight Sun: A History of the Yukon*; and Cornelius Osgood's *The Han Indians*. In particular, I owe thanks to Bina Freiwald, Renée Hulan and the Olynyk family.

I'd also like to note that the first story Jason tells Aileen, beginning on page 97, is based on a traditional Yukon creation myth but departs from it, as Minnie points out, near the end. From that point on, all the stories are Jason's inventions, though they occasionally allude to figures and traditions from Han culture.

It is a great blessing to have an editor whose faith in your book is unshakable and whose ability to root out its weaknesses, unfaltering—and I've had two. Thank you, from my heart, and beyond measure, to Jennifer Lambert and to Jane Warren. Thank you also to my eagle-eyed copy editor, Stacey Cameron, and to Thomas Grady, Kelly Hope, Allyson Latta, and Maylene Loveland.

To Ellen Levine, my agent and champion, a very special thank you.

I gratefully acknowledge the support of the Nova Scotia Department of Communities, Culture and Heritage and the Social Sciences and Humanities Research Council.

I have had a lifetime of wonderful teachers, to all of whom I owe my thanks. A few in particular have been necessary parts of this book: thank you, Stephanie Bolster, Terence Byrnes, and Mikhail Iossel. This book also greatly benefited from the suggestions of its first readers: especially Mary Katherine Carr, Catherine Cooper, Oisín Curran, Sarah Faber, Michael Helm, stef lenk, Susan Paddon, Jocelyn Parr, and Johanna Skibsrud. Thank you to Michael Redhill and the editors and staff of *Brick* magazine—shining examples, labourers of love. Thank you to my family, Margaret Silver, Ian Slayter, and Lisa and Sarah Silver Slayter, for a lifetime of support. And thank you to Conrad Taves, whose conviction never fails and is, fortunately, contagious.

And lastly, most importantly, thank you to the people of Dawson City, for sharing your stories and your extraordinary community with me.